THE UNSEELIE DUKE

DEAL OF SHADOWS: BOOK ONE

KATHRYN ANN KINGSLEY

Copyright © 2023 by Kathryn Ann Kingsley

ASIN: B0BY9QBXK1

Paperback ISBN: 9798393850623

KATHRYN ANN KINGSLEY

All rights reserved.

No part of this book may be reproduced in any form or by any electronic or mechanical means, including information storage and retrieval systems, without written permission from the author, except for the use of brief quotations in a book review.

This is a work of fiction. Names, characters, places, and incidents either are the product of the author's imagination or are used fictitiously, and any resemblance to locales, events, business establishments, or actual persons—living or dead—is entirely coincidental.

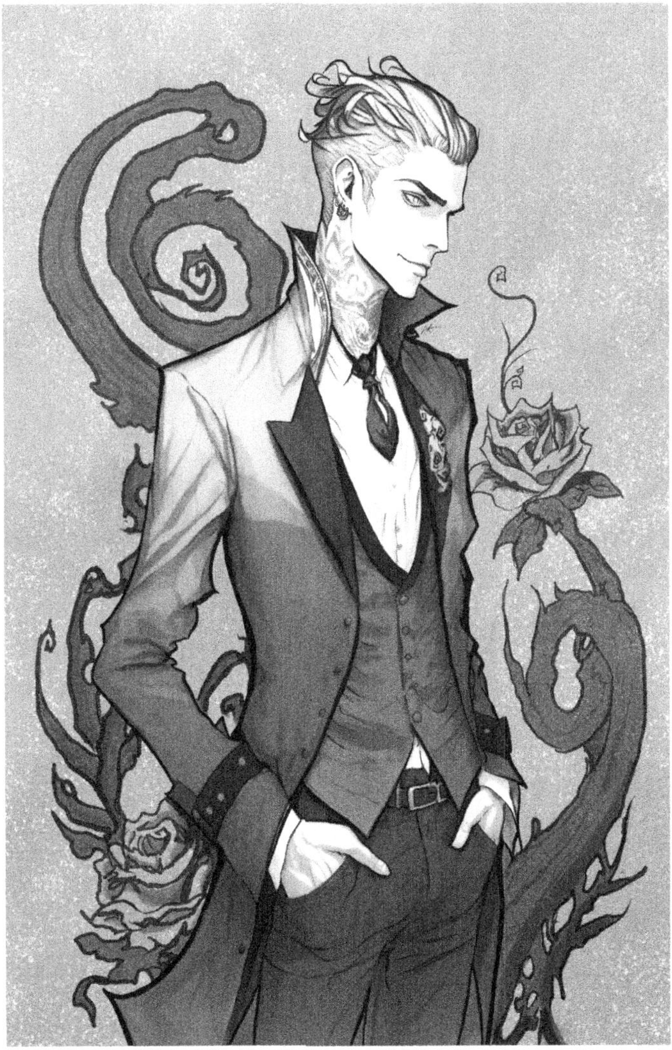

FORWARD OR WARNINGS

This series is an entry point into the world of Tir n'Aill. You do not have to read *Maze of Shadows* to enjoy *Deal of Shadows*.

Every now and then I get a lead male character who demands that I put aside all other things and give him his time in the spotlight. Izael, our Unseelie Duke, is one of those characters. He has been an absolute joy to write, and I hope you find him as fun to read as I had making him up.

This series is a dark fantasy that centers around a love story. I can promise you that there is a happily-ever-after ending; it just might be a little bumpy getting there.

But for the sake of making sure you know what you're getting yourself into, this series will have scenes of graphic (non-sexual) violence, murder, and horror. The sexual content in this series is always consensual, but may involve scenes of mild bondage, breath play, and the like.

He's a constrictor half-snake Unseelie fae with a dubious attachment to reality. What do you think is going to happen?

CHAPTER ONE

Alex had lost everything.

It was amazing how one little problem could send the whole house of cards crashing down.

And what little she had left was going to follow suit *real* fast.

Plucking her cellphone out of her pocket, she checked the time as she made the walk back home from her *former* place of employment. The coffee shop was closing its doors. Business in Cambridge just wasn't what it used to be, now that most of the companies around the Boston area had shuttered their doors to all work from home. At least she hadn't been fired. At least there was that small benefit.

But she was already behind a few months on the rent, and her clunker of a car had finally died three weeks ago. She had barely been able to afford the cost to get it towed out from the front of her place, let alone get it fixed.

Without what little money she had coming in…poof. It was all going to disappear. Her shitty apartment. Her meager life. Gone.

There was no point in even trying to comprehend how

much she owed in student loans. Her BFA diploma in music would make a great umbrella for when she was homeless. She had known there wasn't money in being an artist, but she hadn't known exactly how *bad* it would be.

Her landlord was understanding enough, but that was only going to go so far when he learned that she lost her job. A few random gigs here and there, singing in the local bars, wasn't enough to pay the bills. It wasn't predictable. Tucking her midnight purple hair behind her ear, she let out a wavering breath. She wanted to cry, but she refused to let it happen.

She hated crying. Tried never to do it. And the few times in her life it'd gotten away from her, she'd been furious with herself. No, there had to be a way out of this mess.

Somehow.

Maybe I could start an OnlyFans. She snorted at the idea. It wasn't a terrible one—she had no problem with people who did that. But she'd have to drop a lot of money on the setup, and…it just seemed like a lot of work.

And she'd need money immediately.

She had no family to move in with. Well, no family worth mentioning, anyway. There were no friends she could call to ask for a loan. None of her friends were in the position to help her. And besides, that felt so wrong. Especially seeing as she had no way of guaranteeing any kind of schedule of repayment.

Fishing her apartment keys out of her pocket, she walked up the stairs of the dingy three-family building she called home. Hers was on the top floor, a small one-bedroom that had once been an attic, but it was all she could afford. Or rather—had been able to afford.

Locking the door behind her and flipping the bolt, she collapsed onto the sofa and threw her arm over her eyes. She hadn't even bothered taking her shoes off first. It wasn't like the carpet could get any dirtier. It had been that way when she'd moved in, but she didn't care enough to pester the landlord to get it replaced.

And she certainly wasn't in any position to bargain.

Fiddling with the necklace she wore, she stared up at the flaking paint of the ceiling and tried to think of a way out of her predicament. The ridges of the snake carved out of bone were worn smooth over the years. Fidgeting was a bad habit of hers, and the necklace she'd owned since she was a child was the most frequent target.

There wasn't going to be any solving her problem tonight, she figured. Not when her thoughts were bouncing between dread and borderline panic. Pouring herself a stiff drink, she put a bowl of ramen into the microwave and sat at the vinyl-topped kitchen table that looked like it dated from the fifties. It had that telltale ridged metal trim around the edges, but she wasn't honestly sure when it dated to. It had come with the place. She couldn't complain; it served its purpose.

After eating the world's saddest dinner, she took a shower and did her best to calm down. It was a pointless attempt, and she knew it, but she didn't know what else to do except turn off the lights and enjoy the hot water in the darkness.

Changing into her pajamas, she headed into her bedroom and sat on the edge of her bed. Her frustration boiled over and, with a snarl, she slammed her fist into her thigh a few times. The pain somehow made her feel just a little better. She wasn't sure why.

Letting out a shuddering breath, she decided to grasp on to the only thing she had in times like this—as silly as it would be to outside observers.

She was going to cast a spell.

She had been a witch since she was young, falling deep into the New Age section of a Barnes & Noble, and she had never quite come back out. Tarot cards, crystals, herbs, and trinkets—she collected them all. But the things that decorated her altar the most were bones.

Animal bones, to be specific, ones she found on hikes in the woods. The skull of a fox she had painted and decorated with symbols sat prominently in the center of her arrangement.

Opening the curtains to let the moonlight in, she began her preparations. First, she lit a stick of incense and took her candles out from her dresser drawer and began setting up a circle in the middle of her bedroom. Next was placing a copper bowl down in the middle. She gathered up various herbs, sticks, and leaves from her collection.

To top off the bowl was the skull of a rattlesnake.

Kneeling at the bowl, she shut her eyes and tried to center herself. Once her breathing was slow and regular, she lit the candles around her and held the match in front of her, watching the dancing flame.

It was going to be an unusual spell, but she didn't know what else to do. "I don't know who's listening, if anybody. If you are? I don't really know if I care who you are." She cringed. "But I need help. *Please.* I'm desperate. And I'll trade you for anything I have left. Anything at all." Dropping the match into the bowl of odds and ends, she watched as it caught fire and blazed.

Murmuring words of prayer and thanks to all the old gods she could think of—covering all her bases, really—she repeated it until the bowl was nothing but ashes and a now charred and blackened snake skull.

Tomorrow, she would bury it all in the back yard. Blowing out the candles, she placed the bowl on the windowsill in the moonlight and crawled into bed.

Shutting her eyes, she turned on her side and clutched

her favorite stuffed animal to her chest, and after a long bout of tossing and turning, she finally fell asleep.

AND WHAT DO we have here?

What a terrible little place this is. Is this how mortals live now? Pathetic.

Izael emerged from the darkest shadows of the room. He had heard a prayer, whispered in foolish words. A wish made by moonlight. An open door. And who was he if not the kind of person to step through it?

He loved open doors.

They were the absolute best kind.

Especially those left there by silly mortals.

The room smelled of cloves and sandalwood. The pungent incense made him wrinkle his nose. *Pleh.* He could have done without that nonsense. The odor of recently burning candles almost made him roll his eyes.

Superstition.

Magic was a matter of will. Of focus. Such tools were only toys for the weaker practitioner. He kept his steps silent as he approached an arrangement of trinkets on top of a dresser. A black velvet cloth covered the surface, and it was absolutely cluttered with bits and pieces of everything he could imagine. Dried flowers, crystals and rocks, carved bits of wood, and whatever else the little spellcaster thought might serve their purpose.

But what made him lick his lips were the bones. Sadly, nothing too salient or fresh—and all belonging to little woodland creatures. Damn. But beggars and choosers, and all that.

It was then he noticed the bowl of burnt cinders and a blackened rattlesnake skull in the center of it. A vicious, hungry smile spread over his lips. That would be why the invitation was sent to him in particular. *I wonder if my new friend knows what they've done.* He highly doubted it.

The old ways were not dead. But they were sorely misunderstood.

Where *was* his host, now that he thought about it?

Hearing noise from behind him, he turned. He hadn't seen the mattress at first—it was small. It sat without a frame or supports up against one wall. And on it was...

"Oh, hello," he murmured, his grin growing wider. Was this his new favorite friend in the whole wide world? He very much hoped so.

What a pretty little thing she was. Hair the color of the darkest amethyst pooled about her on the pillow. She was wearing barely anything at all, which he did sincerely hope was the new fashion on Earth. Not that he was ever starved for flesh in Tir n'Aill, but there was something to be said for unwrapping presents.

Her exposed arm was covered in markings—tattoos, he realized. Images of skeletal creatures and monsters crawled through stylized graveyards. Atop one grave was a very stern looking raven. It was an elegant, if entirely morbid, array of art. He wondered if she had any more. He very much hoped so. He wanted to find them all.

She was a beautiful thing, he decided. Curvy in all the right places. Fleshy enough to sink his teeth into, but slender at the waist and perfect for him to coil around and *squeeze.*

Hunger surged in him, sudden and strong. Her scent was all of that in the room—of spices, of clove, a hint of coffee. Of char and smoke. It was delicious.

Kneeling very carefully on her sad little mattress, he prowled over her. He balanced his weight and moved slowly, not wanting to wake her up. Not yet.

She was short. That was fine. Easier to manhandle. He

wondered what color her eyes were. He hoped they were blue. Slowly lowering himself onto his elbows, he bent his nose close to her and inhaled.

A shudder passed down his spine. How he wanted to taste her. How he wanted to *devour* her. But that would have to wait. His insatiable hunger would ruin the fun before it began. And he had the opportunity of a lifetime before him.

He was so *bored* with the fae. The Seelie were droll and uninteresting. The Unseelie were prickish, stuck-up, and irritating. Humans, however? Humans were *fun.* Unpredictable, technological geniuses, and their society was ever-changing. Not stuck in the mire of agelessness like his people, mortals were forced to live fast since they lived short.

He loved Earth.

But ever since the damn fucking miserable *treaty* was signed, it was off limits. Abigail, the Seelie Queen, and Valroy, his liege and the Unseelie King, had finally penned an end to their interminable back-and-forthsy game of fighting.

Nobody was allowed on Earth without an expressly signed contract with a mortal.

And it meant he was *trapped.*

And trapped meant *bored.*

And he hated it.

But this girl presented an opportunity. An ice cream sundae piled with sugary, tasty goodies. His stomach grumbled. It had been eighty years since the treaty was made and he had been able to visit Earth. He did hope they still had ice cream.

The young lady murmured and rolled onto her back, facing him without realizing it.

Why, yes, he would have some, *thank-you-very-much.*

He kissed her. Slowly at first, loving the feeling of her against his skin, warm, soft, and supple. She tasted just as good as she smelled! When she let out a furtive, still-sleeping moan against his lips, he couldn't help himself.

Deepening the kiss, he wound his fingers into her dark purple hair. What a wonderful surprise for her! Waking up with him in her bed. What a treat for both of them. He would make passionate, violent love to her until dawn, and when he had to slink back to the shadows, he would do so, inked contract in hand, and a new mortal plaything to enjoy.

He loved new toys.

When she let out a startled *"mffh!"* against his lips, he knew she was finally awake. He pulled back, grinning broadly. She would surely welcome him into her arms, ready to seal their tryst in more ways than one. "Hello, my—"

He broke off as she screamed in his face.

And promptly brought her knee up into his gentleman parts. He groaned in agony and fell onto his side on the mattress.

So much for that.

CHAPTER TWO

Alex kicked at the man a second time as she flew off the bed. "Holy shit!" She ran for the light switch and turned it on as fast as she could, not wanting to leave her back turned to the intruder-and-probably-rapist for any longer than she had to.

The man was still lying in a heap on the bed, holding his privates where she had nailed him with her knee.

"Ow," he muttered into her pillow.

"Get out! Who the fuck are you? I'm calling the cops—"

She grabbed her phone from the floor next to the bed. It had only taken an instant. But when she looked up, the man was…gone. Just entirely *gone*.

There was only one door in and out of her bedroom, and there was no way he had made it past her. She turned in a circle, searching for him. No one. Anywhere. "What the…?"

Picking up a candlestick from her dresser, she held it over her head like a weapon. "Where'd you go? Come out! Stop hiding!" But nobody answered. Fighting panic, she searched her apartment. All the windows were shut and locked. The door was still bolted. There was no way anybody could have gotten in.

Had it been a nightmare? She was shaking, the adrenaline still crashing through her system. She had gone into full *fight* mode, but now in the aftermath, she wasn't so sure. Maybe it had been a night terror. Or sleep paralysis. She'd never had anything like that before, but she was under a lot of stress.

But the man had felt so real.

She checked all the doors and windows a second time. Checked every closet. Even looked under the sofa, as stupid as that was. Nothing. No sign of anyone. It must have been a nightmare. There wasn't any other option. People didn't just vanish into thin air. She left the lights on in the rest of her apartment, just in case, as she went into the bedroom and plugged her phone back into the charger.

Straightening, she turned around to turn off the light.

And walked right into someone. *"Boo."*

Screaming, she shoved at the person, but they barely budged an inch. She balled up her hands and punched at him, going straight for the face. She didn't even stop to see who she was hitting. She didn't care.

"Gah!" The man pulled back to dodge one of her swings. "What a little hellcat you—*ow!*" He snarled as she kicked him in the leg.

"Get out! Get *out!*"

Hands grabbed her wrists. The man was twice her size and far stronger than she was. Before she could react, he spun her around and placed her back to his chest, his arms banding around her and pinning her to him. "You want me to leave? But you just summoned me here." His voice was sharp but low. "How confusing you humans are."

"Let me go!"

"So full of demands!" He chuckled. She could feel his

breath on her ear. "And we have not even been properly introduced…"

She stomped on his foot. But he was wearing shoes and she was barefoot, and all she managed to do was hurt herself. "Let me go, damn it!"

"Fine, *fine.*" The man obeyed and released her.

She went for her phone, but it was gone. "What the—"

"What a wonderful little toy. What does it do? Besides call the police, like you said. Oh, dear, is this a telephone? How fascinating! You must show me how it works!"

Turning, her eyes went wide. She took a step back, bumping into the wall. "What…"

The man in front of her was easily the strangest she had ever seen. First, he was tall. And *long.* Everything about him seemed just a little out of proportion, and a little sharper than it should be. He had cheekbones that could cut glass. His hair was a bright turquoise-teal, almost a sea green. It was shaved up to the temples and the rest would have reached his chin, if it weren't swept back and yet also sticking out at rakish, unkempt angles.

His clothing looked like a suit from the 1940s if it had been tightly tailored. It was old-fashioned, black with a teal windowpane pattern stitched into it. She could see a pocket watch chain running from his vest into the pocket.

A tattoo of snakes tangled into knots ran up the side of his neck in a deep bluish green. He was studying her phone, poking at it with nails that were too long, too sharp, and pitch black. When he glanced up at her, her confusion and fear only deepened.

His eyes were bright, shining teal. So bright they seemed to actually *glow.* She had seen them over her in the darkness and hadn't registered them at the time. To make matters worse, instead of round black pupils, they were slitted like a snake.

Whatever he was, she had the sudden and sinking suspicion…that he wasn't human. "Who are you?" She swallowed the lump in her throat. "What are you? What do you want?"

"Three very good questions!" He grinned. His canine teeth were also too long and too sharp. He had fangs. Goddamn *fangs.* He slipped her phone into his pocket. There went her only chance to call for help. "Now, which do you want to know first?"

"This isn't possible. This—this isn't possible." She pressed her hands over her eyes. She needed to wake up. "This is just a nightmare."

"Hardly." His voice was closer to her.

She jolted in surprise. He was only a foot away from her now. She squeaked and pressed harder against the wall. "Back off."

"Or? You'll what?" His grin turned sinister as he leaned in closer, clasping his hands behind his back. "You'll—*ow!*"

She had punched him right in the nose.

He pulled back, holding his face. "Violent little thing, aren't you?" He let out a *harumph* and then a sniffle as he checked to see if he was bleeding. "We'll have fun with that later."

"Get out of my home."

"Not much of a home, is it?" He wrinkled his nose and glanced around. "Not that I'm judging—oh, yes, fine, I'm judging." He strolled from her bedroom into the living room like he owned the place. Plucking up one of her throw pillows from the sofa, he turned it over before tossing it back down. "Is this truly where you live? Or perhaps one of your servants? Tell me this belongs to a thrall of yours."

"I—what? No. This is where I live." What the actual fuck was happening?

"Peh. Witches do not garner the same respect as they used

to, I see." He nudged at one of her lampshades, rocking it on the wire support.

"Who are you?"

"Hm? You want my name already?" He arched a thin, dark-teal eyebrow at her. He was wearing black eyeliner. He was, for lack of a better word, *pretty.* Extremely pretty. But he instantly reminded her, with or without the slitted eyes, of a snake. Gorgeous but deadly. "How forward of you. But I suppose if we are to be *friends,* I should trust you with it." He placed a hand on his chest, fingers splayed. He wore several shining rings adorned with various jewels, sometimes two per digit. "May I have yours first, friend?"

"We aren't friends. You broke into my apartment—somehow—and—"

"Broke in?" He gasped dramatically. "You insult me, madam! I did not *break* in. I was invited. By you. Did you not burn an offering? Make a prayer to the goddess in the pale moonlight?" His smile grew devious and vicious. "And lo, I have arrived to answer your summons. A loyal *servant.*" He bowed.

Oh.

Oh, fuck.

Oh, fuckity fuck fuck.

"I didn't think it'd work—I didn't think—" She shook her head. "This was a mistake."

"You said, and I believe I'm quoting here directly, 'But I need help. *Please.* I'm desperate. And I'll trade you for anything I have left. Anything at all.' Or am I mistaken?" He even mimicked her tone of voice. It was almost mocking.

Glaring at him, she edged across the room and went to grab the candlestick again. It was heavy and brass and would at least give her something to smash him in the face with if she needed it. "What are you? Let's start there."

"A wiser choice than my name, if I must be honest. Far

more pertinent to the current situation." He leaned against her table and nearly fell to the ground as it almost tipped over on him. It was half broken. He huffed and brushed his hand off on his suitcoat before regaining his composure. With a dramatic flair, he confirmed her worst fears. "Why, I am Unseelie, my lovely witch."

Unseelie. She had managed to not only summon a fae—which was a very, *very, extremely bad thing*—but an Unseelie. They were evil. Cruel. Devious and murderous. She suddenly felt like hitting him so many times had been an insanely terrible idea.

Seeing her obvious terror, he smiled toothily. "The legends still live. How wonderful. Well. Now that you have a slightly better sense about who you are dealing with, may I have your name?"

"N—no." Names were power. And names meant he could control her. "No, you can't have it."

He laughed and clapped his hands once. "Good! I was hoping it wouldn't be that easy. Then I shall ask to simply know what to call you, my vicious little hellcat."

Trying to consider every possible loophole he had at his disposal, she swallowed the rock in her throat. "Alex." It was short for Alexandra, so it wasn't even her real first name. And she wouldn't give him her last name. Not like it wasn't on all her bills in the apartment. She'd have to hide them.

No. She should be getting rid of him.

"Alex," he repeated with a hum. "I like the sound of it. You may call me Izael if you wish. I am the Duke of Bones, serving the court of the Unseelie King himself." He took the lapels of his suitcoat and tugged on them, clearly quite proud of himself.

A fae. An Unseelie fae. And an Unseelie fae *duke* from the fucking *court*. "Shit, shit, *shit!*" She held the candlestick tight in her hands and took another step back. "Go away. I unsummon you. It was a mistake. I didn't mean to."

"Oh, really?" It was clear he didn't believe her. "Tell me, what were you so desperate about that you summoned anyone at all in the whole wide universe to help you?"

"No reason. No reason at all." It was a bad lie. A terrible one.

He snorted. "Right." He wandered into her kitchen and opened her fridge. "I love refrigerators. *Whirrrrrrr* all day long. What do you have to eat?" He plucked out a container of Chinese food she had gotten a few days before. He sniffed it. Picking out a cold spare rib, he popped into his mouth. Letting out a happy grunt, he kept going.

An Unseelie fae *duke* was eating all her Chinese leftovers.

What the fuck was happening with her life?

"Go away."

"No." He talked with his mouth full. "Not at least until you tell me why I'm here. Oh! Or maybe you want me to guess? I *love* games." He walked to the sofa with the container of leftovers and flopped down onto it so hard that he bounced. "If it's your love life, I have a very easy solution to that."

His grin was suggestive and sinful.

She might've been flattered if she wasn't so damn afraid for her life. As it was, she doubled down on holding the candlestick in front of her like a half-ass weapon. "No."

"Murder, then? Murder is so much fun."

"No!"

"Not love, not revenge…" He hummed thoughtfully as he stuffed a piece of beef teriyaki in his mouth. Glancing around the apartment, he seemed to put it together. "Of course. The forever curse of being mortal. Money. You're short on money. I should have guessed that first, what with this pathetic hovel you live in." When she hesitated just a split second before lying and saying no, he snapped his fingers in success. "There it is!"

Wincing, she tried to cover. "No, you're wrong. It isn't—"

"Liar, liar," he teased. "Do you not have a skill that you can use for money? Or a husband to care for you?"

"I'm not married. And my skill doesn't make money."

"Well, that's silly. What are you trained in?"

She didn't like all the questions. But he didn't seem to take no for an answer. "Singing."

"Oooh, a little angry songbird? A violent sparrow. How charming. More and more, I find myself intrigued." He chuckled. "No family on which you can rely?"

"I haven't spoken to my parents since I moved out. We don't get along. At all." She shook her head. "Look, I don't owe you any explanations, you can just get—"

"Ah, well." He interrupted her, clearly done listening to her. "Overrated thing, family." Staring down into the box of leftovers, he made a face. "This stuff is vile, disgusting, greasy, and far too salty. I hate it." He paused. "I need more."

That made her laugh despite herself. Just the once, but it was enough to spark a light of hope on his face.

"Here's my proposal, lovely Alex. You and I are going to set forward upon a wonderful journey where we help each other. You get what you want, and I get what I want. But I understand that I am a bit…terrifying." He stood in one smooth movement that once more reminded her of a serpent.

Placing the now-empty container on the coffee table, he walked up to her. She pressed her back to the wall. Fishing into his pocket, he pulled out her phone. "First, this. You may have it back." He handed it to her. "But you *must* show me how to use it later."

"F—fine." There wouldn't be a later. Not if she had anything to do with it.

THE UNSEELIE DUKE

"And in exchange for you ordering me more of that terrible food when I return tomorrow night, I will give you these." He pulled two of the jeweled rings from his fingers and held them out to her. They looked antique. "Do not pawn them. Take them to someone who will give you what they're worth."

It was the solution to all her problems. Right there in front of her. Those rings had to be worth fifty grand a pop. It would set her up for a year, maybe longer.

Seeing her obvious temptation, his voice became a purr. "I can always offer you more. But certainly, this is good enough to whet your appetite, hm?" He grinned, twisted and more than a little deranged. "I know mine certainly is…"

He was Unseelie. And fae. And extremely dangerous. And she was a fool.

But she was desperate.

It was this or homelessness.

She didn't want to be on the street. She wouldn't survive for long out there. Not without terrible things happening to her.

Biting back the urge to scream or cry or both, she held out her hand, palm up. Just some rings in exchange for some Chinese food. That was fine. She could do that.

"And don't think about running off. It's you who summoned me, not this hovel you live in." He dropped the rings into her palm. They were heavy and lukewarm from his skin. "I will find you. I do not take kindly when my bargains are broken."

"I…I won't." It wasn't like she had anywhere to go.

"Good! Now. I will leave you to your slumber, my angry little songbird. Ta!"

He disappeared in a swirl of black smoke. Right before her eyes.

Alex slid down to the floor and sat there, her knees close

to her chest. She stared at the rings in her hand and kept waiting for them to shimmer and disappear like the bad dream they *had* to be.

But they stayed where they were.

All she could think of was the same question, over and over again, repeating in her head like a broken record.

What have I done?

CHAPTER THREE

Alex searched the internet for a whole lot of things the next morning.

She started with Izael the Duke of Bones. And wound up with *nothing*. She quickly gave up on that.

Next, she moved onto more practical things. Like capital gains taxes on the sale of jewelry—inherited or not. Or how much money somebody could deposit into a bank at once, and so on. She was going to owe tax on the rings, no matter what. Chewing on her lip, she sat at her laptop, drank her coffee, and turned the rings over in her hand. They hadn't vanished in the morning like she had expected them to. No, they were very real.

And her leftovers were still very missing.

Which meant that Izael hadn't been some twisted fever dream.

She drank the rest of her coffee and supposed that if she had been stupid enough to trade…whatever the fuck she had agreed on trading, which *appeared* to just be Chinese delivery, but she suspected it was going to be much more complicated than that…she might as well enjoy her half of the deal.

Dressing up as fancy as she could and tying back her purple hair so she looked *eccentric* but maybe possibly *not* about to be homeless, she headed downtown. There were a few fancy antique jewelry dealers. After looking at a few, she decided a place called E.B. Horn was going to be the first she visited.

Taking out her phone as she made the walk from her apartment, she debated texting her best friend, Olivia. Alex could take the bus, she supposed, but it never ran during the right times, and honestly, she could use the chance to clear her head.

Olivia and Alex had been buddies since high school. They fell into witchcraft together and stayed in close touch even though Olivia had moved to Toronto for school and settled down there. She was the only person in the world who might believe the nonsense that had happened to Alex in the past twelve hours.

But what was she supposed to say? *Oops, I accidentally summoned an evil Unseelie fae who is obsessed with Chinese food and paid me in antique rings.* Or *Oops, I accidentally summoned an evil Unseelie fae who snuck into my bed and made out with me.*

Either way, it was unbelievable. Even with the antique rings in a little black velvet bag that was tucked into her knee-high boot. She didn't dare carry them in her pocket. It was her luck that today would be the day she got mugged.

She felt like she should tell Olivia something, just in case she went missing. But she didn't want her friend to call the police on her for a wellness check, thinking she had lost her mind, either. So, she sighed and tucked her phone back into her pocket, giving up on that whole plan.

No, she was stuck in this on her own. At least until tomorrow. She was going to cash out the rings, buy the creepy fae his Chinese food, and then move on with her life. It would just be a weird moment in her life that might entirely be a hallucination caused by a mental break from stress.

Maybe I do need a wellness check.

Her thoughts were still whirling when she reached the jeweler. Straightening herself out, trying to look as professional as she could, she took the black velvet bag from her boot and walked in.

"Can we help you, miss?" the lady at the door asked. It was clear she didn't look like the usual customer of a place that dealt in very, *very* expensive jewelry.

She put on her best smile. "Yes, actually. I have a pair of rings I just inherited from my family, and I'd like to have them appraised."

The woman blinked. "May I see them?" She probably assumed Alex had walked in with a used Ring Pop or some shit.

Keeping a beatific expression plastered on her face as best she could, Alex took the two rings from the pouch and held them out for the woman to see. When the lady's eyes went slightly wide, she nodded. "Oh. Yes. This way. I'll fetch the floor manager."

That sounded important. Maybe they were worth something after all. Tucking the rings away again—not wanting to flash them around, even with the armed guards at the door—she followed the lady to a desk by the back.

It was only a few minutes before a man in a perfectly tailored suit approached. He had dark hair swept back from his face. When he extended his hand to shake hers, Alex felt like she had just shaken a microwaved but dead fish.

"Hello, I am Mr. Taylor. And you are, Miss…?" The man smiled thinly. He sounded like he had a German accent that was fading with time in the States.

"Hammond. Alex Hammond." She folded her hands in her lap, trying to look prim, despite the purple hair.

"Melissa says you might have some rings that you would like me to take a look at?"

"I just received these from my great uncle in the mail. He says they've been in the family forever. They're lovely, but student debt and all that jazz." She placed the two rings on the table in front of her.

The man hummed and picked them up. He took one of those funny little jeweler's microscopes out of the desk drawer—the kind a person just squeezed into place with their eyebrow. He turned them over. "Do you…know anything about their history? And how they came to be in his possession?"

"No clue, sadly."

He let out a breath. "Miss Hammond, these are, well, Tiffany. And quite spectacular." He took the magnifying glass from his eye and set it down. "It's extremely rare for pieces like this to appear without paperwork to accompany them."

Alex shrugged and made up a story on the fly. "His father or grandfather, I don't remember which, was overseas in France in World War II. It's possible he got them then? Hard to get paperwork from that era."

"Perhaps they were stolen, then."

"Maybe. But that has a twenty-year statute of limitations on it, doesn't it?" She smiled at him. "And if they were stolen in World War II, we're well past that point."

That was another thing she had searched that morning.

He hummed. "Yes, I suppose so. Are you interested in selling these rings, then, Miss Hammond?"

"I am."

"May I take these rings into the back? I would like to see the owner regarding what we could offer you for them."

She didn't really like the sound of that. But the odds of the guy going "what rings?" were pretty slim in a place like

THE UNSEELIE DUKE

this, she figured. Nodding, she watched as Mr. Taylor headed into the back.

Maybe she'd get twenty thousand dollars. Oh, man. That would be *life changing.* She could pay her rent for a few months while she got back on her feet doing…something. Somewhere. Maybe she could even get another car or move out of the city where the rent was cheaper.

When Mr. Taylor came back a few minutes later, she felt her nervousness lessen as he placed the two rings in front of her again. He took out a piece of paper and a pen and wrote two numbers on them. "This is what we could offer you for each ring."

He slid the paper over to her.

And it took every ounce of her stage training not to slide out of the chair and collapse to the floor.

One ring was worth over *two hundred thousand dollars* alone. Together they were worth almost six hundred! She must have gone beet red in the face with how her heart was pounding and with how warm she felt.

She swallowed, took a breath, and somehow managed to keep a straight face. "Is that what you're expecting their resale value would be? I assume this is pre-markup, since you have your own margins to think about."

He paused. "That's correct."

"How much would you expect to get for them at auction? What percentage more?" She didn't want to be a hardass. But she also didn't like getting taken advantage of. That was what happened when you had funky colored hair and tattoos—nobody ever took you seriously.

Mr. Taylor stared at her blankly for a long moment. And she stared right back at him and waited. Finally, she won the contest. "Twenty-five percent."

"So, you're expecting to profit…" She opened her phone and pulled up the calculator function and typed in some quick numbers. "Roughly one hundred and forty-six thousand dollars from this? I'm pretty sure whatever auction house I end up going to will charge me a lot less than that. I have to pay a twenty percent tax rate on this either way. I have to keep that in mind as well."

The phone next to Mr. Taylor rang. He picked up the line, listened silently for a moment, and then hung up. That meant that whoever he had just spoken to was listening to the conversation. Chances were the whole place was bugged.

Cute.

Mr. Taylor took the piece of paper with the numbers, scratched out what was there, and amended it. He slid it back over. "Would twenty percent be more amenable to you, Miss Hammond?"

That meant she'd get an extra sixty grand. Before taxes, but…uh. Yeah. Yeah, that was plenty. "It is. Thank you."

The jeweler let out a breath. "I will send Melissa to the bank to have a cashier's check made. It should take half an hour. Do you wish to wait here?"

"Sure." She didn't dare leave without the rings. And he probably wouldn't want her taking off with them, either. So, they gave her a spot to sit by the wall and wait as Melissa went to get the check made.

And a half hour later, she was walking into the bank with a check made out to her with the largest sum of money she had ever seen in her life. She had a receipt for the sale made up to explain to the nice bank teller that *no,* she wasn't committing fraud.

And an hour and a half later she was walking into her apartment, feeling entirely numb and emotionally drained.

She kept staring at the balance on her bank app. The amount was going to take a while to fully move over, but they had given her fifty thousand of it while the rest cleared over the next few days.

It was the most she'd ever seen in her account.

Literally ever.

Sitting down on the sofa, she just kept staring at her phone. It didn't feel real. And maybe it wasn't. Maybe she was wearing a straitjacket and bouncing off the walls at Brigham and Women's.

Curling up on her side, she hugged the throw pillow next to her. She shut her eyes and must have dozed off. Because the next thing she knew, *someone was kissing her.*

She screamed and punched the form over her. He grunted and sat back onto his heels. "Is that simply how humans greet each other now?"

It was him.

The fae.

She yelped and scrambled to the other side of the sofa. He was kneeling on the ground beside where she had fallen asleep and was rubbing his chin where she had socked him. And the look on his face was almost comically dejected.

"Can you not keep doing that?" She glared at him. "It's an invasion of my personal space."

"But you—were just—I mean—how could I *not* try it a second time?" He grumbled and stood, brushing off the knees of his suit pants. "Maybe you were so grateful for my gifts that you changed your mind."

"No."

"Clearly." He grinned. "Where's my food?" His expression fell. "You didn't forget, did you?"

"No, I didn't forget." How the hell could she forget something like that? She reached for her phone and flicked it open.

He stood there silently for a few moments. "Well?"

"Ordered." She put her phone back down.

He blinked. "Pardon?"

"The food's ordered." She hugged her other throw pillow

to her chest. She didn't know why. It would be useless as any kind of armor. "It'll be here in, like, twenty minutes."

"This place has room service?" He glanced around. "Odd priority. I would have, perhaps, repainted the walls first, but *c'est la vie*."

"No, it—" She squinted at him like he was an idiot. "Somebody comes and just brings it to us from the restaurant. It's delivery."

"Oh." He huffed and planted his hands on his hips. "Don't look at me like that. It's been a long time since I've been allowed on Earth! I didn't know paying the serfs to bring you food was a new hot trend."

"They aren't—" She rubbed her temple. He was going to give her a headache. "They aren't serfs, they're just not paid what they should be. When was the last time you were on Earth? And what do you mean by *allowed?*"

"The 'why' isn't important. Long story. Wars and treaties. Yadda, yadda." He waved his hand dismissively at her. He had new rings on. He must have a huge collection. "And I believe the year was 1945."

"That explains the suit."

He frowned down at himself. "I like my suit. What's wrong with it?"

"Fashion's changed. A lot."

"I assumed so, since you like to wander about half naked." He tilted his head at her. She was wearing a tank top and a jacket. Not exactly skimpy. But she guessed maybe it was for the times. "Not that I mind," he continued.

"Knock it off."

"Why?"

"I don't trust you."

"Didn't really ask you to, now, did I?" He sat on the sofa, once more bouncing as he landed, and kicked his feet up on the coffee table. She noticed the tattoos on his neck seemed to have changed. They were in a different spot—she swore they were, anyway. To be fair, the first time she had met him, she had been in a panic. "Did you sell the rings?"

"I did."

"Hopefully for more than some magic beans." Izael draped his arms over the back of her sofa, looking perfectly at home.

"More than that, yeah." She really didn't trust him. And that included trusting him with any details whatsoever.

"Aaaaaaaaaand?" he crooned.

"It'll solve my money problems."

"For now." He shrugged. "Money is finite. And you're mortal. It'll be gone sooner than you think. It won't solve your problem."

"Yeah, it will. I can get on my feet with this. Pay off my debt—"

"Ooo! I didn't know there was debt!" He clapped his hands. "You didn't mention that. Who did you owe? Illicit lover? Abusive father? Drug lord? Pimp? *Please be pimp—*"

"Holy *shit,* stop." She laughed in disbelief. He was like a child. An evil child grinning at her like he wanted to eat her. But his glowing, slitted, sea green eyes were lit up in enjoyment at seeing her laugh. She shook her head, trying not to let that register. "No, student loans. From going to college."

"Where you trained to be a songbird."

"For what good it did me, yeah." She shrugged. "No work being a singer. Or not enough to go around."

"Maybe you aren't any good."

She glared at him, trying to set him on fire with her mind.

"Oof, that look!" He pressed his hand to his chest as if she had shot him. "I am struck by agony."

Again, she laughed despite herself. Getting up from the sofa, she went to the fridge to get a pair of beers. She could at least be somewhat hospitable to the monster. He hadn't hurt her. He just was a bit of a creep.

So far. "You haven't heard me sing. How would you know?"

"I don't. You could sing for me and prove me wrong."

"Nah."

"Why not?" He almost looked like he was pouting.

"Because you're fae, and I don't trust fae." After popping the caps on the hook she had mounted to her wall, she walked back to the sofa and handed him the beer. "And I don't perform for them, either."

"How lovely." He took a sip and mumbled something into the neck of the bottle that she didn't quite catch. "My point being," he continued after he lowered the bottle. "You will run out of money and need more. And I can provide."

She shook her head. "No. I'll fulfill our agreement and give you the Chinese food. And then this ends."

"Ends?" He laughed. The sound of it sent a shiver of cold down her spine. And her fear redoubled as he flicked a serpentine, bifurcated tongue from his mouth. "Oh, no, my dear…we've only just begun."

CHAPTER FOUR

Izael tried not to laugh at his songbird's terror. He tried and he failed. "What?" He kept his tone innocent but couldn't help sporting his favorite fiendish smile. Alex jumped up from the sofa, putting as much distance between them as she could in the dingy, disgusting little flat of hers.

"What *are* you?" Her eyes—which *were* wonderfully blue —were wide as saucers.

"You know what I am. I've already told you." He flicked his tongue out again, knowing quite well that had been what had spooked her. But he couldn't stop himself. The taste of her fear on the air was simply too delectable. "Did my eyes not give it away?"

She began to fidget with a necklace she usually had tucked under her shirt. He had seen it while she was sleeping on her sofa. It was part of the reason he had to try to kiss her a second time. It was a snake devouring its own tail, carved from bone. He knew the symbol—it belonged to his cousins who hailed from the land of sand and sun.

And it was simply further proof that she belonged to *him* and always had. This moment was destined by the fates. He simply had to convince her of the fact. He pondered how best to approach the matter. Humans were usually simple in their wants—money, sex, power. But she wasn't a fool. She wouldn't be so easily tricked.

He had offered her more money, and she was turning it down. *For now.* She was too afraid of him in that not-fun kind of way.

He was clearly offering her sex, and she kept kneeing him in the privates. He also blamed that on the un-fun fear.

Perhaps power? But she didn't seem like the egotistical sort.

"If you're referencing my *true* form, however, it is truly something spectacular to see." He stretched out on the sofa, sipping his beer. He preferred wine, but beer would certainly do. "But you're already afraid enough as it is. I'd hate to make matters worse."

"Are you going to hurt me?"

"I wasn't planning on it." He sniffed dismissively. "Not unless you want me to." He let that fiendish smile crawl over his face again. "Do you want me to?"

"No!" She leaned back against the wall by the door. She took a hefty swig from her beer. Taking her hair out of the ponytail it was in, she combed her hand through her purple locks, and he desperately wanted to do it for her. "What do you want from me?"

"Simple. I want to stay here on Earth. My world is so… dreadfully *boring.* I like being a big snake in a small pond. And I am not allowed to stay here unless I have an active contract with a mortal. So, I seek from you an active contract." He was probably giving too much away all at once, but he wanted her to trust him—just a tiny, itsy-bitsy amount.

She studied him curiously. His small bit of truth had

exactly the intended effect. It had piqued her interest. "But Earth can't be any more interesting than your world."

"Sure, your creatures are far more mundane and far less *murdery* than ours, but by the Morrigan, nothing ever changes!" He groaned in dismay. "A painting can be the most beautiful one in the world, and after a while you're going to get sick of staring at it. I love humans because you're always coming up with something *new.* I want *new.*"

He didn't just want new things—he needed them.

And he also needed her sitting on his lap, entirely naked, riding his cocks.

Or beneath him.

Or chained to the bedposts.

One thing at a time, he supposed.

He sipped his beer.

She was studying him, as if waiting for him to peel off his face or jump at her to rip her limbs off. But he did no such thing. "You just…want to explore Earth."

"Mm-hmm." And that was, for the most part, entirely true. "I am not like our King Valroy. I have no need to see humans exterminated. Where would the fun in that be? No, let you all run amok in your pigpen and watch what fascinating toys you come up with."

Her expression turned annoyed at the pig reference, but she let it slide. "And you want to make a deal with me so you can stay here."

He smiled hopefully.

"No."

He frowned, dejected. "But why?"

"You're fae. You're *Unseelie* fae. I can't trust you farther than I can throw you. I'm not going to get into some complicated mix-up with you. It'll cost me a lot more than it'll cost you in the end. That's what you people do." She pointed at him.

"And you are suddenly the expert on my people, are you?" He smirked. "A songbird witch hard on her luck is secretly the holder of all the knowledge on the ways of the Unseelie?"

She arched an eyebrow. "Well, am I wrong?"

"Not in the slightest." He barked a laugh.

She sighed.

Gods, she was *adorable* when she was put out. She opened her mouth to argue with him some more, but the doorbell rang.

He jumped to his feet. "Food!"

Alex had ordered food for four people.

And she quickly ordered more. It was clear it wasn't going to be *nearly* enough for Izael. The strange, freaky monster was sitting on her sofa, devouring a Pu Pu Platter like it was his goddamn *job*.

She sat on the other side of the sofa from him, watching in awe. He seemed to have no interest in the fried rice, so she sat there and ate that contentedly while he plowed through the rest. She couldn't help but stare at him as he devoured the Chinese food.

He somehow managed to make going totally nuts on a box of takeout look graceful. She couldn't help but stare at him for a whole mess of reasons. But on that list, for some dumb reason, was the fact that every time he sucked the grease from one of his fingers with a quiet grunt, it sent a shiver down her spine.

He was gorgeous. In a weird, terribly frightening, probably-wanted-to-eat-her-alive kind of way. But there was no denying he was extremely attractive. Even *with* the freaky snake tongue and slitted eyes.

He picked the vegetables out of the spring roll to eat the

fried wrapping.

"Can you eat veggies?" She stuck her fork into the bin of fried rice.

"I suppose I could if I had to. But they're disgusting. Why would I bother when I have so much glorious meat in front of me?" He gestured his hands wide at the spread in front of him.

She shrugged. She wasn't, despite his teasing, an expert on the Unseelie. She wasn't going to judge the man for being wired the way he was.

That was right until he got to the box of chicken wings. He cackled in glee as he devoured the meat from the bone.

And then sticking the bone in his mouth, bit it in half with a loud *crunch.*

She wailed.

He chewed the bone loudly before swallowing it, and then ate the other half. He looked at her and blinked, confused at her expression of horror. "What?"

"Holy *fuck!*" She grimaced. "You eat bones?"

"I told you my title. Duke of *Bones.* Booooooones.*" He narrowed an eye at her. "Were you not listening?"

"I was, but—" She shook her head and wedged herself farther away from him into the far corner of the sofa. "Holy shit, that's disgusting."

He huffed, as if insulted. He picked up a second chicken wing and ate that one whole. Without chewing it. She watched the lump of it go down his throat. "Is that better?"

"No. Not really. No." She cringed and repressed a shudder. She was working on her second bottle of beer. Now she wished she had broken out something much stronger. Getting drunk around the strange man was probably a very bad idea, but also probably very necessary.

He shrugged and went back to chewing the bones. She shuddered and decided she really wasn't very hungry anymore. But her misgivings didn't bother him at all. Pretty soon, both the first *and* second orders of food were gone.

He frowned down into the empty container and almost looked like he was going to pout. "Did you order more?"

"I…I can, I guess." She wrinkled her nose. "Am I going to end up ordering you food for the rest of time?"

Sighing dramatically, he put the empty box down. "No, no. It's *fine*. You upheld your half of the bargain." He twisted on the sofa to face her. "Now, let's discuss our next bargain!"

"There won't be a next bargain." She narrowed her eyes at him. She wasn't stupid. She didn't care what he offered her. "Sorry."

"Come, now. There must be something in this whole wide world you want!" He propped his feet up on the sofa next to her. "Think of it—anything you could possibly dream of. What do you wish for the most?"

"I gave up on all my hopes and dreams. I don't have any wishes." She probably shouldn't have been that honest with him. But whenever she said that to people, they always laughed it off. She expected him to do the same.

But instead, it looked like she had broken his heart. He looked so *sad* for her. "None at all? Truly?"

She shook her head. "I don't get to be famous, or rich, or anything. I'm happy if I can pay my bills. And I can do that now because of our first deal. I'm not meant for anything more. I accepted that a long time ago."

"But…*why?*"

"That's a really long conversation I don't particularly wanna have with you." She sipped her beer again.

He stuck out his bottom lip. How somebody could be so terrifying while pouting, she had no idea. "You really are no fun."

She shrugged. "I do my best."

Tilting his head to the side, he watched her with fascination as if he'd never met a human quite like her—as if she were a true mystery or a fluke to him. She didn't know if that was a compliment or an insult.

"Well. Then. I propose that is the problem we try to solve first." He crossed his legs at the ankles. "I would like to find a way to rekindle your desire and joy for life."

"I never said I didn't have any j—"

He kept talking like she hadn't interjected. "So! I will show you what life *could* be like if you were sensible in signing a contract with me. Here is the game that I propose. For seven days, I will stay here on Earth where you shall show me all that humanity has done in the last eighty-some-odd years. Museums. Cinema. Food. History. Food. And for seven nights, I shall take you to the world of the fair folk, where I shall show you all the wonders that we have to offer. What say you? Do you agree?"

"Not so fast. You said 'game.' A game has stakes."

"Mmh. That it does." He leaned back against the arm of her sofa, eyes lidded and sultry. "Clever songbird. You will be a hard one to trick, won't you?"

"I hope so."

"Well. I seek to discover what it is you wish for. You claim you have no desires in this world. I want to prove you wrong."

"Okay? You still haven't told me what the prizes are for this dumb game of yours."

"Simple! If you have a wish in your heart by the end of the seven days, you must agree to sign a contract with me for its fulfillment." He smiled. "Simple as that. We could call this a… test run of our new working relationship."

"And what do I get if I win?" She folded her arms over her chest.

"Enough money for the rest of your life that you needn't work a day unless you choose to. Enough to procure yourself some…" he looked around the apartment and wrinkled his nose, "better lodgings, at least."

"No."

His expression fell. "Why not? It's perfectly reasonable."

"Because if I lose and I'm forced to sign this new contract, I get no say in the new stipulations. I'm not going to agree to a game that gives you carte blanche to do whatever you want if I lose. That's suicide." Probably literally. She couldn't imagine the serpent-like man ate *only* chicken bones. She shivered at the idea of him devouring her alive.

"Damn." He mumbled something about wishing she hadn't noticed and tapped a finger to his chin as he thought it over. "Very well. Should my new contract proposal be unappealing to you, you will have one attempt to offer terms in return that I find acceptable instead. A counteroffer, if you will."

That was tempting.

And she wasn't used to things being tempting.

Seeing the land of the fae? For real? Seeing *real* creatures and magic? "And these seven nights I'll spend in Tir n'Aill. I won't be harmed, assaulted, accosted, or otherwise mangled in any way during that time?"

"You will be left entirely unharmed by myself or any other of my people. I cannot speak for the Seelie, but they are banished from Tir n'Aill while the sun sets. You will be safe from them as long as we tread about only while the moon is high." He shrugged as if it were a non-issue. "My home will be safe enough, however, should we be surprised by the dawn."

She didn't like this idea of being forced into a new contract. "What about three attempts at a counteroffer? And I promise to negotiate in good faith. No lies." *What am I doing?* But the idea of being set up for life on a pile of cash was…extremely tempting.

THE UNSEELIE DUKE

He took a few seconds to consider it. "Very well. But on one condition—you allow me a single spell upon your person to divine when you are lying to me. Call it an assurance of your good faith."

"And the spell will only do that? Only specifically tell you when I'm lying? It won't do anything else to me?" She arched an eyebrow. That seemed just as dangerous.

But her life was…empty, dull, and boring. Full of never-ending days working at a shitty coffee shop or something similar. And full of nights that were as occupied as the void. The idea of what he was promising her—a chance to see another world—was almost second to what he was offering her if she lost.

A chance to *want* again.

A chance to look forward to tomorrow again.

He had proposed to her a game that she didn't know if she wanted to win.

"I give you my word as the Duke of Bones—the spell will do nothing harmful to you." His lips curled into a sinister smile. He could sense he was winning her over.

This was stupid, and she knew it. This was going to end her life.

But her life was worthless. It wasn't really a huge loss.

Letting out a sigh, she reached a hand across the sofa toward him. "Deal."

"Wonderful! You will not regret it, my lovely songbird." He took hers and shook it firmly before leaning over and placing a slow, sultry kiss to her knuckles. "Now…shall we begin?"

She barely had a moment's warning before he sank his fangs deep into her hand.

CHAPTER FIVE

"*Ow!*" Alex smacked at Izael with her other hand, afraid of ripping her flesh open if she yanked her injured one back. "What the *fuck,* you—"

He removed his fangs from her hand and held her hand up. "Shush." Turning her hand to the side, he squeezed it, forcing some blood from the punctures and sending it dripping into his other palm.

The blood sizzled and swirled. He blew on it, and she watched as it took on the appearance of molten glass. Letting go of her hand, he began to turn the shape over in his palm. It grew and changed, and before long was a perfect sphere of red-hot material.

It must be the spell.

He blew on it again, and it began to cool, until it was a perfect ball of crystal-clear glass about the size of her fist. He smiled. "See? Not so bad, was it?"

She got up off the sofa to go wash the wound in the sink. "You aren't infectious, are you?"

"Infectious with what?" He blinked in confusion.

"Being an asshole. I don't know. Fae shit." She glared

THE UNSEELIE DUKE

at him.

Laughing, he leaned back on the sofa again and held the glass ball up on his fingers, perching it between his pointer, middle, and thumb. "I am not infectious with any 'fae shit.' I wouldn't worry." He flicked the ball from the back of his fingers, and then rolled it back over the top of his fingers to his palm and back again. "Tell me a lie."

She rolled her eyes. Whatever. "My real name is Walter McSlappypants."

The glass sphere glowed a slowly pulsing bright teal.

"Well, it works." He grinned. "Perfect! I am so glad you agreed, my songbird." He flicked his wrist, and the glowing glass ball disappeared into thin air. "I will come fetch you tomorrow night and we shall begin our adventure then, hm?" He stood and brushed himself off, picking a bit of sofa lint off his sleeve and flicking it away. "How is it you do not even own a cat? How dreary."

"I'm glad I don't. You'd probably try to eat it."

He went to argue, then laughed. "You're probably right. I'm off to conduct some business before we meet again." He bowed low with a wide sweep of both arms. "Until then, my darling. Ta!" He disappeared in a puff of dark teal smoke.

Alex's eye twitched.

Gods above and below, she was beginning to hate the fae. Or at least that one. Definitely that one. Sinking down onto her sofa, she stared at the demolished boxes of Chinese food that should have fed a family of twelve and had instead fed one weirdo.

Who ate bones.

Putting her head in her hands, she let out a sigh.

And she had just signed up for a *lot* of trouble.

She had a sinking suspicion she was an idiot.

IZAEL RETURNED HOME feeling like a genius. He hadn't returned to Tir n'Aill in such a good mood in *ages*. He was humming a song to himself as he strode into his home with a literal skip in his step.

He was proud of his home. He couldn't wait to show it off to his violent little songbird. The marble floors were checkered black and white. Growing up through the center of it was an enormous ash tree that stretched a hundred feet overhead. There were no walls—but why would he need them? No, the marble floor served as a perfect definition of the edges of his home.

He was whistling as he took off his suitcoat and threw it over the back of a chair at his dining table.

He was happy. He couldn't remember a time in the past eighty years he had been so thrilled.

That was, he was happy right until he saw that he wasn't alone. He skidded to a halt, his joy collapsing as he saw a man leaning against the trunk of the ash tree. He looked like a long-dead sailor who had been left to rot on the bottom of an ocean, only to be dredged up.

He was slight of frame, but Izael knew better than to think his visitor was weak. No, this creature was anything *but*. He was, in truth, an enormous sea monster. And he had the dubious distinction of being second in command to King Valroy of the Unseelie.

Ah, fuck.

Izael quickly hid his shock and momentary fear behind a broad smile. He threw his arms out at his sides. "Uncle Anfar, to what do I owe this pleasure?"

The creature masquerading as a man rolled his eyes. "For the last time, I am not your uncle. And I am not here on a social call."

"I know that. On both accounts. But seeing as *you* are very scaly, and *I* am very scaly, it makes us related, does it

THE UNSEELIE DUKE

not?" He grinned. He knew he was insane. It wasn't like it was subtle. Izael figured it added to his charm.

Anfar sighed drearily. "Where have you been disappearing to? I have reports that you have been traveling to Earth."

Ah, double-fuck.

He figured he had more time! He grimaced. "I have been procuring a contract with a mortal."

Anfar arched an eyebrow and said nothing. His eyes were pure black from lid to lid. All he did was stare at Izael and wait.

The sea monster always gave Izael the willies. He smiled as sweetly as he could and gestured his hand aimlessly. "A young witch who did not realize what she was doing. She summoned me to make a bargain. I traded her two of my rings for dinner on Earth. You know how much I miss my freedom."

"Yes. And that is precisely why I am here. Your activities have not gone unnoticed, and I wished to make sure you were not *starting a war.*"

"Who, me?" Izael placed his hand to his chest as if insulted. He wasn't. Not really. Izael didn't give two shits if the Unseelie and Seelie broke their idiotic truce. He just wanted his freedom to wander Earth unchecked. Was that so much to ask? "Never!"

Anfar grunted and shut those black eyes as though Izael was giving him a headache. "And is your business with this mortal concluded?"

Izael changed the subject. "How did you know I had been traveling to Earth? I thought I was being quite clever."

"Is your business with the mortal concluded?" Anfar wasn't falling for his tactics.

Folding his arms across his chest, Izael huffed. "I have followed the rules. The treaty states that if I do not have a contract with a mortal, I cannot linger on Earth. And *she* summoned *me*. What is the issue?"

"The issue, Duke, is that you are a lunatic and cannot be trusted not to start trouble." Anfar glared at him. "Whether or not you are following the letter of the law. So, I will ask again. She summoned you for money. Has your deal concluded?"

Izael tried not to laugh. Poor Anfar. Because he despised "the game," he never played it well. Izael put on his best disappointed expression and let his shoulders slump. "Yes. She has paid me for an evening of dinner, and I have given her two of the rings from my collection. That contract has ended."

And it had.

There was just a second contract involved, that was all.

Anfar hadn't asked about *that*. Not specifically. Therefore, Izael hadn't lied. Not specifically. Therefore, he was in the clear.

"Good." Anfar pushed away from the tree and walked away. The sea monster had been and always was brusque in his mannerisms. Izael didn't take it personally as Anfar opened a puddle in front of him and jumped into it, disappearing into the inky darkness without even a word of farewell.

Once the sea monster had gone, Izael sighed and stripped out of his clothing to take his true form. It was tiring having legs. Using his tail to climb the tree, he went to his bed—a large boat that had been sailed to Tir n'Aill by humans many centuries ago. Izael had filled it with pillows of every kind, a habit that was not uncommon to the fae. Slithering into the pile, he lay down and shut his eyes, and pondered.

He would have to be careful. Very careful. They would be watching him closely. He would likely have to use different gates between the worlds, instead of traveling directly—and to concoct excuses for his absences. He needed some manner of project or someone to cover for him.

But who?

Izael had few friends and fewer allies. That was the way of things in the Unseelie Court. Rolling onto his stomach, he summoned the glass orb he had created from his songbird's blood. He waved a hand over it and watched as it shimmered. An image appeared in the center of it.

Silly witch. The orb did a great deal more things than show him when she was lying.

It was his link to her now. A contract signed in her blood. Alex was cleaning up after their dinner, stuffing the used paper boxes into a trash bag. Her brow was knit in confusion and worry. She didn't trust him—and she was right not to.

He was already plotting her life as his human pet. He would spoil her rotten—she would live a blessed life at his side. His desire for her flared as he watched her work. He would treat her like his little duchess and lay the whole world at her feet.

But she would belong to *him* and *him* alone.

Running his pointed nails along the surface of the glass, he wished it was her skin instead. He wanted to touch her. To ravish her. To watch her break. To watch her scream in delight and ecstasy and pain as he brought her a world of new experiences as his lover. As his pride and joy. As his toy.

He would have to bargain with someone to hide his comings and goings. And he knew he would give a great deal to continue his scheming with the young mortal.

The question was…who?

And *how?*

There must be a way.

There had to be a way.

He simply had to find it.

Then, it hit him.

Oh, it was a *dangerous* ploy. But it was the only one he could guarantee would work. The only one that would ensure he would succeed. But it would risk it all. If his plan went awry, Izael would become a scaly smear on the stones within seconds.

Izael did not fear many people.

But this one?

This one, he feared very much. And for good reason.

Pushing up from the pillows, he let out a groan and vanished the glass orb. His head whirled with how complicated his life was going to become. But he did adore complicated games, did he not?

And this was going to make it a tangled mess of strings.

Cracking his neck to one side and then to the other, he wandered from his nest of pillows and struck off into the woods of Tir n'Aill.

There was only one person who could ensure he would not be discovered in his comings and goings. One person who might appreciate what Izael was trying to do.

Or he'd rip off Izael's head and feed it back to him by shoving it down his stump of a neck. One of the two. Fifty-fifty shot, really. Izael usually didn't like playing games he didn't know he could win. But everything that was worth it came with high stakes.

Moving through the shadows, he traveled through the darkness to appear at his destination. The person he was coming to see was sitting at a table, staring down at a pile of papers. A half-drunk goblet of wine perched between his pointed nails. The man looked…tired. Weary with whatever he was looking at.

Rulership was not all it was cracked up to be, it seemed.

Izael put on his best smile and bowed his head. "Greetings, King Valroy. May I have an audience?"

CHAPTER SIX

Izael approached the king, gliding along the grass and stone before stopping by the cluttered dining room table Valroy was occupying. The king was seated in a chair that had the back cut in such a way that his large, dark blue, leathery wings were unencumbered—the arms were not attached to the thin back, notched for his extra appendages.

It looked as though it had been grown, not carved—a delicate collection of thin wooden vines that twisted about each other in a fantastical and beautiful pattern. Izael suspected it was a gift from his wife—Abigail, the Seelie Queen.

And that was Izael's only hope in this situation.

Valroy sighed heavily and placed a hand over his eyes. "What do you want, snake?"

Izael smiled as beatifically as he could, wrapping the end of his long tail around the legs of one of the other unoccupied chairs at the table. "Why, King Valroy, you seem almost unhappy to see me."

The searing, faintly glowing blue gaze that met him

would have withered a lesser man. Or perhaps one who was less insane. But Izael considered him neither little nor sane, so it was of little concern to him. He kept the same expression plastered on his face as Valroy continued to stare in silence.

"May I beg a moment of your time?" Izael curled his tail to allow him to rest on the coil of muscle. He very much disliked sitting in chairs in his true form. "I assume that since I have already interrupted you, it would not be much more of an imposition…"

Valroy rubbed his fingers along his temple. Taking a piece of paper in front of him, he flipped it over. "Make it fast."

Izael waved a hand in the air lazily. "It has come to my attention that it has come to *your* attention that it has come to Anfar's attention that—"

Valroy grimaced, baring his fangs at Izael. "I said fast."

Izael had a great many problems. But being stupid was not on that list. It was clear the king was in a particularly foul mood, and if he wanted to not have his hide turned into a pair of snakeskin boots, he should do as the man said.

For Izael was one of the strongest fae to grace the Unseelie Court in many centuries. But the king was hardly a fae at all. He was much, *much* worse than that. Bred from the Morrigan and an archdemon, but what lurked in the truth of his soul was as deep as the void itself.

Because that was precisely what King Valroy was.

The void given flesh.

Izael smiled. "I have struck a contract with a mortal girl. I intend to make her my pet, and I will enjoy my time on Earth as the treaty allows. Your sea monster has taken umbrage with this."

"Anfar rightly knows that when you have your fingers in things, trouble follows." Valroy sat back in his chair. "And the Seelie are eager for any reason to start a war."

"As are we, to be fair." Izael shrugged. "This peace is against both our natures."

The other man huffed a single laugh. He mumbled something about his wife and rubbed his temple again. "What is the nature of this contract of yours?"

"She claims to have no wishes or wants in this world. That all her dreams have died. I have seven nights and seven days to prove her false." There was no lying to the king. Not if one wanted to avoid becoming a fashion choice. Besides, Izael had an angle. He was just waiting for the right moment.

"And then what?" Valroy was also no fool.

"Then, she must agree to another contract where we negotiate on how best to grant her wish." He let his smile turn sinister. Desire boiled in him. He wanted the girl. He needed to watch her squirm in his grasp. He wanted to hear her cry out his name in bliss and agony.

And he *would* have her.

War or not.

"It is all perfectly legal to the letter of the law, my king. She has agreed to all of this. I have not even had to resort to any coercion besides simply the power of words. And my natural charm, of course." He batted his eyes.

Valroy rolled his. "My answer is no, Izael. Cancel the contract. You are to stay here in Tir n'Aill."

Izael felt his shoulders droop. "But…but I have done nothing wrong."

"Yet. My answer is no." Valroy sat forward and flipped the paper over to resume his work. "You are dismissed."

Looking away, he grimaced. He knew better than to bare his fangs at the king. He fidgeted, thinking. This was the wrong way to play his hand. But he had no choice. "She is a witch, my king."

That regained the king's attention. Valroy turned his head toward Izael, just slightly. "Explain."

"She summoned me. She was desperate for money, lest she lose her home." He knew the story of how Abigail had come to make a terrible bargain with Valroy, some few hundred years ago. Witches seemed to have a proclivity for falling upon hard times. "I made a simple trade with her—a few of my rings for some hospitality. I must have her, my king. I *must*. She wears a snake of bone upon a necklace. Her fear of me is delicious and raw. She is meant to be mine. This is fate." His hands were tightened to fists now. He said the worst word in the world. The one he loathed above all others. *"Please."*

Valroy tilted his head, studying Izael with a calculating stare. After an extremely long stretch of silence, he finally spoke. "I am saving myself centuries of your whining. That is all."

Relief flooded Izael, and he bowed low in deference to the king. He did not give thanks, however.

"I will ensure your movements are shrouded from the eyes of others. But I know nothing of this. Should your activities come to light, you will be presented to the Seelie as a roasted and stuffed snake dinner. Do you understand?" Valroy's words were cold as ice.

It was not a metaphorical threat.

Izael nodded. "Yes, my king."

"Now go away."

Izael did not hesitate to leave the presence of the king, returning to his home eagerly for several reasons. Least of which, anyone taking the risk of speaking to Valroy had a fifty percent chance of walking away mutilated and another twenty percent chance of not walking away at all.

He had become even more of a moody bastard since the treaty had been signed.

That damnable treaty.

That damnable loss.

Curling back up in his nest of pillows, he stretched out and shut his eyes, letting his mind wander to images of what it would be like to have his tasty little witch there beside him, slumbering at his side.

He was tempted to touch himself, to bring himself pleasure, imagining her body atop his, riding him. But he would save the blaze of his hunger for his new pet. He wondered if she would let him put a collar on her.

He wondered if she would like it.

Rolling over onto his stomach, he grumbled. He wanted her *now*. But he had to be patient. And there was joy in such a dangerous game as this. Her life had always been on the line. But now, so was his. That came with an edge of danger that he deeply appreciated.

But he was not a man who played games he had a chance of losing.

If only that were advice King Valroy had taken to heed those eighty years ago.

Damnable treaty.

It had been a risky maneuver—to try to use the chaos of the humans' second "world war" to attempt to overthrow the balance between the Seelie and Unseelie. Valroy had thought he could subdue the Golden Court's presence on Earth once and for all.

And they had lost.

If it had been Queen Titania who still wore the golden crown, Valroy would be long dead. But Abigail, who for *some* reason loved her husband Valroy, spared him at the cost of forcing the Unseelie King to sign the miserable excuse for a deal that had banned Izael and all the rest from meddling with humans.

It was only by a stroke of idiocy on the queen's part that gave them the option to procure contracts with the mortals. Honestly, Izael believed it was Valroy who had rightly pointed out that if they were not allowed to contract with mortals, Valroy and Abigail would have never fallen in love.

The king was not above using sentiment to win arguments when necessary.

And neither was Izael.

Summoning the glass orb he had made with Alex's blood, he let it shimmer and change to show him what she was doing. She was asleep on her little mattress on the floor, blankets thrown half over her as if she had been tossing and turning in restlessness.

He hoped she was dreaming of him.

He hoped she was having nightmares of him.

He would lay the whole world at her feet. She would be a spoiled duchess, wearing the finest of clothes—mainly so he could tear them off her—and be fed the most perfect of treats. She would have servants to wait on her hand and foot. He would lavish her with gifts. With praise. With pleasure.

With terror.

Because Alex belonged to him. And she would come to understand it. And she would embrace him with open arms in the end.

Or else her end would be of a very different kind.

She did look so tasty, after all…

Laughing, Izael stretched out and shut his eyes. He yawned and let sleep come for him. For tomorrow was going to be the start of a wonderful game.

And either way?

Izael would win.

ALEX WOKE to the sound of pots and pans knocking over in her kitchen. She was standing on her feet and had the brass candlestick from her altar in her hand before she even registered what was happening.

She shouldn't have been surprised.

But when being woken out of a dead sleep by the sound of somebody rummaging through her kitchen, her first thought was naturally not going to be "oh, it must be that psychotic fae asshole."

But there he was. Izael. Wearing a full, vintage-style black suit. It had a damask pattern printed on it also in black, giving it a bit of a shimmer as he moved around. She rubbed at her eyes, trying to blink the sleep out of them. "What're you doing?"

"Oh! Good morning. I am trying to figure out what *this* is." He picked up her microwave. He had unplugged it. "It is strange. I'm wondering if there is something about it that I'm missing." He grinned at her.

"First, you unplugged it."

"Well, yes, of course. I wanted to take it apart." He frowned. "I know what electricity is, I'm not stupid. It tingles. Smarts if you get too much of it."

"Don't take my stuff apart. Jesus Christ." She sighed and walked back into her bedroom to get dressed.

"I'm flattered you think I am the son of a god," the fae called from the kitchen with a laugh.

"Very funny." She pulled on her clothes and walked back out, combing her fingers through her hair. "It's called a microwave."

He put the object back down on the countertop. "Oooooh —I think I heard of these! They were just barely coming to market when I was banished from Earth." He pushed the button on the front, causing the door to pop open. With an amused snicker, he shut the door and popped it open again.

It was almost cute. *No, he's evil. He eats bones. And do you know what has a lot of bones? People. Therefore, he eats people.*

Alex sighed and walked to her cabinet to pull out a can of chunky beef stew. Pouring it into a bowl, she plugged her microwave back in, put it where it was supposed to go, and put the bowl of stew onto the glass tray.

Izael reached for the door button.

She slapped his hand away. Pressing the numbers for a minute and a half, she hit start, and the object whirred and lit up.

"Oooooooohhh..." Izael leaned over to peer into the frosted glass door. "Fascinating. Why have you turned breakfast into a Macy's store display? Why does the soup need to feel fancy?"

That made her laugh. "It's heating it up."

"But...how? There's no heat." He put his hand on the top of it tentatively, as if it were going to scald him.

"Some kind of, well, microwave radiation makes the water molecules bounce around and heat up. I don't know. I'd have to look it up." She went to make herself some toast. The toaster, he seemed to understand and didn't feel the need to prod at.

Fuck, she needed coffee. It was way too early to put up with his nonsense. She sighed, figuring she should be at least a *little* nice to the monster who could probably eat her alive. "Do you drink coffee?"

"I do, yes."

"How do you take it?"

"As black as my soul." He leaned against the counter and shot her a cheeky grin. "But as sweet as my amazing personality."

She mimed throwing up.

Izael cackled. "In other words, no cream, plenty of sugar."

"I gathered." She smirked. "What's on the docket today, fae boy?"

"Fae *boy?*" He huffed in mock insult. "I am a fae *man*,

thank-you-very-much." When the microwave beeped to say the time was done, he jumped. He poked the little button, and fetched the bowl of soup, studying it curiously. "Goodness. How wonderful."

"Wait until I show you the internet." *Oh, no. What if he finds porn?* Maybe at least that would get him out of her hair for a little while. The idea almost made her laugh. Almost.

He didn't need the encouragement.

As if he knew right where everything in her kitchen was —which he probably had done plenty of poking around before waking her up—he fetched a spoon and began to eat the stew, rightly assuming the meaty breakfast was for him. "As for what to do today?" he said through the chunk of beef in his mouth. "It's been a very long time since I've been on Earth as far as humans go. I want to see what you have done with your eighty years since I have been back."

She poured him a cup of coffee with more sugar in it than she figured anybody would want and slid it to him. By the time she was done making herself some—cream no sugar— her toast was ready. "How about the Museum of Science? You just have to promise me you'll behave and not eat the dinosaur skeletons."

He laughed loudly and leaned over. Before she could stop him, he kissed her cheek. "We are going to get along swimmingly, you and I."

Somehow, that was what she was afraid of.

CHAPTER SEVEN

Alex was fairly convinced after the second hour of Izael leading her about the Museum of Science that he was, in fact, a deranged toddler from another world. He had demanded they eat *all* the terrible tourist food —from hot dogs to weirdly salty lemonade to frozen Dippin' Dots and more.

But fuck if he wasn't clearly having a blast the entire time. Every exhibit he looked at with the energy of someone trying to absorb every piece of information. He had a million questions about everything—why was that like this? Who discovered that? What happened to this thing? Why was this invented?

But it wasn't until she took him to the planetarium show that she found herself staring at him more than she was looking up at the projected stars.

She had never seen such a look of wonder or amazement in her life.

He was dangerous. He was definitely a murderer. Yet his eyes—which he had the good sense to somehow make notglowy when around other people, though they were still slitted—were as wide as disks.

And it made her realize, as she watched him stare at the projection in amazed silence, that he wasn't lying about his love of Earth. He really *did* want to be here. Oh, she still didn't trust the snaky bastard as far as she could throw him. And she definitely wasn't going to turn her back on him if she could help it.

Maybe he was a brilliant actor, and all of this was some massive show to try to win over some sympathy from her. And it was entirely possible. But something in the way he watched the fake sky and listened to the corny narrator as if everything that was playing out before him was pure majesty told her that…no. He meant this.

It almost made him a little endearing.

Almost.

They headed from the planetarium and went meandering through some more exhibits before they got to the dinosaur bones. And as she predicted, he licked his lips as he looked up at the triceratops skeleton on display.

"I'm pretty sure it's fake." She folded her arms across her chest and eyed the skeleton. It seemed like it would be much more useful to put a replica on display where anybody could throw slushies at it than a real skeleton. But what did she know?

"I could take a bite and let you know." He grinned fiendishly at her.

"No." She glowered up at him. "No eating the dinosaur."

The fae let out a harumph. "Well, then, tell me what's for dinner."

She thought it over for a moment. "Barbeque? We can get you a few racks of ribs. Or a whole-ass cow."

He arched a dark teal eyebrow. "Is this a new mutation of a normal cow that is entirely made out of arses?"

She burst out in laughter. He honestly meant it. "No, it's just a turn of phrase. You've heard of half-assing something, yeah?"

"Yes?" He seemed not to follow.

"So, if you can half-ass something, you can whole-ass something." She waved her hand at him and his comical confusion. "Never mind. We can get you ribs. Just don't eat the bones in public. People will freak out."

He sighed. "That's no fun. But *fine.* You are my human sherpa, I suppose." He eyed the dinosaur again. "Wonderful creatures, these were. A shame they didn't last."

"Eh, I'm fine without them around. I don't generally like the threat of being eaten on a second-to-second basis." She didn't mean it as a dig. But she figured it was applicable. "How dangerous is Tir n'Aill?"

"Extremely. But you will be with me, and nobody tampers with the toys that belong to the Duke of Bones." He smirked.

"I'm not your toy." That earned him another glare.

"When you are in my home, you are. If you were not, someone else would come by to gobble you up. A tasty little morsel like you? You would last *seconds* around my people." He hummed. "Four. Precisely four seconds."

She couldn't exactly argue with him. She didn't figure the dark world of the Unseelie fae was full of free hugs that didn't end with you being swallowed whole. And in the case of Izael, probably literally. "So…why do you eat bones?"

He blinked. "Why do you eat anything?"

"Do you need bones to survive?"

"They give me power." He shrugged. "It is simply the way I am and how I have always been."

She supposed she couldn't fault him for being the way he was born. Wolves ate sheep. Wasn't the wolf's fault. It was just super shitty to be the sheep. And in this situation, she knew which one she was. "So…are you a snake?"

"I am Izael. Really, you're adorably dense sometimes." He poked her in the forehead with a grin.

Swatting at his hand, she led him from the exhibit and on to the next one. "Right, but the tongue thing. And the eyes."

"Did you like the tongue thing? I can do a great many things with it…" His sensual purr turned to a laugh when she slapped him in the stomach as hard as she could. "So violent! I love it."

"You're such an ass."

"Hm. No. I'm insane. But I see your point. What am I, you ask? Well, I am as much of a snake as you are a monkey, I suppose. The similarities are there, but sorely missing the point." He wrapped an arm around her shoulder and pulled her to his side.

She went stiff but didn't push away from him. Namely because people were staring at them. They made a really odd pair walking around—probably the strangest goth couple anybody had ever seen. Him with his elaborate suit and dark teal spiky hair and snake eyes they'd mistake for contacts, and her with her purple hair and black leather coat with a few too many zippers on it.

If she pushed him away, people might call the cops on them. So, she stayed there, rigid as she was, and settled for glowering at the ground in front of her. "Well, then, what are you?"

"I'll show you tonight. How's that sound? When we're back in my own home and not so likely to attract…unwanted attention." He squeezed her lightly. "I know that is the only reason you're letting me touch you, isn't it? You don't want to make a scene. I'm not above taking advantage of that."

"Don't let it go to your head."

"Far too late for that, I'm afraid." He smiled contentedly off into the museum and let out a small breath. "I am enjoying myself, Alex."

"I'm glad." She guessed she kind of was, too? He did seem to honestly be enjoying himself. And watching him marvel and wonder over the most mundane of things was weirdly entertaining and endearing. She even had to give him a penny and some change to get one of those stupid flattened-pennies-with-a-logo-on-it things.

And when it was time to leave, and she got sucked into the gift store?

Holy shit, the credit card receipt almost gave her an aneurism.

Hey, at least she figured she had *plenty* of cash now, and it technically was because of him, so no, she wasn't going to tell him he couldn't have the expensive Da Vinci thermometer.

They headed back to her apartment, helping him carry the bags of toys he had bought. She didn't trust him in a public restaurant not to just straight up eat the bones in front of people. It was a lot less risky—for the general public, at least—to have him sequestered inside her tiny home.

Her feet ached by the time they got back. And he was skipping along, happy as a clam, ecstatic to be back out and about on Earth. She had to smile at his exuberance, even if she didn't want to admit it to him.

Pulling out her laptop, she opened the page for delivery food while she watched the deranged toddler unpack all his toys and start playing with them. And in some cases, she meant that literally.

"What're you going to do with all that?" She looked up from the delivery food page.

"Add it all to my collection, of course."

She started snickering.

He frowned. "What?"

"Paart of yoooour wooooorld," she sang with a roll of her eyes. "Okay, Ariel."

Now he looked entirely lost. "I…do not understand what is happening right now."

And that was how she wound up watching *The Little Mermaid* with a deranged, evil, snake-like fae, while eating a few hundred dollars' worth of barbeque. Which was mostly for him.

This time she didn't feel as nauseated when he started eating the pork rib bones like they were Kit-Kat bars. But it wasn't exactly pleasant to witness, either. But he watched the movie, glued to every second of it, fascinated and amazed by what he saw. He said he had seen cinema before, but nothing like that. They moved on to *Aladdin.* And it was halfway through *Lion King* that she must have fallen asleep.

She woke up when someone gently nudged her. She hummed sleepily and shifted. It was right then that she realized she was lying on the sofa with someone underneath her. She was lying against Izael, and his arms were draped around her.

Her first reaction was thinking about how comfortable he was. If weirdly lukewarm.

Her second reaction was to punch him as hard as she could in the stomach. Luckily for him, her leverage was bad. He groaned all the same.

"Damn it, human—" He cringed. "Why do you have to keep doing that?"

"Because I didn't ask to wake up like this." She sat up and straightened her clothes. "Do you have to be so fucking *grabby?*"

"Actually, yes." He rubbed his stomach where she had punched him. "I do. And I am. And I will not apologize." He grumbled. "You looked so sweet, and comfortable, and I didn't *hurt* you or do anything wrong, I just wanted to hold you. Is that so wrong?"

"Actually, yes," she echoed him. "It is."

"Why?"

"Because I didn't say you could. You took advantage of the fact I was sleeping."

"I mean…I could have done a lot worse." He shrugged.

"Yeah, you could have. But you shouldn't do those things, either." She sighed. It was like arguing with her coffee table. Her table wasn't really going to understand. *Fucking fae.* She rubbed her temples with both hands.

Izael's sigh was less frustration and more sadness. "I didn't mean to upset you."

She glanced over at him. He actually looked crestfallen. He was watching her with those glowing sea green eyes, and it was like she had just scolded a puppy for sleeping on the bed, when all he wanted to do was cuddle.

Shutting her eyes, she rubbed her brow with the heels of her hands, trying to work out the tension and the pain. "It's fine."

"Does that mean I can do it again?"

"No!"

"But why?"

She groaned. "Fuck me—"

"Can I?" He grinned.

She smacked him in the arm. But that time it was half-hearted. "No. And stop being a wiseass."

He laughed, knowing precisely what he was doing. He moved toward her, and she turned to face him just as he crawled over her, forcing her to lean back against the arm of the sofa. "I wish to kiss you."

"No."

"Why not?" His gaze lingered on her lips. "Am I not attractive to you? Am I not beautiful?"

"I—I mean, sure. Fine." He had an orb that told him when she was lying. There wasn't any point in denying how pretty he was. "But you're also a dangerous monster who definitely murders people."

He hummed. "Doesn't that excite you? Even just a little?"

She swallowed the rock in her throat. "No?" It kind of did. And she didn't want to admit it.

He grinned, seeing through her bad fib. "Oh? Are you so sure about that?" He leaned closer. "Come, now…just one. And if you don't like it, I won't ask again." Reaching up, he trailed his sharp nails over her cheek, sending a shiver down her spine and her skin exploding in goosebumps. "And you have my word on that…"

"You said you wouldn't ask again. Not that you wouldn't simply *do* it again."

He chuckled. "I did. Clever thing, you are." He leaned in a little closer. The warmth of his breath brushed against her. "I did not steal a kiss while you were sleeping this time. Do I not get a prize for that?"

"I—"

He closed the distance between them, clearly done with waiting for her. He kissed her, and her mind almost sank into white noise at how searingly passionate the embrace was. His hand cradled the back of her neck and pulled her close, deepening the gesture as he growled deep in his throat.

It felt like she was water, and he was a man dying of thirst. It was like he was trying to swallow her whole—and for all she knew, he could. He moaned against her, slipping his body closer with all the lithe strength of the snake he resembled.

The prick of his nails against her scalp made her shudder. Despite herself, her eyes slipped shut, and she couldn't help it. He tasted how the woods smelled after it rained—crisp and earthy, of leaves and grass and the untamed wild.

It was incredible.

When he broke away, she was breathless, and her head

was reeling. She blinked her eyes open. For a moment, she wasn't angry.

And then she saw the smug look on his face.

With a glare, she brought her leg up between his legs and nailed him in the crotch.

Izael's eyes went from smug and pleasured to wide and pained as he doubled over onto the sofa next to her, his face pressing into the cushions. He groaned. "I hate it when my balls are on the outside…"

That sentence made no sense to her, but whatever. "I said not to."

"Technically true," he said, still muffled into the cushions. "But you also clearly enjoyed that."

"Technically true. And you're also a total asshole."

He pressed up with a huff and stretched, cringing at the lingering pain from her blow. "And you are extremely violent. I hope we get to put that to good use someday." He huffed as if he was trying to keep down all the food he ate. "And not by trying to re-seat my nuts into my stomach."

She nudged him. "Time for you to back off a step."

"Not yet." He smirked. "It's nighttime now." He pointed toward the window. And sure enough, the sun had fallen.

Oh, shit.

"And you know what that means," he purred.

Her stomach fell as if she had been dropped off a cliff. Yeah. She did. She thought she had wanted to see the magical world of the fae. But now? Now, she wasn't so sure. "Um… can we rain check? I'm pretty t—"

Alex didn't even get a scream out of her mouth before the whole world dropped away from her and she fell into a swirling abyss to the sound of Izael's maniacal laughter.

CHAPTER EIGHT

Alex became aware of herself face-down in damp grass. Letting out a small grunt, she pushed herself up onto her hands and knees and then sat back on her heels. And when she had the wherewithal to open her eyes, she froze at what she saw.

Any question in her mind—any at all—that Izael was some fancy prank and wasn't actually a fae from another world was dashed away in an instant. Because wherever she was…it was *not* Earth.

The grass that surrounded her was midnight blue, glistening silver with dew in the pale moonlight. Even the moon was wrong. The marks on it were different, and the stars that surrounded it were entirely changed from anything she would have ever recognized. The grass transitioned around her, back and forth, between the swaying long blades and a smooth black and white marbled floor, arranged in a stark checkered pattern.

It was anybody's guess which was there first—the marble or the grass. It seemed to follow no rhyme or reason in how it transitioned. Surrounding the space was a strange and haphazard collection of bits and pieces of fancy Louis the XIV-style architecture. Sections of walls that made no sense—a door here, a window and some plaster and some fancy wainscoting there—an elaborate white fireplace that had no chimney or wall surrounding the mantel. A fire was burning quietly, casting an orange glow across the marble and grass.

Bursting up from the center of the space was an enormous ash tree—or maybe it was a birch. She didn't know. Its bark was white and seemed to almost glow in the moonlight. Branches sprawled out high overhead, filled to the brim with glistening leaves that swayed in a delicate wind.

From two of its main branches hung a large rowboat or a skiff. It looked ancient, but she couldn't date it. It was suspended some ten or fifteen feet off the ground by heavy ropes. And all around her were bits of furniture that reminded her of some bizarre open-concept home.

A dining room table set out for guests that looked Japanese in the way it was set low with cushions instead of chairs. Piles of paper and books, knickknacks, and bookshelves overflowing with *stuff*.

Slowly standing, she stared in awe at everything before her. The air itself seemed to shimmer with life. Like little bits of glowing things were suspended on every breath of wind that drifted by.

It was breathtaking. It was eerie. It was the single most beautiful thing she had ever seen in her life. But something about it sent a shiver down her spine. Even with its stunning nature, something about it felt…dangerous.

And as she turned around, her worries were confirmed.

Standing behind her was a monster.

His lower body was that of an enormous snake, the coils of muscle undulating around him almost as if it had a life of its own. The scales were a silver-bluish-green, glinting like the feathers of a peacock or mother of pearl. But his underbelly was a dark and vibrant teal.

Shrieking, she turned and tried to run. And tripped over what at first looked like a log from the birch-ash-whatever tree in the center of the space. But as the log wound itself around her ankles and dragged her sharply back toward the monster to the tune of his sinister laughter, she knew it was part of the monster that had scared her.

When the ground disappeared and she was lifted into the air—upside down—by the creature, she swung her fists uselessly in the air at his grinning face.

It took her right until that moment to realize who she was trying to pummel.

Growling in rage, she swung another fist at his smug expression. "Izael! Put me *down!*"

The fae continued to laugh. He planted his hands on his scaley hips and tilted his head to the side as if trying to look at her from her perspective. "And why should I? This is absolutely delightful."

"Holy fuck, put me *down,* you psychopath—" She squeaked as he did as she said, if only for a split second, letting her drop abruptly toward the marble. "Not like that!"

He cackled. "Oh, sweet songbird. It's just delightful to see you so far out of your element. Promise not to run, and I'll put you down *gently.*"

Blood was starting to rush into her head, making her ears throb. "Fine. I won't run."

"Promise?"

"Promise." She really did want to punch him in the face. But she could promise not to run. Now that her *oh, no, monster* panic had worn off, she needed to at least understand where she was going to run to before tearing off into the darkness of a foreign, dangerous world. She was fairly—

somewhat—maybe a little—convinced Izael didn't want to eat her at that exact moment in time.

There was no such promise about whatever else lived in his world.

He set her back down, carefully as he had promised, and she scrambled away from him. At least as far as she could, before bumping into one of the coils of his tail.

His hair was still spiky and weird, sticking out from his head at odd and unkempt angles. From the waist up, little had changed about him. He had no shirt on, and she was intrigued by the strange markings that flowed up him. His tattoos definitely had changed again, the twisting snakes in different positions. And a single teal line ran up from his snake-half all the way up his midsection to his throat and to the underside of his chin.

His faintly glowing eyes were far more spectacular now, though it might have been because of the dim lighting. Scales started around his navel and took over his body as it would have transitioned to his waist and hips. The snake half of him was easily some twenty-five to thirty feet long, coiling around him and her in graceful, easy movements.

He was gorgeous.

But he was a predator.

Like normal snakes, she supposed. Elegant, powerful, stunning, and some of the most efficient killers on the planet. And the man—the *fae*—in front of her, was no different. She slowly managed to climb back to her feet, almost afraid that any sudden movement would trigger his instinct to kill.

And every movement she made seemed to delight him more than the last. He slithered closer to her—literally slithered. His forked tongue flicked out of his mouth as he tasted the air. "Your fear is delicious, songbird…"

"Not helping—" She took a step back and bumped into a

coil of muscle that had risen to around her shoulder height, clearly meant to block her in. "Not helping at all."

"Who said I want to help?" He tilted his head to the other side, clearly fascinated and rapt with her reaction to him. It wasn't comforting.

"Please—don't hurt me—"

He chuckled again. He slipped closer to her. And without any way out, she was frozen there as he moved into her space and threaded his fingers into her hair. His long nails scraped against her skin. It sent goosebumps flowing down her arms. Judging by his quiet hum, it was clear that he noticed her reaction.

"I won't hurt you." He leaned in a little closer, his breath washing over her cheek until he was whispering in her ear. "Not unless you want me to." His tongue flicked against her lobe, causing her to jolt. "And I think you might."

Pressing her hands against his chest, she tried to push him away. He was too much. This was all too much. "No, please—"

He sighed and leaned back, giving her some needed space. He looked almost...disappointed was the wrong word. *Hurt.* "What is wrong, songbird? What have I done?"

She shut her eyes. He was too surreal. This all felt like a strange dream. When she shut her eyes, she could pretend she was still at home, safe, and this was just the product of a bad fever. "This is all overwhelming."

"Ah." He retreated another few inches.

She could hear the sadness in his voice. And even though she *knew* she shouldn't...she felt bad for hurting his feelings. "I'm sorry. I know this isn't your fault. You're not—you haven't done anything wrong. You haven't hurt me, and you haven't done anything that I know you could. It's all just a lot. You're just a lot. You're who you are, what you are, and

I'm not going to ask you to change. But I'm sorry. I'm processing it as best I can."

When she opened her eyes, he was smiling at her. It was a strange, almost dreamy expression. Kind, and far away from the malice and deviousness she had seen just a few moments before. "Oh, Alex." He stroked a hand over her hair. "You are truly precious. Do you know that?"

"I—" Nobody had ever looked at her like that. Nobody had ever spoken to her like that. No, she didn't know. So, she fell back on her old habits. An armor made of prickly defense. "What do you want from me?"

He blinked. "Pardon?"

"What're you after?" She pulled her head out of his grasp. Or tried to, at any rate. It didn't seem to stop him from simply going back to touching her. It wasn't that she didn't like how it felt—the problem was the opposite. She liked it. And it was dangerous. "What do you want from me, really? If you win this contract of ours, what'll you ask for in exchange? I want to know."

"I've told you, haven't I?" His smile turned just a little sinister once more. "I want to experience Earth. I miss it dearly."

"But that's not all you want." She narrowed her eyes at him accusatorially. "This contract has a price. What is it?"

His smile widened, revealing his fangs. "Is it not painfully clear to you by now how badly I wish to make mad and wild love to you, to throw abandon to the wind, and give you pleasure unlike anything you have ever known? Or are modern women simply that dense these days?"

"Holy—" She slapped a hand over her eyes. "People don't just *say* shit like that!"

"Why not?" He took her wrist and pulled her hand away from her face. "What is so shameful in telling you how I wish to *ravish* you? To wind you in my coils and show you the heights of bliss?" He smirked. "If only simply because it seems to embarrass you so."

"Yeah, cuz—" She shoved him. "People don't—no! The answer is no."

He snorted. Actually snorted. "I don't believe you."

"Why I—" She wanted to punt him in the nuts. And suddenly his comment about having "balls on the outside" made sense. He didn't. This must be his true form. She growled and leaned back against his tail where it was still keeping her caged in. "Izael. No."

"Why not?"

"Like I said. You're too much."

He cackled.

"That's not what I meant!" She smacked his chest. But despite herself, she was smiling. Yeah, she walked into that one like an idiot. "Goddamn it." She ducked under the coil of his tail at her back and then hopped over another section of him. She was trying not to laugh. "Again, seriously, do you have to be so grabby?"

"It's a snake thing." He shrugged with a smile. And sure enough, she had to dodge the tip of his tail that tried to wind itself around her ankle. "And I like touching you."

"Clearly."

"Why is that so offensive to you?" He moved closer again. She kept backing away from him. But he was herding her toward that central tree, and if she wasn't careful, she'd have no escape path before long. "And why do you curse a god in whom you do not believe?"

"It's just part of the English language now." She hopped over a tree root in an attempt to keep him from catching her. But the more she dodged, the more amused he seemed to become. "This isn't a game."

"Isn't it?" He laughed. "I am having very much fun."

"Well, knock it off."

"Hmm." He tapped his chin with a sharp-nailed fingertip as if considering it for a moment. "No."

And then she learned how fast a snake monster like him could move. He dashed out at her, and before she could even get out a squeak, he caught her. She felt a thick coil of his tail wrap around her midsection, pinning her arms to her sides. Her feet were left dangling uselessly in the air. When she tried to kick, another coil wrapped around her calves, keeping her still.

"Let me—"

He pressed a finger to her lips. "Shush." The coil around her tightened, just a little, reminding her how very little power she truly had in this situation.

She did the smart thing for once.

She shut up.

He smiled and leaned in, that forked tongue of his flicking out and tickling her cheek. "You want to know what I want from you, songbird? You want to know what my endgame with you *truly* is? Very well…I'll tell you. But you must understand how much of a disadvantage this is for me. So, in exchange, I want another kiss. A proper one."

She stared at him, her eyes wide. When he waited for her answer, she stammered for a moment. "I—just—just one?"

"Just one." He brushed his knuckles over the line of her jaw. "You will find I am an equitable and generous businessman." His glowing eyes focused on her lips. "Especially for you."

His other hand slid around her waist, just below the coil of the tail that was keeping her trapped there. His fingers wandered under her shirt to rest against the bare skin of her lower back. Damn it if it didn't send a thrill through her.

This was wrong. All of this was wrong.

I'm so fucking stupid. Swallowing the rock in her throat, she finally muttered her answer. "Fine."

He grinned and wasted no time before claiming her lips. Dragging her closer, her feet touched the ground again as his tail released her, only to wrap around them both, pinning her to his chest.

She pressed her hands against him, trying to get some kind of purchase—trying to hold on for dear life as he devoured her like a starving man. It was possessive. It was wild. It was needy and demanding. He tilted his head to deepen the embrace, his one arm now banding her close to him with his other threading through her hair.

Gods above. Gods below. Whoever was listening—it was *incredible.* And it had no right to be. It lit a dangerous fire in her. She shouldn't be doing this. She certainly shouldn't be wanting it.

When she moaned against his lips, he snarled, primal and low. The fingers in her hair tightened into a fist and yanked her head back, the sting in her scalp making her gasp against him.

He took the opportunity to slip his tongue into her mouth, forked and strange, exploring and conquering. It was bizarre. It was terrifying. And it was the most amazing kiss she had ever experienced in her life. It coiled around her own tongue, too long and agile to be human.

When her head was spinning from lack of air, she smacked his chest. He relented, breaking the embrace. She was panting, her chest heaving, and everything tasted and smelled of him. Of the woods after a rain. Of spice and something crisp.

"If you liked that, imagine what else I can do with my tongue." It flicked out of his mouth again to tickle her cheek.

All she could manage was an exasperated noise that made him chuckle. She shut her eyes and leaned her forehead against his chest, needing anything—even the source of her confusion—to support her. "Damn it, Izael."

"People say that to me a lot. I've never quite understood why. But it's fine." He stroked his hand soothingly over her hair. "We'll take it slow, pretty girl. I can be patient when I'm sure I'm going to win…and I'm positive in this case."

She wished she could argue with him. But if he kept kissing her like that? It probably was a losing battle on her side. For better or worse.

"Now. For my side of the bargain?" He kept petting her hair. "Here is your answer. I wish to enjoy Earth for as long as I can—to see the sights. To explore. To spend my days with you at my side, showing me the world that I have missed so very much."

He slid his hand to her chin to gently cup it and tilt her head to look at him. "And when that game must end, and I am driven back home to Tir n'Aill? I will do it with you at my side…"

Fear twisted in her stomach. "What?"

He smiled. Sadistic and sweet in the same moment. "Do you not understand? I intend to keep you. You will belong to me." He smiled. "I will take your soul."

Alex did the only thing she could think of.

She punched him in the nose.

CHAPTER NINE

Alex pried herself out of the coils of Izael's tail as he rubbed his nose with a pathetic *"owwww-uh."* The whine would have been adorable if he hadn't just told her what his endgame was.

"No. No, absolutely not. No." She finally managed to step out of his coils and put some distance between them. "I want out of this deal. Right now."

"But why?" He blinked those glowing teal eyes, honestly looking confused. "What is so upsetting to you?"

She laughed in disbelief. "Are you kidding me? I'm not going to be your pet. There's no way I would sign up for that. You can't have my soul!"

"And why not?" He planted his hands on his hips. "I would pamper you—lay the whole of two worlds at your feet. You would live the life of a queen. I would care for your every need, your every want. And in return, all I would ask would be your companionship."

"And slavery."

He shrugged. "Do cats resent their owners for the food, shelter, love, and comfort that they receive? I think not."

"I'm not a fucking cat, Izael." She tugged her tank top down. At some point, he had pulled it up to expose her stomach.

"You're right. You aren't." He wrinkled his nose. "Fucking a cat is just wrong on every level."

It was nice to know that even Unseelie fae had standards. "I'm not going to be your pet. No. I refuse."

He turned his gaze up to the starry sky and sighed as though he were begging some invisible force for patience. The idea that she was being at all unreasonable made her want to throw things at him. He shook his head. "You will come to see reason in time. That is why we are playing this slowly, my dear violent songbird." He rubbed his nose again, checking it for blood. "I do wish you would stop punching me in the face."

"Stop deserving it and I'll stop doing it."

"No real chance of that happening." He snickered, and shifted closer to her. "Come here, Alex. I will not hurt you."

She staggered back to keep more distance between them. "I don't believe you."

He extended a hand to her, his palm up, those pointed black nails looking as vicious as ever. But his expression was soft, almost pleading. "You will always be safe with me."

She glowered. "We have very different definitions of safe."

"It is very rare that I take a human to keep." He let out a small breath. "For two reasons. One, it seems to make you all so very miserable, though I cannot seem to understand why. And two, so very few of you ever pique my interest. I am not a man who takes pets lightly."

"If you're trying to flatter me…"

"I am, actually." He chuckled. "I see it's not working. Give me time to convince you, songbird. Besides—*when* you lose this game of ours, you will not have a choice in the matter. You will make a wish, and in return, you will belong to me."

THE UNSEELIE DUKE

Ah. There it was. If she lost and had a desire by the end of the seven days, he'd grant it—in exchange for her belonging to him. Therefore, she had a very good reason not to lose. "And what if my wish is not to belong to you?"

He opened his mouth and paused, before shutting it again and fixing his lips into a frown. "Well, that's not very sporting of you." He huffed. "I was trying to be nice and calming your fears, and now you're using it against me?"

"Yes. I am." She took another step back. She wanted to run for her life. But where would she go? She was in a strange world filled with stranger monsters. She'd make it—what had he said?—four seconds, tops. "Because I know you don't play fair, either."

"I play perfectly fair!" He folded his arms across his chest, looking offended. "I have not once lied to you."

"Right." And another step back.

"And for another matter, do you *really* wish not to belong to me? Or am I simply ruffling your human sensibilities?" He wiggled his fingers at her with the last two words.

"I wish not to belong to you."

He gestured, and that glass-looking magical orb appeared in his hand. With a fiendish grin. "Want to make a wager that you're lying?"

"What?" She furrowed her brow.

"Simple. I will ask again, and we will use this magic to see if you are lying or uncertain. If you are—then we shall skip to the end. You will be my pet, and I will get to keep you until age and death take you. If you are telling the truth, and this truly *is* your wish—then you win, and I shall shower you with treasures and you shall never want for money again." The smile on his face was like the Cheshire cat—wide, pointed, and deeply unsettling.

And it had her questioning herself.

75

What if she was lying? She didn't think she was. Being a pet to a fae was a terrible thing. She didn't want that. Right?

Right?

"I…"

He laughed, low and insidious. "Not so certain of yourself now, are you? Are you picturing yourself, tangled in my coils, gasping my name as I take you? As I make you *mine?*"

"Knock it off."

"I think you are."

Well, she was *now*. "I don't want to belong to you."

"But do you *wish* it?" Perching the glass orb atop his pointer and middle fingers and his thumb like a tripod, he refused to give it up. "Prove it. I dare you. Let us see if you are attempting to convince both of us."

Alex suddenly discovered something about herself that she wasn't quite certain she had known before.

She really fucking hated losing.

Snarling in frustration, she turned on her heel and stormed away across the checkered marble floor. "Fuck you."

He howled in laughter, celebrating his victory. "Oooh, poor, sweet witch. Don't be frustrated with me. Don't you see how you win, no matter the outcome of this game of ours?"

"Do tell." She turned her back on him, needing to get some space. She put her head in her hands and tried to think everything through.

"Well, it's quite simple. *Either* you win, and I shower you with gifts for the rest of time—or you lose, I shower you with gifts, and you live a life of love and comfort as my prized pet." He sounded so sincere. He honestly believed what he was saying was true. That it wasn't slavery. It was somehow a benefit.

"I'm not a house cat."

"You're better than one." His words were close to her

THE UNSEELIE DUKE

ear, and she jolted. Whirling, he was only inches away. Damn him, he could move fast and silent like a—well, like a snake. That glowing, snakelike, turquoise gaze of his wandered down her body, slowly and pointedly, taking in the view. His voice was a low, sinful growl. "Far better than one."

His obvious hunger sparked something in her she wanted to kill with a flamethrower. "I—"

The heat from his gaze vanished without warning. She watched as his tattoos shifted, swirling over his body into a new position. The Celtic-knot snakes suddenly looked very angry. And now, so did he.

He hissed, baring his fangs, and vanished into thin air in a swirl of black smoke.

She jumped at the sudden disappearance "What the—"

Someone screamed from the woods to her left. Turning, she watched as Izael emerged, his tail coiled tightly around the waist of a man, effortlessly holding him aloft. "Hello, interloper."

The stranger was kicking his legs in a futile attempt to escape. His hair was a dark green, and his skin was a paler shade but not by much. For a moment, it struck her that the guy resembled the Jolly Green Giant, at least in coloration. But this fae was built like a stick—long, gangly limbs with little to no muscle on them.

The man was stammering. "Release me, Duke—you cannot—this is—"

"You are spying on me. You snuck into my home, unannounced. By right, your life is forfeit." Izael grinned sadistically. "And you know it, little interloper."

"No! I—Anfar—"

"I know who you serve." Izael cracked his neck from one side to the other. "And should he come looking, he knows the law you broke well enough indeed."

The man wailed. "No, please! Duke, mercy—forgive me, I was only doing as I was told!"

"And I am only doing what is my right." Izael laughed once more.

Alex only looked on with a sort of detached sense of horror at what was happening. Somebody named Anfar had sent a spy, that spy had been captured, and now Izael was… what? Going to kill him? Snap his neck, maybe? Stab him?

If only it were that mundane.

Her eyes went wide, her breath stopping in her chest, as she suddenly discovered what the teal line that bisected his chest was for. And how precisely he went about eating people.

His torso opened. The line that ran from the underside of his chin down to the scales at his waist simply…parted. Opened like a Venus flytrap, revealing rows and rows of jagged, pointed teeth like a shark or a leech. The inside of his body was a dark teal, but squishy like flesh. The rest of what had been Izael's torso simply folded back and out of the way.

The man screamed.

Alex couldn't say that she blamed him.

And with that?

Izael swallowed him whole. Head-first. The rows of teeth undulated as they forced the man deeper, his screams now muffled. There was a strange, wet, squelching sound as Izael grabbed the man's legs and began stuffing him farther down his…throat.

Izael wasn't a man with the legs of a snake.

He was a snake with the head of a man's torso.

It took a moment that felt like eternity as Izael swallowed the man whole. It felt like something from a nightmare as Izael's body simply…closed back up, like someone zipping up a hoodie. He ran a thumb over his bottom lip as if wiping away a bit of barbeque sauce from their dinner.

THE UNSEELIE DUKE

He blinked. Made a face. And then with a *"kak"* like the sound a cat makes when it hacks something up, he coughed something into his palm. "Ugh. I do hate how those things taste. Oh, look!" He peered down at whatever he had coughed up. Holding it aloft, it was a ring. "Would you like to sell this one? I'll give it to you, free of charge. You'll be helping me hide the evidence, and you can—Alex?" He blinked. "What's wrong?"

She was standing there, numb, staring at him. She had started to breathe again, but she was pretty sure that was out of desperation and not because she wouldn't still be entirely unmoving if she had a choice.

He slowly slid closer to her, as if he were worried she were about to burst into flames. There wasn't even a bump where the man should be. It was as if the spy had simply vanished. "I'll wash it off before you sell it, if that's what you're concerned about."

She held up a finger, asking him to pause. Just a moment. That was all she needed. Just a second.

He blinked but stayed unmoving.

Turning around, she walked away from him. Slowly. She wasn't in a rush. She had nowhere to go. She just needed some space.

Alex took a deep breath.

Held it.

And promptly fainted.

———

Izael watched, utterly confounded, as Alex collapsed in a heap on the marble tile. Why had she fainted? He frowned. Really, she could not possibly have been surprised at what she had seen. She knew he was a snake; didn't she understand how that worked?

How was he supposed to eat people, otherwise? With a knife and fork?

Silly humans.

I suppose I'm not getting laid tonight, then, am I? Gliding over to her, he reached down and scooped her up in his arms. Maybe he should have warned her. But it wasn't like he had a choice. The spy needed to be dealt with, and it was such a shame to waste a good set of bones.

Moving up the tree to his hanging boat that was his bed, he placed her down on the pillows and decided she looked utterly perfect lying amongst them. She belonged there, in his bed. There was no question about it. Her amethyst hair blended with the jewel tones of his pillows.

He curled around her, over her, under her, before taking her into his arms and holding her close.

She was so warm—so wonderfully, perfectly warm. He was a snake and had little heat of his own, to be fair. It didn't take much to impress him. He pulled a blanket over them both, not wanting her to catch a chill in the evening air.

He had wanted to show her the beauty of Tir n'Aill. But he supposed a little horror was good enough. It was not all Tir n'Aill had to offer, but it certainly was not inaccurate. He was not the only monster that lurked in the darkness, after all.

He kissed her cheek, knowing how she would fuss about it, if she could argue. Hugging her to him like a child's teddy bear, he smiled. "You'll see how wonderful I can be in time, songbird. You'll see that you belong with me. I can be very persuasive." He kissed her cheek again.

Yawning, tired after such a wonderful snack, he shut his eyes and nuzzled into her hair. She smelled so wonderful. "Very persuasive indeed."

CHAPTER TEN

Alex woke up feeling as though she had taken a nap underneath her favorite weighted blanket. She was cozy, she was warm, and she felt snug and *safe.*

It was approximately twenty seconds before she remembered what had happened. And that she wasn't home, wasn't underneath her blanket, and definitely wasn't safe.

Her eyes shot open.

For a moment, she couldn't figure out what she was looking at. Blinking, lifting a hand to wipe at her eyes, she tried to focus. It was pillows. A ton of them, in every single color, pattern, fabric, and style imaginable. And over it was a thick fur pelt that had been turned into a blanket. That was what was over her. But that wasn't the only thing.

She was also under coil after coil of a thick, gigantic snake. Izael. One of his arms was thrown over her waist, and she could feel the muscle of his other arm beneath her pillow. He was cuddling her, big-spoon style.

Whatever they were in was swaying slightly. She turned her head—it was that boat that had been hanging from the limbs of the tree. It must be his bed. There was a weight against her back, and she realized it was Izael's forehead, pressed against the back of her neck. She shifted, trying to worm her way out from under him.

Murmuring, he tightened his grasp and pulled her back to him. "No moving. Warm."

Sighing, she shut her eyes for a moment, praying for patience from whomever was listening. "Izael, let me up."

"No. Warm." He hugged her, nuzzling his head into her hair. His words were still slurred, and he was clearly half asleep. "Cold blooded."

She rolled onto her back. He seemed fine with that, instead resting his head on her shoulder. His coils of tail shifted, some worming under the blanket and some on top. It occurred to her that if he wanted to kill her, he could. Easily. Very easily. She supposed he always could have.

He had eaten a man.

Whole.

She decided to remind him of that. "You ate that man."

One faintly glowing turquoise eye opened to peer at her. Grumbling, he shifted until he was over her, supporting his weight on his hands on either side of her shoulders. She didn't like him caging her in—but realistically, she was no more trapped now than she was a second ago.

He yawned, almost comically so, revealing his sharp teeth. "When will you mortals understand?"

"Understand what?"

"That humans and fae may resemble each other, from time to time, to some degree." His forked tongue flicked out his mouth, accentuating his comment. "But we are *not* the same. Your values are not ours. And they never will be."

That was very true. She had to give him that. She didn't know anything when it came to the fae—what they did, how they viewed murder. How they viewed *eating people whole*.

"Let me guess, what you just did wasn't even scratching the surface of what the fae do to each other?"

"Bingo." He lifted a hand to poke her on the nose with a pointed claw. "Especially the Unseelie. Do you want to see how we make goblins?" His grin was excited in the way that made her answer very obvious.

"No. I don't think I do."

He pouted. "You're no fun. I—" He paused. His tongue flicked in the air again, clearly smelling something. His expression went to one of…well, there was no other word for it. *Fear.*

His tattoos swirled and changed to a new pattern. He looked down at her with an intensity in those slitted eyes that was both urgent and vaguely panicky. He covered her mouth with his hand before lifting it and putting a finger to his lips. The message was obvious. Be silent, or else.

She nodded.

Straightening, he yawned again, stretching his arms over his head with another loud yawn, before turning and draping his arms over the side of the boat. "Hello, Uncle Anfar! How lovely to see you."

Another fae?

And one Izael was frightened of.

Yeah, she was going to lie there and not goddamn move or make a noise. She wished she could see through the slats of the boat, but it was in good condition and had no cracks.

"You caught me in the middle of a nap. What can I help you with?"

"Where is Ginzer?" Whoever it was, this "Anfar," their voice was deep and sullen. It was obvious he wasn't amused by Izael's antics and friendly demeanor.

"Oh, your spy? Dead, of course. As is my right for someone lurking about my home." He hummed. "I coughed up his ring, if you want it."

"No." Anfar let out a long sigh. One of very clear centuries of annoyance. "You are up to something, Duke of Bones. I *know* you are. And I will find a way to prove it."

"I am up to nothing that is not sanctioned by our laws or our treaties, Uncle Anfar." Izael shrugged. "So even if you could, I'm hardly in the wrong. You know me—I always follow agreements to the letter."

There was a pause.

Izael huffed. "Well, goodbye to you, too, then." He mumbled something that was probably impolite and pushed away from the railing. Smiling down at her, he shifted his tail to coil under himself a bit more. "Look at you! Having a sense of self-preservation."

"Who was that?" She sat up, a little nervously, before peering over the edge of the boat.

"That was Anfar, the second in command to King Valroy. A sneaky bastard who wants to make sure I stay here, trapped in Tir n'Aill, *bored out of my fucking skull.* I swear, he hates me."

"Do you deserve it?"

"Absolutely." Izael cackled. He smoothed a hand over his unruly hair, doing a little something to calm it down but not much. "He's convinced I'm doing some kind of trickery to make a deal with a human so I can go galivanting around Earth. He's absolutely right, of course, but I'm not going to tell him that."

"Are you not supposed to be doing this?" She pulled her legs out from one of the thick coils of his body. The end of his tail came around a second later and wound around her ankle. She tried to shake her foot out from it, but he just cinched tighter. She gave up trying.

"Oh, it's not breaking the treaty. Anfar is just overbearing. Besides, to make sure, I even have permission from King Valroy to pursue you. But—"

"Wait, wait, *what?*"

"I...mean...I talked to him and..." He blinked. "What's wrong? I told you, you belong to me, and—"

"Izael." She glared at him. "I do not belong to you."

With a dramatic sigh, he stared up at the sky. "Fine! You don't belong to me *yet.* Once six more days and six more nights pass, and you tell me your wish, you *will.*"

And her soul would belong to a *man-eating monster.* She needed a plan to get out of this mess. She needed to think of something clever. Something so clever, a probably-centuries-old fae duke wouldn't see it coming.

Which had about the same chance of happening as a snowball taking over as King of Hell. "I need a drink." She sighed.

"I can help with that!" With no other warning, he darted forward and scooped her up like a bride about to be carried over the threshold.

"Whoa! Hey!" She smacked his chest. "Put me down!"

"Do you want to climb down? I think not. I could throw you overboard, but you'd complain about all your broken bones. Sit still, songbird." He chuckled. "I'm merely being practical. For once."

Resisting the urge to punch him in the face, she folded her arms over her chest and settled for glowering at him.

"At least you cannot kick me in the sack in this form." He smiled, completely ignoring her annoyance as he slithered out of the boat that was his bed, easily drifting lazily down the tree until they were on the ground. "And I doubt you would know where to aim for my cocks, either."

He put her down.

"I'm pretty sure I know enough about the anatomy of snakes to know where your—" She hitched on what he had just said. "Hold on. Hold on. Back up." Plural. He had used *plural.* "Do snakes..."

The shit-eating grin on his face was one for the ages. Holding up two fingers, he wiggled them back and forth.

"Oh, my God, no." She walked away from him, putting her hands over her face. "You have *got* to be kidding me."

He bellowed in laughter again. "What? First of all, don't knock it 'til you've tried it. Second of all, if it *really* bothers you…I'm sure we can come up with a workaround."

"No. Nope. I'm good."

"Sooooo…you're saying you *do* want to try taking both at the same—"

"Oh, my God, stop!" She laughed, unable to handle his constant goading. It was clear he was teasing her. "You're impossible."

"I've been told that." He moved in front of her. Damn it if he wasn't graceful as sin, and hypnotic to watch. "I take it as a compliment."

"You're not supposed to."

"I know." He smiled. There was a softness in those glowing turquoise eyes. As if he was really enjoying his time with her.

She should be running away in terror. She should be crying uncontrollably, cowering in a corner, whimpering because she was in the presence—and the focus of—a literal man-eating monster.

But in the weirdest way, she trusted him not to hurt her. He needed her to explore Earth, for one. And two, she honestly didn't believe that was his goal. Whether or not he was a bit of a sadist was to be determined—she leaned into assuming he was—but he hadn't actually hurt her or harmed her in any way.

He just wants my soul, that's all.

He just wants to keep me like a goddamn pet.

Would that honestly be so bad when it came down to things? To be totally taken care of?

No, don't even consider it, you fucking idiot.

Izael snapped his fingers, thankfully jarring her out of her thoughts. "Booze!" She watched, fascinated, as he glided across the marble tile toward what looked like an antique wardrobe. He opened it, and it was filled with glassware and bottles of every kind. "What's your poison, darling?"

Darling.

She shook her head. "Whiskey."

"Nice choice. Spicy, smoky, hits like a brick—kind of like you." He flashed her a smile over his shoulder.

She rolled her eyes at the clear attempt at a pickup line but decided it didn't warrant a snarky retort. Instead, she found herself fascinated by one of his bookshelves. It was filled with…well, everything. All kinds of nonsense. Added to his collections, scattered around, were all the bits and pieces he bought from the Museum of Science.

He really was a spooky, snaky, man-eating, monstrous Ariel.

It had no business being as endearing as it was.

Don't trust him.

Don't ever trust him.

"What would you like to see first? The underground enchanted waterfall, the bleeding trees of Nor, the chasm of endless screams?" He approached, holding a glass of whiskey out to her.

She took it. "Uh…are those places real?"

"Well, the first two are." He chuckled. "I made up the last one."

"What a relief." She took a sip of the alcohol. It burned. Good. She needed that. "How about the waterfall? That sounds the least horrifying."

"That's because you haven't seen it yet." He grinned with that vicious twinge that he favored.

"Do you have anywhere…not about murder, or screaming, or corpses, that we can go see?"

He thought about it for a second. "Sure, but those are all the boring places."

"How about tonight we start boring, and tomorrow we move on to the not-boring places?" She shook her head. "I don't think I can handle much more than that tonight."

"Sex is out, then?" He laughed as she glared at him. "I'm joking, sheesh." He paused. "So…sex is—"

"Izael." But she couldn't help it. She smiled. Damn it.

And he grinned in triumph. "Finish your drink, songbird. And I shall take us somewhere beautiful."

She sipped her drink and turned back to his collection, pretending to be curious about all the random antique-store-worthy knickknacks and other nonsense he had. But it was mostly to give herself a chance to think. And to process the fact that she was looking forward to wherever he was planning on taking her. If only just a little.

Deep down, she knew he was like a constrictor. Once she gave him an inch, it wasn't an inch she'd ever get back.

And she had already given him far, far too much.

Yet she knew he wouldn't be happy until he had it all.

CHAPTER ELEVEN

Izael was whistling to himself as he walked up to his large wardrobe where he kept his collection of clothes. He shifted back to human form, a little disappointed that Alex wasn't watching, given his nakedness.

He opted for a dark teal pinstripe suit and matching vest, with a white undershirt and a black tie. Slicking back his hair, he grinned at his reflection in the mirror on the door of his wardrobe. Slipping on a pair of socks and shoes, he was humming some high-energy swing piece as he danced back up to his wonderful new pet human.

Even if she was struggling with that realization. He understood why she took umbrage with the idea. Humans were so bullheadedly independent creatures, even if they very *clearly* couldn't handle themselves when they were free. They always resorted to destroying everything around them. At least the fae were mostly concerned with bickering and warring between two factions—they had to do *something* to pass the time, after all—but not seemingly dead set upon ruining everything else while they were at it.

Humans. Wonderful, fascinating, and entertaining on their own. *Unflinchingly* stupid in large numbers.

Alex was poring over the contents of one of his bookcases, her brow furrowed in that adorable way she was prone to doing when she was trying to work out a dilemma. He had seen it plenty of times before, and he figured he was going to see it plenty of times in the future. In their very long, very inevitable future.

He took her by the hand and pulled her to him without warning. She squeaked and went rigid, but he wasn't having it. He began to dance with her, laughing at how locked up she was. "Relax! I'm not going to eat you."

"Now that I know that's a very real possibility, sorry if I'm a little *jumpy* about it." She glared at him with those wonderful blue eyes of hers.

"Pah. Trust me, songbird—there are plenty of things I want to do to you. Swallowing you whole is not one of them." He grinned, knowing how wolfish he looked. It was a point of pride. He spun her, finding himself more entertained than not by her begrudging sigh as she allowed herself to be thrown about.

"Is dancing still a thing on Earth?"

"Yeah. Swing is out of fashion, but people still do it."

"We should go to a club! That would be so very much fun." He tugged her close and banded his arm around her lower back. "Don't you think so?"

"S—sure." She leaned away from him to try to put some distance between them. "Maybe you'll find a new shiny object to play with that isn't me."

"Doubtful." He let his gaze fall to her full lips. They did taste so wonderful. "Once I decide I want something, there's no stopping me."

"Great." She sounded less than enthusiastic.

That was fine. He was winning her over. She smiled and

laughed at his antics and moaned at his kisses just enough to tell him all he needed to know. "I thought of the perfect place to take you. But we'll need to fashion you a glamor first. Can't have you wandering about all *mortal* and all—someone is likely to see and get covetous of my prize."

"Or tell Anfar."

"Or tell Anfar." He smiled. She was a quick one, his new songbird. It made her all the more fun to play with. A game of chess versus an easy opponent provided little challenge, if some semblance of victory. No, he preferred a game of wits with a more suitable match.

"You're going to make me look like a fae?"

"Indeed." He let go of her and caught a few strands of her amethyst hair in his fingers. "Pardon me." He pulled them free, winding the strands around his finger.

"Is this how a glamor is made?"

"It's how *I* make a glamor. Magic isn't about rituals, songbird. They are about will. Two painters might seem similar at first blush but have entirely different methodology. Yet they both create art." He blew on the strands, watching as they shimmered and glowed a brighter shade of magenta. They hardened into something not unlike glass or spun sugar. Palming the strands in his other hand, he clenched his fist and broke them into dust. "Shut your eyes."

She did as she was told.

He blew the dust from his palm onto her like the dust was so much glitter.

Terrible stuff, *glitter*.

The use of it should be classified as a war crime.

Neither here nor there.

He commanded the glamor to change her. He watched as her skin grew pale, the tattoos on her arm disappearing. Before his eyes, her hair turned so dark purple it was almost black, her skin tinged only just barely with a purplish tone.

When she blinked open her eyes, they were a wonderful cyan.

"Did it work?"

He grunted. By the Morrigan, she was *beautiful.* He needed her. Needed to taste her. Needed to bed her, to *fuck* her, to—

He reached out and grasped her by the back of the neck and yanked her forward, dragging her abruptly into a kiss that was violent in his sudden and wild need. She tasted like the midnight dew on fresh grass, of moonlight and woodsmoke, of warm spices and coffee. Just a bit like herself, but somehow *more.*

Invading her mouth with his tongue, he wound it around hers, hungering for more. Pulling her hips to his with his other hand, he desperately sought the pressure—the friction.

She moaned. Furtive. But it was there. She clung to his lapel, holding on for dear life. How he wanted to claim her. To *take* her.

Everything in him screamed that she belonged to him. That this was the natural law of things. *She is mine. She is mine!*

When she slapped her palm to his chest, he ignored her. When she whacked him again, harder, he finally relented and allowed her to breathe. She gasped in air, her chest heaving, those wonderful, plush breasts of hers squished up against him.

"Was—that part of the magic?" She was still reeling.

He paused. "If I said yes, do I—"

"Izael."

He sighed. "No. I just…couldn't help myself. You are like moonlight given flesh." He leaned in for another kiss. When she turned away, he ran his tongue up the tendon on the side of her throat. "Let me have you. Even just a little."

THE UNSEELIE DUKE

"I don't think there's such a thing as 'just a little' with you."

"How quickly she learns." He growled low, and playfully scraped at her skin with his teeth. She shivered. "I know you want me. I know you want to see what I can do to you—in human form or my true self. And I so very desperately wish to show you."

"What do I get in exchange?"

He pulled back to arch his eyebrow at her. "Besides a night of bliss unlike any you have ever known?"

Her pale whitish-purple cheeks went just a little redder. "Yeah, besides that."

"Hm." He smiled, a little wryly. "You are saying you can be bought. Is my little darling songbird for rent?"

"That's not—" She sighed. "I didn't mean it like that."

"Oh, no, no. I am not judging. Merely surprised at your honesty. Everyone has a price for everything in this world. No one is above a good deal." He flicked his forked tongue over her cheek, loving how she squirmed in uncertainty and anticipation. "Give me some time to come up with an… amicable arrangement."

"I seriously wasn't—" She closed her eyes for a moment and seemingly counted back from ten. "I was joking."

"No, you weren't. But if you'd like to pretend you were, that's fine." He let her go, but not before bringing her hand to his lips and pressing a very slow, sensual kiss to her knuckles.

"What if we break off this deal—this wish wager? We could remain friends with benefits—"

"Is that what they're calling it now?"

"Kinda. Used to. Maybe still do. I don't know—anyway." She was getting flustered. And oh, she was adorable when she was flustered. "We break this deal off. You and I can…I don't know, find our own way forward, without a contract."

"Sadly, I will have to refuse. For two reasons—one, without a contract, I am not allowed on Earth. And two… what's the phrase? Why buy the cow when you can get the milk for free? Why would I—" He blinked. "Why're you glaring at me like that?"

"I am not a goddamn cow."

"I—oh. Yes. Well. No. You aren't. I wasn't—come back!"

Alex had turned on her heel and stormed away from him.

"I wasn't calling you a cow! It's a turn of phrase." He jumped in front of her, cutting her off. She reeled up short before smacking into him. "My point is—when I win this wager of ours, I still get to have you." He grinned. "But it was a decent ploy."

Alex ran a hand over her fae-ish face. She looked similar to her un-glamoured self, save for slightly sharper features, pointed ears, and the coloration. He wanted to throw her over his shoulder, carry her up to his bed, and show her that she could, in fact, fit all of him.

And because she likely wouldn't believe it after the first time, he would prove it to her about a dozen more times.

Just to make sure.

You know.

To get the point across.

With a huff, she turned again and walked up to his dresser, standing in front of his full-length mirror. "Whoa…" She leaned in, looking closer at herself.

"Do you like?" He followed her, putting his hands on her shoulders. He couldn't help himself. He needed to touch her. And to his immense satisfaction, she didn't pull away. Or punch him. Or slap him. Or knee him in the crotch. Or any other myriad of less fun reactions.

"It's…weird." She touched her pointed ear. "Oh, that's fucked up—I can feel that."

"It is not merely an illusion. You are this shape, more or

THE UNSEELIE DUKE

less—if you were to take the form of a ghost, I would not recommend attempting to pass through walls, but…you get the idea." He smiled. He loved watching her discover something new. Her expression lit up in a way that was so very different from her normal skepticism or annoyance.

Which was likely just because he was around.

That happened to him a lot.

"Cool." She smiled. She looked pleased—even just a little. It warmed his heart in a surprising way. Oh, goodness. Was he already falling for his songbird?

He supposed he might be.

How wonderful!

He kissed the back of her head, loving the scent of her hair. "Shall we? I have just the place to show you. Then, I shall have a feast prepared for us, and we shall revisit the topic of my ravishing you until the dawn."

She elbowed him hard in the stomach.

With a groan, he doubled over. Mostly to make her feel good about herself, not truly because it hurt that badly. But he would count it as progress that it wasn't his more sensitive area that she had targeted.

And that she was smiling.

That indeed was progress.

"Where are we going?"

Straightening, he tugged on the bottom of his suitcoat to straighten it, muttering about wrinkles. "Because of your love of the morbid and strange, I thought perhaps Monument Forest."

"You say that like I know what you're talking about. Do the fae bury their dead?"

"Oh, absolutely not. We return to the world around us." He waved his hand dismissively. "Burning the dead or burying them is just…so strange. But that also means that there is little to mark our passing. We, the Unseelie, create monuments for those who have passed. The Seelie prefer trees and other living displays." He offered her his elbow.

"Huh." She put her hand in the crook of his arm without complaint. He headed off toward a doorway that was only a jamb, attached to two ruined walls with no ceiling. But as he approached, the world on the other side of it changed, revealing a gateway to somewhere new.

Alex pulled in a breath, her cyan eyes going wide.

"Magic is all around you, my dear." He placed his other hand atop hers. "I cannot wait to show you more of it."

"It's…just going to take some getting used to. You're sure this is okay to do? Just wander around?"

He chuckled. "You are safe with me."

"Safe. With a man-eating Unseelie snake fae who is extremely horny and probably a little insane. Sure. Safe."

His chuckle turned into a laugh as he stepped through the gateway. "Oh, my dear, sweet, wonderful Alex. I'm more than just a little insane. You don't know the half of it."

"Fuck me," she groaned.

"That is, in fact, my plan." He grinned like the cat who ate the canary. "But *somebody* keeps fussing about it."

"Are you always this infuriating?"

"Yes." He straightened his shoulders. "It's a point of pride."

"I think I'm starting to side with Anfar."

"Bah. You would hate being trapped with him. Brooding. Grumpy. Altogether far too serious. No, I think you like me more than you are trying to let on. But I understand the game you're trying to play."

"Game?" She arched an eyebrow at him.

"Hard to get, of course."

"God, I hate you." She sighed. "I'm not playing hard to get, I'm trying to get out of this with my soul."

"Overrated things. You don't really need it."

"Izael."

"Yes, yes. One thing at a time." He loved their banter, however. It was so entertaining! She had so much more life to her than his usual companions. Letting out a contented breath, he smiled up at the stars and the moon overhead. It was beautiful, lighting the trees around them and the path in a gentle glow.

Yes, he was going to fall for his songbird.

If he had not already.

"Ah! Here we are." Monument Forest was surrounded by a thick, almost impenetrable wall of trees of every species imaginable, their limbs twisted together to create a barrier except by the main pathways.

But if she liked cemeteries?

She was going to love this.

He stepped inside with her and found himself watching her expression. When her jaw dropped open, her eyes going wide once more, he knew he had been right.

Amazement.

She wore it so beautifully.

And he decided, right then and there, that he would ensure that she wore it more frequently as well.

You will be mine, Alex. There is no way around it anymore.
I think I might already be a little bit yours.

CHAPTER TWELVE

Alex knew she was making a terrible mistake. It wasn't like the signs weren't all there. But she'd be lying to herself if she didn't admit she found herself attracted to Izael. All right, fine. More than a little attracted. There was something about him that was hypnotic. It was dangerous, and she knew it was going to get her killed. Or turned into some pet on a leash.

But damn it if his touch didn't *do* things to her in a way that she hadn't felt in a very, very long time. If ever, if she were honest. She had always found herself awkward in relationships—she was too rational, too level-headed. She approached friendships and dating like business transactions, and that tended to send people running the other way.

Izael seemed to take it as a challenge.

Then again, he also seemed insane. And was after her soul —or her life—or whatever it was that he was really gunning for.

Despite the horrifying fact that he *ate people alive,* and that Tir n'Aill seemed to be filled with monsters just like him, there was something…alluring about him and the world he came from. She couldn't help but gape at the scenery around her.

Tir n'Aill was, simply put—astonishing.

The trees around her swayed in the breeze, the leaves glistening in the moonlight that cast them in highlights of pale blue. The moon was high overhead and larger than it should be—and it took her a moment to realize it wasn't even the same *moon.* The markings of the craters were all different.

She was also trying to avoid thinking about the sensation that she was being watched. There was a reason Izael had put her under a glamor—and it wasn't just because he apparently thought she was hot as a fae.

Which, okay, fine, she did look good as an Unseelie fae. But that was very much beside the point.

He was bringing her to Monument Forest—which was apparently the closest thing they had to a graveyard. It was flattering, in a weird way, that he wanted to bring her somewhere she would appreciate like that. It meant he noticed her tattoos and figured out what she liked. It meant that, maybe in just the smallest way, he *cared.*

It was a dangerous thought. He was a snake—literally— and was trying to lure her into a false sense of security. That was all it was. But her debate about Izael's intentions was instantly washed away when they stepped through the gates to the forest. The trees had clearly been commanded to grow the way that they had, their branches twisting together in an ornate but chaotic pattern that formed the arch.

Taking in a sharp breath, she held it for a second. She had seen photos of royal gardens, but nothing she had seen came close to touching what was sprawling out before her. Twisting hedges formed spirals and arches as raised beds of flowers glistened with dew in the moonlight. Jutting up were statues like cemetery angels—made from every material she could imagine. Stone, wood, twisting vines, and more. Each figure was more outlandish than the last. And each one stood resplendent in a dramatic pose or in stoic silence.

"Wow…"

"Mm-hm." He took her hand. "Oh! Let's start here!" Abruptly, he took a hard left and yanked her along behind him like she was a balloon on a string. She almost tripped over her own feet and honestly didn't think he noticed.

He's a deranged toddler. A deranged, murderous toddler.

Izael came to a skidding halt in front of one of the large statues. "This is Bres!" He gestured up at the figure carved from what looked like obsidian. He had leathery wings at his back, and in his hands, he clutched two daggers. A crown sat atop his head. "The former Unseelie King."

She tilted her head to the side, studying the figure. The man represented was caught in an eternal sneer. He was kind of scrawny, to boot. "He looks like a shady jerk."

"That he was." Izael snickered. "And got himself murdered by Dagda, the Seelie King, and his half-brother. Seelie are always trying to control us—to tamp down on what is rightfully ours. Things didn't improve after Bres fell, and we were without a king for a thousand years." He sighed, and tugged her along, taking her down another path. At least this time, it was at a reasonable pace.

"What about King Valroy?"

"Oh, there's the fun part." Izael smiled and tucked his other hand into his pocket. For all intents and purposes, they could have been on a leisurely date night stroll.

He eats people. Remember that. Whole people.

"King Valroy is…complicated." He hummed. "Where to start? Well. After Dagda came Queen Titania and her mate Oberon."

"Like the play?"

"Like the play. Meanwhile, the Unseelie were without a

King or Queen at all. The Morrigan mated the fallen archangel Asmodeus and gave birth to Valroy. But he is far more than simply a half-demon welp of the goddess." He shrugged. "He is the void given flesh."

"Wait. What?" She blinked. "How's that work?"

"There are creatures much larger than even our gods. They are strange, ancient, *terrible* things that linger in the spaces between worlds. Apparently, this one got bored." He cackled, his sharp features splitting into a manic grin. "I can sympathize! He wished to know what it was like to be, well, 'real.' So, here he is. But the Morrigan put a stipulation upon him that he must be married before he could take his throne. She knew that on his own, unchecked, Valroy would burn Tir n'Aill and Earth to cinders."

"Why would he do that?"

"He can't help himself. It's in his nature." Izael's glowing turquoise eyes were brighter in the darkness, and she found herself getting trapped in them again, even at the expense of missing some of the beautiful scenery. "We fae are true to that which we are, above all else. It is only you humans who try to trick yourselves into thinking you are either more or less than what you really are."

"Wolves and sheep and all that jazz."

"Precisely." They rounded a corner down another wildly twisting path. The flowers around her were so dark purple that they were black, shining in the moonlight. They looked like lilies, and they were absolutely gorgeous. She reached out to touch one, but Izael caught her hand. "Ah-ah. Look, don't touch."

"Why not?"

"Deadly nightshade." He smiled. "And while in your world, it's merely poison…here? They take their title quite seriously. One touch, and you are dead."

"O—oh." She quickly pulled her hand back. "Don't touch *anything.* Got it."

He kissed her cheek. "I will be here to warn you."

That would have been flattering, if it wasn't for the fact that she knew he was protecting her out of a sense of ownership. She let out a breath. "Izael, I don't belong to you."

"Yet. But you will. Six days, and you will be mine."

"No, six days, and we end this contract of ours. Remember, I get three counteroffers to whatever your proposed exchange is for my wish." She poked him in the arm.

"What would be so very wrong about belonging to me? I really do fail to understand your problem with the situation. You're merely being stubborn and indignant because you are a mortal." He huffed.

"I am—" She shut her eyes and checked her anger. She wasn't going to get anywhere with him like this. "Whatever. I don't want to argue about it. What's the story, then, with Valroy being king?"

"Well, he found himself a lovely little mortal witch named Abigail."

Gee, that sounds familiar.

"And stole her away from Earth. He trapped her within his Maze of Shadows and tormented her until she loved him." He grinned. "Which set just an absolutely wonderful example for the rest of us, let me tell you."

She glared at him. "Great."

"Well, Abigail became the Seelie Queen. And just when we all believed there would be a bloody, terrible war between our people once again, they settled their differences and simply decided to…coexist. With fighting at the edges, mind you—we are always spying and scheming. But there was no genocide."

"What a relief." She shook her head. "So, what about the treaty?"

THE UNSEELIE DUKE

"When you humans pitched your world into true death and chaos—not once, but *twice*—Valroy could not resist the smell of blood. He helped sow chaos as best he could, wanting to encourage your lot to murder each other. Abigail could not abide such violence, and we went to war once more. Valroy could not murder his love, however—he could not strike her down. So, in the end, the Seelie were victorious." He grunted. "Cheaters."

"I don't think that's called cheating."

"But it is, though! Think about how cruel it was for Abigail to use the man's *one* weakness against him. Especially when she is that weakness." He grimaced in disgust. "Typical Seelie. No honor. No dignity."

"Then she made Valroy sign the treaty?"

"Precisely."

"What does it say, exactly? Besides the fact that fae need a contract to be on Earth." She passed several carefully grown rose bushes that had taken the form of a giant woman who had the lower body of a spider. *Could be worse. He could be a spider guy.* She shuddered at the thought.

"What does the treaty say? Honestly, I am not quite sure. I never really *cared.*" He let go of her hand, and his coat draped over her shoulders a moment later.

He thought she was shivering from the cold.

It smelled like him—like crisp cologne and the woods. She smiled up at him faintly and knew better than to thank him. That was something you never did with his kind. But it still struck her—what a weirdly thoughtful, psychopathic, murderous, fae snake lord.

He smiled back at her before turning another corner and down another row of statues. He named off the figures as they passed, saying a little bit about the ones he remembered, though there were quite a few that he couldn't recall who they had been in their lives. Honestly, it all began to sort of run together for her as well. His world was old, and therefore it had a lot of heroes and important figures. But there was one thing that connected all the Unseelie.

They were all beautiful.

But they were all *monstrous*. Dangerous horrors that somehow managed to cross the line into elegance. Creatures with all manner of extra limbs, missing eyes, or that looked like half of every kind of insect and animal that she could recognize, and several that she couldn't. Even those who looked fully human, if a bit elven, had a haunting nature about them that told her they were just as vicious as the others.

Until they reached one statue. It was of a woman, made entirely out of quartz. The moonlight made it seem to glow from within. She was absolutely the most beautiful woman Alex had ever seen, sitting atop a tree stump that was made from marble. Izael came to a stop in front of the figure. "This is Lady Astasha."

The way he said her name, she could tell she was in for a doozy of a story. "Oh?"

"She tried to save us all from the cruelty of King Valroy, by agreeing to marry him. Valroy wanted nothing to do with her. In the midst of all that nonsense, Anfar fooled himself into thinking he was in love with her." He shrugged dismissively. He looked just as sharp in a vest and a shirt as he did while wearing the suitcoat. "He was in love with the idea of her. Not the woman herself."

Frowning, she looked back up at the statue. "How sad."

"And even worse when Valroy executed her. Drove nails through her eyes and into her skull. Well, that's not quite true. That didn't kill her. He made Anfar finish her off."

"Note to self. Do *not* piss off Valroy." She made a face.

"That is a very good idea." He shook his head. "Even I

don't cross him. He's threatened to turn me into a pair of boots on more than one occasion."

A stranger's voice broke into the conversation. "Likely because you deserve it!"

Izael seemed to know who it was instantly, and he clearly wasn't happy about it. Snarling in rage, he turned and hissed at the voice.

"Oh, step off." The voice laughed. She turned to see one of the other statues—this one of a man carved out of granite, feathery wings spread wide. He truly resembled a cemetery angel. Draped on the stone figure's shoulders was a young man who looked skinny, without looking frail. He was kicking a foot idly back and forth where it dangled. "I'm not here for you, nope-rope. I'm here to talk to the girl."

"No—" Izael was fuming. He took a step in front of her, his hands balled into fists. "Begone, you half-breed bastard. She is *mine.*"

"Doesn't seem like she agrees with that yet." The man twisted around on the statue and was sitting with one leg on either side of the figure's head. He folded his arms atop it and rested his chin there, completely unconcerned with Izael's anger. He had bright, shining, silver hair and matching silver eyes. He was pale as a ghost but had a wild and mischievous grin.

She furrowed her brow at the man. *Apparently fae know memes. Okay. Cool.* "Who're you?"

"Little old me?" He laughed. "Oh, well. No one, really."

She tried again. "May I know what to call you?"

He winked at her. "She learns quick, this one. No wonder you like her, snake. Sure!" He blinked out of existence, vanishing into thin air without warning.

She shrieked as he appeared next to her just as quickly. He took her hand and bent at the waist to kiss the backs of her knuckles. "Robin Goodfellow, at your service."

CHAPTER THIRTEEN

"What're you—" Alex never got the rest of the sentence out.

Robin Goodfellow snatched her by the wrist and the whole world folded away from her. She felt an awful lurching sensation, like being on the worst kind of rollercoaster. When the terrible movement was over, she fell against a nearby stone wall and struggled not to be sick. She had no idea where she was.

Or if she was about to get murdered by none other than Robin Goodfellow. By the literal *Puck*.

Speaking of. The little bastard was sitting on another rock nearby, grinning like an idiot and snickering. "Humans. You really don't take to that well at all."

Oh.

Oh, fuck.

He knew.

"I—I mean—um—I'm not—" She straightened. Her eyes flew wide when she finally took in where she was. The whole room was an enormous cavern, the walls, floors, and ceiling entirely made out of a strange, iridescent, and softly glowing blue crystal. Everything around her hummed with a strange power.

"Oh, it's fine. I don't care. The glamor is a good one, I just already know who you are, Alex." He sniffed dismissively. "And it's not why I need to talk to you. And to answer what you're probably super curious about—we're in the crystal mines of Nir Talae. It's complicated enough that it'll take that snaky bastard a couple minutes to catch up with us."

"Great." She leaned her back flat against the wall and took another slow breath. Her stomach was finally settling down where it ought to be. "Are you going to kill me?"

"Nope."

"Maim me?"

"Nope." He smiled. "Too much time with the Unseelie, I see."

"Sorry. I'm being dragged around by the wrist by a guy who literally *eats* people." She shook her head. "This is all too surreal." It felt like a dream. Nothing had really sunk in yet about the reality of her situation. She half expected to wake up at any point and learn that she had been in an accident and had been in a coma.

"You'll get used to it. If you live that long."

"Gee. I appreciate that."

"Nothing personal." He shrugged. "Anyway. I came to give you a warning."

"Oh?" She tucked a strand of her purple hair behind her ear. Which was still pointy. Which was still super weird.

"It's about Izael and this contract you have with him." He kicked his bare feet. He was always moving.

"I know. If I lose, he'll grant my wish in exchange for my soul." Grimacing, she folded her arms across her chest. "I'm not exactly thrilled."

"Yeah, but it's more than that." He took in a breath and let it out with a groan. "Something you ought to know before we really get going—I exist in every second of every possible moment of my entire life, including all branches and outcomes."

"What?"

"I am every*when* I'll ever be. So, I know the future. Every future. Kind of. Ish. It's fuzzy. I also live in every possible every*when* that could possibly ever happen." He wrinkled his nose. "It gets complicated."

"No shit." She blinked. That sounded awful. "I'm sorry." *That explains him calling Izael a nope-rope.*

"Meh. I'm used to it by now. Any*whooozle*. I wanted to warn you about the possible outcomes of your contract. If you win, Izael dies. And if you lose, Izael dies."

"How?"

"Can't tell you. Doesn't really matter. But yeah—if you want to save Izael's life, you can't win or lose the contract." He hopped off the crystal, clearly getting ready to leave.

"Wait—wait. I can't win *or* lose, or he dies? What other option is there?" She took a step toward him.

"That's your problem, not mine. I'm not really supposed to be meddling in human affairs, anyway. That whole treaty thing." He blew a lock of silver hair out of his eye.

"Is Izael dying a bad thing?"

"Well, if you're trapped here in Tir n'Aill if you lose, I can't say it'll go great for you." He chuckled. "Not that there aren't plenty of other lords and ladies who would be happy to pick up your leash once he was dead. It won't change much for you except who's railing you from behind." He cackled and mimed grabbing a waist and thrusting his hips forward.

She fought the urge to shout at him. Whatever. Fae were horny creatures. She figured they would be. Instead, she rolled her eyes.

"But whether or not you want to find a way to save him?

That's up to you." He shrugged. "I'm just telling you what'll happen. So, I—" He froze. "Whep! Time's up. See ya later, alligator!" With that, he disappeared in a blink.

And in that same moment, Izael appeared in a swirl of smoke. "Where is that little—"

"He just left."

Izael rushed up to her, catching her by the upper arms. He almost looked frantic. "Did he hurt you? Did he touch you? What did he do?"

"He just talked to me. That's all."

"No." Izael grimaced. "That is not all. He never *just* talks. He is a manipulator and a Seelie spy. He works for the Queen. What did he tell you?"

She shook her head. It didn't feel right to tell him. "It's probably all just a lie. It doesn't matter."

"Tell me."

She lifted her chin. "It isn't important."

"Alex. Tell me what that half-breed told you." He stepped closer, looming over her, and backed her into the crystal wall behind her. "Tell me right now."

She lifted her chin. She was trapped and woefully outmatched. But damn it if she was going to just roll over for him. "And what'll you give me for it?"

His expression cracked into an unfriendly smile as he laughed darkly. "A better question will be…what will I do to you if you don't?" He trailed his sharp-nailed hand up to her throat, resting it there, his fingers on one side and his thumb on the other. He didn't squeeze. But he didn't need to.

Her stomach twisted in anticipation and fear. "I'm not going to tell you what he said. It was a message for me, not you."

Those turquoise, glowing eyes of his flashed. "You are playing a dangerous game, songbird. You are *mine*. No one else's. Do you understand?"

"I don't belong to you, either. I belong to myself." She pressed her hands against the crystal behind her. Without warning, something ripped through her. She felt like she was plugged into a live socket. Electricity coursed through her and slammed into Izael. The force of it knocked him through the air with a deafening *crack* and the smell of ozone.

Izael smashed into the far wall and crumpled to his knees, groaning in pain. There was a blackened hole in his shirt.

"Iz!" Before she could stop herself, she ran up to him. She honestly didn't know why. "Are you okay? I'm sorry—I didn't mean to—"

He laughed, if weakly. "That's what I get for forgetting you're a witch." He stretched his legs out, leaning back on the wall with a grunt. "Oh, that stings. Good shot, songbird."

"How—I don't even know—" She knelt beside him, cringing at the burn on his chest. "I wasn't trying to do anything."

"You can tap into the magic of the world around you. And this place is filled with it." He smirked. "Are you concerned about me? I think you are."

"No, I'm not." She sat back on her heels. Was she? *Shit.*

"You are." He chuckled. "You even called me *Iz*." He reached up and poked her on the end of her nose with his pointed nail. "You *like* me. Admit it."

"No. I don't. And Izael is just too many syllables in a pinch." She glared at him. "And I'm only concerned because I don't have any way out of this place, and without you I'm trapped and dead."

"Ah. Yes. Clearly." He obviously didn't believe her. "You could kiss it and make it better." He pointed at his chest. "Or kiss somewhere else if you—"

"Izael."

"Yeah, yeah." Grunting again, he used the wall to get back to his feet. She certainly wasn't going to help him after all

THE UNSEELIE DUKE

that. "Can't fault a snake for trying." He took a step away from the crystal surface. His knees buckled.

Instinctually, she caught him, almost dropping him because of his weight. He was a lot heavier than he looked. He draped an arm over her shoulder and smiled at her, if just a little bit through a veil of pain. "See? You *do* like me."

"Just shut up and get us out of here, will you?"

"Fine, fine..." He gestured and a portal opened in front of them.

Alex didn't know how else to describe it—just a swirling hole. In space. Just sitting there.

It had been one *fuck* of a night. And something told her it wasn't close to being over. "Can I go home yet?"

"Are you kidding me?" Izael walked toward the portal, still leaning on her. She wondered if he was faking it. Really, she ought to just drop him and walk through the portal on her own. But she had no idea if it worked without him, or honestly where it was going to go. "It's barely past midnight! We haven't had our dinner yet, and I haven't even had a chance to seduce you."

Going through a portal was a lot less jarring than being teleported, she decided. At least it didn't make her want to throw up. "I'm not going to dignify that with a response."

"Sofa." He gestured at the plush piece of furniture over by one of the bizarre, ruin-esque walls that defined the edges of his home.

"Are you faking being hurt for attention?" She helped him over to the sofa either way, glad for the literal weight off her shoulders when he sat down. He stretched out sideways, and she watched, amazed, as his form shimmered and changed into that of his "true" form, the long coils of his tail draping up and over the back, over the arm, and curling around on the floor. And then promptly curling around her ankle.

Grabby bastard. She flicked her foot, trying to shake him off. But it was no good.

"Why would you think I was faking it for attention?" He brushed the soot off his chest.

"Because you've been doing that since we met. I saw you with that spy you ate. There's no way in hell that when I punch you it actually hurts." She shook her foot again. "And will you let go?"

"Fine, yes, I was faking it. But it wasn't for attention. Mostly for humor." He chuckled. "I don't want you to be so afraid of me. Well—all right, I want you to be afraid of me, but in that…sexy fun way. Not the unsexy unfun way." His tail pulled her closer to the edge of the sofa. She had to hop along with the motion, otherwise she would have fallen over. "Sit with me."

"I don't trust you."

"I didn't ask you to." Another coil of his tail wrapped around her waist, and she officially didn't have a say in the matter anymore as he dragged her down to the sofa. "Sit."

The coil around her waist tightened. "Izael, knock it off." She wormed her arms down in between herself and his tail, trying to wriggle out of his grasp.

"You haven't told me what that treacherous Puck told you." The coil of muscle undulated around her, and he wrapped a second layer around her chest.

"Izael—wait—" She had made a mistake by putting her arms between her chest and his tail. A very bad mistake. Suddenly, she couldn't stop him from wrapping the smaller, narrower end around her throat. He didn't squeeze that part yet—but it was very clear that he could.

He shuddered, the muscle around her tightening in a wave and then relaxing. "You feel so good…and you look so beautiful—see? That look right there in your eyes. That's exactly what I was talking about." He sat up, the coil of his tail forcing her onto her back on the sofa. He loomed over her, resting his weight on his hands on either side of her head. "I think you like this. Don't you? Hm?" His forked tongue flicked out of his mouth, tasting the air. "Yes, I think you do."

"Iz—" She didn't get to finish his name. He kissed her, taking the opportunity to slip his tongue into her mouth, winding around her own as he claimed her. She was helpless. Entirely helpless.

The coils around her tightened in a slow wave again, just a little harder than before. She couldn't deny how sexual it was. How weirdly and wonderfully erotic it felt. Even if she could speak, she wasn't sure she could deny how each time he tightened and relaxed, it sent a shiver of pleasure through her.

When he parted from the kiss, his glowing teal eyes were lidded and stormy with desire. He hovered over her, watching her as he continued the pattern of squeezing and releasing. "Tell me what the half-breed told you."

"N—no." She gasped. "It was for me, not for"—she broke off as he tightened the coil around her throat, momentarily making it a little hard to breathe—"you." Why did it feel so good? It shouldn't feel good. But it did. And the look on his face told her there was absolutely no point in trying to pretend it didn't. He already knew.

"Tell me and I'll stop." He smirked. He ran a hand across her hip, splaying over her abdomen, his fingers slipping under her shirt. "Unless…" he purred, his tongue flicking against her cheek, "you want me to keep going, anyway…"

She should just tell him. What did she care if he died? She shut her eyes, leaning her head back against the sofa, feeling the very tip of his tail wrap around her throat. She should demand he stop.

But she didn't do either of those things.

CHAPTER FOURTEEN

"Pretty girl." Izael could not believe his luck. His feisty, beautiful little spitfire of a human pet was almost *glowing*, she was so needy. "That's it, pretty girl…let go." He wondered if he could bring her to climax just from squeezing her. And she felt so damn good, her racing heart and her stuttering breath—it took all his willpower not to tighten harder and make her whimper for air.

Or to stuff her full of his cocks right here, right now.

No. He would have to get her used to him first—step by step—before he did that. He wanted to "punish" her for keeping secrets. He was worried about whatever that bastard little fuck Goodfellow had told her. But if he could get a taste of his songbird in exchange for her guarding her secrets? He'd make that exchange.

He'd learn the truth eventually. He always did.

"Izael," she murmured as he tightened his coils again around her, miming the tempo to a dance he would do with her soon enough. But not tonight. She was frightened—in that sexy, fun way he'd been talking about—and she was also

THE UNSEELIE DUKE

uncertain, likely torn between what she wanted and what she knew she "should" do.

He stroked her warm skin, loving the feeling of her beneath his palm. He flicked open the button of her pants, lowering the zipper. She squirmed, wriggling in his grasp. Chuckling, he loomed over her again as he began to tug down her pants. "I love it when you struggle—keep fighting. It feels amazing."

"What're you going to—" She gasped and arched her back as he squeezed her just a little tighter. He held it for a moment longer before relenting. "You—you can't—"

"I can. And you want me to." He scraped his teeth over the edge of her jaw. "Don't worry. I won't take you tonight. I plan on making you suffer, not rewarding you." He grinned and sat back on the main coil of his tail.

Human clothing was so irritating to remove sometimes, even if the modern clothing she wore was so wonderfully form-fitting and revealing. He tugged off her jeans, tossing them aside. She squeaked and struggled, kicking her legs. Laughing at her pathetic attempt, he spread her legs on either side of his chest.

"Hey!" Oh, how she glared at him. So wonderfully indignant, considering her obvious state of arousal.

He tutted and ran his fingers over her underwear. He vanished his long, sharp nails. The last thing he wanted to do was hurt her. "You humans, you find so much shame in pleasure. Why? It is natural—it is beautiful. You revel in violence yet balk at this. I will never understand."

"I—" She groaned as he ran his thumb over her sensitive bud, through her underwear. She clearly bit back whatever other noise she wanted to make.

"Sshh, pretty girl...Just take your punishment." He grinned. "Or you can tell me what Puck said, and this ends." Something he knew she didn't *truly* want. And neither did he. He had given her an easy way out, and he was so happy to see she took it.

He pulled her underwear aside and bent his head down to her, running his tongue along her, loving the heady taste. She whimpered as he squeezed the coils around her. But that whimper turned into a cry as he drove his tongue deep inside.

You will want to be mine when this week is over. Mark me, Alex.

ALEX MUST HAVE BEEN LOSING her mind. She must have gone insane. That was the only explanation for what was happening. She was trapped in the tail of a giant, evil snake fae who was currently *eating her out.* Which had new meaning, seeing as she had watched him literally devour a man whole.

Her vision was swimming as she threw her head back, her body spasming with pleasure as he wriggled his long, very flexible tongue inside her. It felt unlike anything she had ever experienced before in her life. His thumb didn't let up the pressure. It was only seconds before she felt her ecstasy climb and begin to peak.

He stopped, snickering. "That was fast." The urgency began to abate. "Been a while?"

Picking up her head, she glared at him, and it only made him laugh harder. "I swear to *fuck.*"

"I told you this was punishment, didn't I?" He ran his fingers over her, exploring her body, stroking her thighs and her abdomen. "Hm. Yes. I think I want you to beg me."

"I'm not going to beg."

He chuckled. "Oh, we'll see about that." He lowered his head to her again, his tongue wriggling inside. She bit back a moan. The pleasure began to build again, climbing steadily, and just as she was about to be pushed over the proverbial cliff, he stopped.

She snarled in frustration.

And he only laughed.

This was going to be his game.

The goddamn motherfucking *bastard.*

"I wonder how long you can hold out." He hummed as he stroked her body again. "What do you think? Eight times? Nine times? Oh, let's make it an even ten. I'll tell you what—make it to ten times without begging me to finish you, and I'll give you a reward."

"Why does everything have to be a game with you, you—" She broke off as the coil around her throat squeezed. She shuddered, unable to help how good it felt.

"Fae." He grinned. "It's kind of our thing. Well, you've already made it to two. Let's do this in earnest, shall we?"

Alex could only mutter obscenities under her breath as he did exactly that.

THREE. Four. Five times, he brought her to the edge before stopping. She was sweating now, her body covered in a thin sheen of it. Her eyes were shut, and each time he let up the pressure on her, she would let out a stream of curses that would make a sailor blush.

He loved it.

By the Morrigan, he was going to become addicted to her, if he wasn't already. His precious, wonderful, amazing, violent little songbird. He wouldn't let anyone else touch her —no one. She would be all his, and his alone.

He wanted her. His body was painfully hard in his sheath, throbbing with *need.* But he wouldn't take her. She was already being receptive. He wanted her to accept her desire, not be ashamed of it. She needed to trust that he wasn't going to hurt her before he tried to squeeze all of him inside her.

And it would really be a squeeze.

He was looking forward to it. Immensely.

Six times, and she let out a frustrated sob, tossing her head from side to side.

"Giving up already, pretty girl?" He couldn't help himself. He was almost preening with pride at his achievement! "Just say it. Say, 'please, Izael' and it'll all be over with."

"No," she ground out through clenched teeth.

"All riiiiight, if you say so..." Seven times, and she was thrashing in his grasp. Eight times, and she was gasping for air. Nine times, and he wondered if he was going to actually drive her insane.

But he was proud of her. Even as she swore at him, cursed him, tried to kick him, tried to seek out her own end by wriggling in his grasp. She was strong willed and a worthy opponent—and a very worthy plaything.

"So close, pretty girl. So close." He stroked his palm over her abdomen. "You are doing wonderfully."

"I fucking *hate you.*" She glared at him, still in her glamor.

"Hm. No, you don't." He ran his tongue up along her again, savoring her. "Last round, unless you want to tap out now."

She snarled, cussed at him again, and threw her head back. "...No."

"Good." And he set to work. When he brought her to the peak and stopped, she almost screamed, she was so angry. But she didn't beg. He howled in laughter. "Well done!"

"I fucking *hate* you, you egotistical piece of shit fae! I'm going to skin you and turn you into a handbag, you goddamn, motherfucking, donkey sucking shit sandwich! Let go of me *right—*"

It was time for her reward. He shut her up by plunging two fingers into her to the knuckles, stretching her abruptly and without warning. He captured her sensitive bud in his teeth, tormenting it as he began to piston his fingers in her at a harsh tempo.

It didn't take long at all.

She wailed in release, her body arching, muscles going taut and clamping down around his fingers. He lifted his head to watch her, to bask in the sight before him as she thrashed in his grasp. He tightened his coils, just a little, loving how it felt to have her writhe.

When she came down from her high, she was gasping. He unwound his tail from her throat and let up the pressure from around her ribs.

"Beautiful," he murmured. "So beautiful."

"Fuck…you," she said between desperate breaths.

"Mm. Not yet." He shifted, grunting a little in discomfort, and slithered off the sofa. "Although, if you will excuse me, I need to—ah—tend to something."

She opened an eye to cast a glance at him. Her annoyed look told him that she knew exactly what he was going to do.

"Do you want to watch?" He grinned.

She grabbed a pillow from over her head and smacked him with it.

Laughing, he left her be, and headed to his hot spring on the far side of his home. "Just think of all the fun we could be having right now, if only you accepted how much you want me!"

"Fuck you!" she shouted back at him.

"Soon, songbird. And then I'll really make you sing."

Her growl of frustration only deepened his amusement.

What the actual fuck was she thinking? What the actual, literal *fuck* had she been thinking? Tugging on her pants, she got up from the sofa and walked to another piece of furniture, needing some distance to try to screw her head back on straight.

That had been the single most intense sexual experience of her life. Apparently, she was into a bunch of shit that she had been entirely unaware of until right at that exact moment. To say she felt a little bit conflicted would be putting it lightly.

She should've just told him what Puck had said to her. What did she care if he died? Right? *Right?*

She shouldn't care. She shouldn't care at all. Izael was after her goddamn soul, and the whole situation was going to get worse before it got better. He was a deranged, people-eating madman. Sure, he was hot as sin and very, *very* good with his tongue, but she needed to put things into perspective. It shouldn't matter how good he was in the sack if he wanted to turn her into his personal lapdog.

But.

She had been worried when she'd actually hurt him.

Even if she wanted to pretend she hadn't been.

And she was...enjoying their time together. Their dates were fucked up and bizarre, and Tir n'Aill was a nightmare world of fantastical monsters and strange sights. But like him, it was undeniably beautiful, too.

And now he was off somewhere else in his home jerking off his *two dicks*. "What the fuck am I doing?" She put her head in her hands and shut her eyes. This was all getting out of hand. Extremely out of hand. She needed to find a way to end it—to break it off with him. But *how?*

If I win the contract, he dies.

If I lose the contract, he dies.

What other option was there? What third way out could

there be? Maybe she should tell Izael what Puck had said. Maybe he'd cancel the contract if he knew his own life was on the line. No, more likely, he'd claim it was all nonsense and just a shitty attempt by the Seelie to make him cut off contact with Earth.

Yeah, she was pretty sure there was no getting rid of Izael. If she let things play out normally, and she won, she'd be on Earth, and he'd be dead—which made her weirdly sad. All things considered, he hadn't been awful to her.

The other option was she lost and he died, and she was trapped in Tir n'Aill and got turned into somebody else's lapdog. And the odds were good that whoever snatched her up wouldn't be nearly as relatively—for an Unseelie—kind to her.

There was only one other way forward. If she couldn't convince him to cancel the contract, she'd need to find a way to nullify it somehow. There had to be a loophole. There had to be another way forward. But *what?*

And the clock was ticking on figuring it out.

CHAPTER FIFTEEN

Tzael took his time returning to Alex. Not because it took him very much time at all to finish himself off—hardly. He had been ready to burst after what they had done. But he figured the poor young witch was going to be overwhelmed and likely needed a few minutes to think.

Sure enough, when he strolled back over to her, wearing legs and clothes this time, she was sitting in a different chair, staring off into the middle distance. That line between her brows was etched there as if it had been carved into stone, her chin in her hand and her elbow on her knee.

She didn't even notice him approach. He walked up beside her and bent to kiss her on top of the head. She hummed and looked up at him, finally seeing him, before sitting back in the chair and letting out a long breath. "Sorry. This is all a lot to process."

"I know. I certainly have not been patient with you." He stroked a hand over her purple hair. It was so soft. "Why don't I take you home? I think you have had well enough of me this evening." He smiled. "I don't want to tire you out—we've only just begun, after all."

THE UNSEELIE DUKE

With a half-hearted, exhausted laugh, she pushed up from the chair. "Yeah. I could use a nap."

"And besides! It's time to see your reward." He felt like a child on their birthday, but he was the one giving *her* a gift. He couldn't wait to see her face as she realized what he had done for her. Extending his hand, he waited for her to take it.

"I thought…" She trailed off, obviously not knowing how to describe what they did in a couth manner.

"Hm?" He chuckled. "Oh, hardly. *That* wasn't your reward. That was something else entirely. He flexed his fingers, urging her to hurry. "Come, now! I've been sitting on this all night."

Quizzical, but with that begrudging look she wore around him more often than not, she placed her hand into his. He bent to kiss her knuckles before leading her to the edge of his home. With a gesture, he opened a portal back to Earth and stepped through it with her.

They appeared in the living room of a stately apartment. It was a little over a hundred years old, or so the date on the outside of the building said. The brick "brownstone" had been cut up from one massive estate into several smaller but no less elaborate "condominiums." Whatever the shit that meant.

Humans make things so unnecessarily complicated.

The home was already furnished with expensive taste. Turning to face Alex, who was now staring at where they were with a truly perplexed expression, he thrust his arms out at his sides. "Tah-dah!"

"Where are we?"

"Why, your home, of course." He flopped down onto one of the leather sofas and stretched out, loving how big it was. He rarely fit in most furniture.

"I…this…I don't live here." She stated the obvious.

"No, you do." He loved this moment—revealing how

clever he was. "This place has been in your name for six years, in fact."

She gestured for him to rewind. "Start over, please. I'm too tired to figure this shit out on my own."

He cackled. That was fair. It had been a wild twenty-four hours for her. The sun was just beginning to rise on Earth, the darkness that was hampered by the electric glow of lamps just beginning to turn pale and battle back the unnatural orange that never faded.

"This is my gift to you." He gestured again at the condominium. "Your reward. I cannot have my precious pet living in squalor, now, can I? This is *far* more respectable for one of my belongings."

"I don't—" She grunted. "I'm not arguing with you about that right now. Okay, explain to me *how* this happened."

"You'd rather not know."

She fixed him with that stare that said she was not going to budge on the subject. "Now you really need to tell me."

Taking in a breath, he puffed it out in one long string. "It was simple, really. I made a deal with the businessman who owned this. I would grant his deepest wish in exchange for his home and everything in it. Seeing"—he took a dramatic inhale before continuing—"as he told me he owns four other houses, it was hardly a high price for him to pay."

She narrowed her eyes. "Where is he now?"

"Elsewhere." He smiled.

"What did you do to him, Izael?"

"I granted his wish." He loved watching her try to figure out how to corner him. It was such a wonderful game of cat and mouse that they played. He hoped it would never end. He didn't want to crush her soul—he simply wanted to *own* it.

She stared up at the ceiling with its elaborate molding

and took a long breath, clearly taking her time to calm her temper. "What was his wish, Izael?"

"That he should be admired by society for hundreds of years to come." He huffed. "He believed simply having money was enough to earn the respect of his peers. He was annoyed he had not yet procured it."

"Welcome to Earth." She walked over to a polished antique bar that was against the wall. He had moved her altar from her dingy hovel from there to here. She straightened one of the stones that rested atop it. He had thought he had done it perfectly, but apparently it was just a little off. "How, exactly, did you grant his wish?"

"You…really don't want to know, songbird." He knew that was just dangling the baited hook in front of her.

Her glare was enough to prompt him to give in. She had been clever to be very specific about her questions. He supposed he might as well stop the dance.

"He is now a painting in the Museum of Fine Arts." He smiled, almost preening at his own wonderful wickedness. "Quite clever of me, don't you think? He shall truly have the admiration of others for centuries to come."

She was not nearly as impressed. "Jesus *fuck* Izael, you killed him! I'm not living here. It's not mine."

"But it is! A little magic, a little influence, and this has been in your name since the very beginning. It's entirely paid off. There is nothing to worry about."

"Except the fact that you killed the guy who lived here!"

"He was foolish enough to ask for such a ridiculous thing." He shrugged. "It is not my fault he didn't think through his request. He could have asked for anything, and he decided to feed his pathetic ego."

She seemed entirely unhappy about the situation.

Frowning, he sat up. "Would it help you if I said he was a terrible person?"

"Was he?" She arched an eyebrow at him.

"Probably."

"Goddamn it, Izael." She walked into the kitchen, threading her hands into her hair. "What happened to my old apartment?"

"All your things are here now. Anything that was worth keeping, really. I left the ugly furniture behind. What good is having a table I can't fuck you on without risking snapping its legs? Pah. Useless." He hopped off the sofa and headed after her. She was scoping the place out. One bedroom, one bathroom, a large kitchen, an office, and a living room. Hardly ostentatious, in his opinion. Simply much higher quality than her previous sham of a home.

She sighed at his comment but didn't reply.

"I was only thinking of your safety. I doubt you wish to be dropped on your head while I'm mid-thrust."

That earned him another sharp expression. He loved that look on her face. It made him want to devour her again. She was so beautiful when she was mad. Watching that anger transition to bliss was one of the most wonderful things he had ever seen.

"Is there any way I can talk you out of this?" She poked her head into the master bedroom.

"No-*pe*." He let out the last part as a pop. "I take care of my things."

She walked into the kitchen. "For the last time, I am not—" She yelped as a small, furry creature jumped onto the counter next to her and mewled. "Geh!"

He beamed. "And here is the other part of your reward."

She stared at the orange tabby cat, who was purring and kneading the countertop. She quickly gave in to the obvious begging for attention and reached out to pet the animal, who eagerly leaned into her hand. "Tell me this isn't his cat."

"Oh, no. Hardly. That idiot had no pets. Likely no family,

either." He shrugged. "This little fella was snooping about the garbage cans outside. I asked him if he had a home, and he said no. So, now he does. He's simply happy to be safe and warm and fed."

"You can talk to cats?"

"Of course. Can't you?" He blinked. "I figured that since you are a witch—"

She slapped a hand over her face.

"Well, I must teach you how to have a proper familiar. He's more than happy to serve. See? Some pets *appreciate* the shelter they're offered by their owners." He leaned in close to her, unable to keep the smugness out of his tone.

She ignored him and picked up the orange cat, who eagerly rubbed his head against her cheek. He was purring loudly enough to be mistaken for a car engine. "Well, he's sweet. I'll keep him. I'll need to pick up supplies for him."

"Already done. Couldn't have him pooping all over your new home, now, could we?"

She shut her eyes, clearly at her wits' end. "Does he have a name?"

"Not one you could pronounce."

She kissed the animal's head, obviously instantly taking to the creature. "How about Pumpkin?"

"He…comes from a long, ancient, noble race of humanity's protectors and guardians, and you're going to name that dignified beast *Pumpkin?*" Izael grimaced.

She rolled her eyes. "How about Lord Pumpkin, Destroyer of Worlds, Ender of Kings, Devourer of Vermin?"

The cat let out a *mrrrpt* and bonked his head against hers.

"He finds that acceptable." He smiled.

"Good." Alex gently put the animal down, scratching his back as the cat wandered off to go find something to play with. She leaned against the granite countertop and took in her surroundings once more. "I won't thank you for this."

Smart girl.

"But I'll accept it," she finished.

Very smart girl.

He scooped up her hand to kiss her knuckles again. "That is all I could ask. Now, you look exhausted."

"Gee, I wonder why." She shot him another withering look. "I'm going to take a shower first."

He opened his mouth.

"Alone."

He shut his mouth. *"Fine.* You're no fun," he muttered as he headed into her bedroom. The bed was enormous, and up on a wooden frame as it was meant to be. Not just a hideous old thing stuffed in a corner on the floor like she had been living with.

She ignored him and headed into the bathroom. He imagined her naked, bathing, the hot water pouring over her body. He had to fight not to slip his hands into his trousers and start fondling himself.

It was twenty minutes later that she walked in, damp and wearing only a towel. She ignored him where he was sprawled out on the covers, already in just a pair of boxers and nothing else. He preferred to sleep naked, but he didn't want to push his luck with the witch. He already intended to share her bed.

But by the Morrigan, the sight of her with her wet hair, glistening with the remaining water from the shower? He wanted to bend her over the edge of the bed and fill her—mark her as his own.

When she went to the dresser by the wall and found a pair of underwear and an oversized shirt, he followed her every movement. She was ignoring him. When she dropped the towel, revealing her bare ass to him, he grunted. "Are we this comfortable with me, now?"

"I figured you went muff diving on me for like half an

THE UNSEELIE DUKE

hour. I can't exactly pretend that didn't happen." She pulled her shirt over her head. It reached down to her upper thighs. She stepped into the thin pair of panties. "No point in being shy about nudity anymore."

"Muff…" It took him a second. "Ah." He snickered. "I like that one."

"I figured you would." She sighed. "So, yeah. I figured we're past the point of modesty."

"Good." He patted the bed beside him, pulling the covers back for her.

"Are you going to keep your hands to yourself?" She arched her eyebrow at him. "I'm too damn tired for a second round."

"I promise." He flopped his head onto the pillow. "I simply want to hold you."

"I just have one question." She glanced at his waist.

"I only have one in this form." He chuckled, clearly seeing the relief on her face. "You will take all of me, sooner rather than later. But I want you to desire it—not fear it." He patted the bed again. "But I promise I am done molesting you for now."

"Good." She climbed into bed, if a little awkwardly. She lay down, a good foot away from him on the king-sized mattress. He wrapped an arm around her waist and tugged her flush to his chest. She grunted but let it happen without complaint.

He kissed the back of her head. "I will take care of you, my songbird. You are safe—you are wanted. And you are valuable."

But he did not miss the troubled look on her face.

Whatever that bastard Goodfellow had told her, it had sown the seeds of uncertainty in her. He would discover what that little half-breed had said soon enough. He would get it from his songbird. But she needed time to rest and—what was the word? "Process" what had happened?

The fact that she had not broken down in hysterics after all she had seen that day was a remarkable feat of strength. She needed her rest. "Tomorrow, I would like you to take me to a music club. I would like to dance and to drink."

"Sure." She shut her eyes. "If you promise not to eat anyone."

"I promise to try not to."

"Izael."

"What?" He couldn't help but snicker quietly. He knew he was an arse. He rather enjoyed it.

With a long-suffering sigh, she shut her eyes. Nuzzling into her hair, not minding that it was damp, he fell asleep with her in his arms.

And felt whole for the first time in a long time.

CHAPTER SIXTEEN

Alex didn't know quite what to do with herself when she woke up in a bed that had belonged to a stranger—who was now an oil painting and very much dead. To say she was conflicted was, again, putting it lightly. Izael's arm was draped over her side, and she could hear him softly breathing from where he was still nestled in close to her, his knees against the backs of hers.

Pumpkin was curled up by her stomach in a perfect orange tabby cinnamon roll.

It felt cozy. It felt perfect. It felt comfortable. And…good.

But he had killed a man to give this all to her. Cursed him to be a portrait for the rest of his existence. And the man at her back wasn't a man at all—he was a man-eating snake who had designs on her soul.

Who would die if she won *or* lost the contract between them. It was starting to become painfully clear to her that she didn't want that to happen. Even though she knew she shouldn't care. But like holding back the tide with a teacup, it was pointless to lie to herself about the fact that, no, she *did* care.

He was weirdly sweet. Considerate. And it was clear that he wanted to protect her. His words to her hours earlier when he told her that she was wanted…it had twisted a knife in her chest.

She had never felt wanted. Her parents had been distant from her at best, and when she decided to follow her now-dead dreams of becoming a singer, they had cut her out of their lives. She was an unwanted daughter.

When she had quickly realized her hopes of becoming a singer were pointless, she was an unwanted performer.

When she had tried to keep a job, she found out she was an unwanted worker.

Everywhere she went, save for her rare friendships, she was alone. And for the longest time, she was fine with that. But not with him. With him, she felt *desired*. And it was a powerfully addictive feeling. Reaching out, she gently petted Pumpkin. He let out a quiet *murrrl* and rolled onto his back, stretching his paws over his head. Smiling, she started scratching his belly.

"I'll roll over too if you'll rub me like that," Izael muttered, clearly still half asleep.

"He's cuter than you are," she teased.

"Peh. Lies." He nuzzled into her hair and hugged her tighter, clearly not wanting to wake up and leave the warm and cozy bed. "He has a big enough ego as it is. Don't encourage it."

And honestly, she was in no rush to move, either. "You should talk."

"Mmph," was all she got in response.

"Izael?"

"Yes, songbird?"

"Can't we just…stay like this?"

That woke him up enough that he lifted his head and propped himself up on his elbow. Reaching his hand that was draped over her waist, he brushed some of her hair away from her face and tucked it behind her ear. "What do you mean?"

She rolled onto her back to meet his turquoise gaze. "I mean, can't we just date? Without all this contract-soul-owning nonsense?"

"You want me to woo you like a human?" He arched his eyebrow at her in disbelief. "My, my. Are you admitting you *enjoy* my company?"

"Don't push it, snake boy."

"Snake *man.*" He smiled, clearly pleased with his victory all the same. "And sadly, no. Without a contract, I am banished to Tir n'Aill. Only when I own you will I be allowed to travel back and forth without strings attached."

"You plan to let me stay on Earth?"

"Why, of course. I want to be here, not on Tir n'Aill. It would be quite silly and self-defeating to make you stay in my realm. As entertaining as it would be to watch all my kindred drool over my shiny new human toy." That smile turned wicked again. It did things to her that she was only just starting to admit to herself.

"I don't want to belong to you."

"I know. But you won't have much of a say in the matter in a few days." He stroked the backs of his knuckles over her cheek. "But do you see what it could be like between us? I will let you pursue your dreams here on Earth, whatever they may be. You will be free to have hobbies, friends, to travel—to see the sights you never thought you could visit. I will worship you. Shower you with gifts. When you age, I shall care for your every need. But you will be mine."

"What happens when I die?"

He leaned down and kissed her cheek. "Your soul will stay with me. And when I return to the ether, you shall join me."

Taking a breath, she held it and let it out in a wavering sigh. It felt wrong. Even without the looming prophecy of his death. "I…please, Izael. Can't we find another way? Another deal to make? Something? Anything?"

"You're simply grappling with the fact that you know you are losing." He rested the pad of his thumb on the hollow of her chin, his pointed nail pricking her lip just slightly. "And that you may, just a little, be desirous of such an outcome. You humans have a wild need to be free—even when it harms you. You will resist chains of any kind simply for that they exist. I understand. It will take time to adjust."

She didn't know what to say. But he didn't give her much time to debate her choices. He kissed her, slowly—but no less passionately than before. It wasn't rough, but it felt just as claiming as ever as he pressed his body to hers.

There was no point in denying that she wanted him.

There was no point in denying that she even kind of *cared* about him.

She just had to figure out what she was willing to do about it.

His stomach grumbled, and she laughed against his lips. Pulling his head back, he sighed in annoyance. "Stupid hunger, ruining the moment."

"Why don't we feed the beast?" She smiled up at him. Pumpkin stood, stretched, yawned, and then jumped off the bed to walk out of the room. "Seems like both of you are demanding breakfast." She shuffled out from under the sheets and stretched. The bed was much nicer than hers, and she didn't wake up with a crick in her neck like she usually did.

Coffee. She needed coffee, and lots of it.

"Any chance I could convince you to cook naked?"

She flipped him off as she walked out of the room to the tune of his laughter.

Finding her way around the kitchen took a few minutes. None of it was really hers. It felt like she was squatting in the home of a dead man—and really, she was. Izael followed a few minutes later, impeccably dressed in a three-piece suit. He flopped down onto the leather sofa, smiling, clearly pleased as punch.

She fed Pumpkin while the coffee was brewing. The tabby purred loudly, rubbed against her legs, and then began to scarf down the cat food at a million miles an hour. It made sense if he was a stray. "Easy, there, buddy—you don't want to puke that all back up." She chuckled. "There will be more where that came from." A thought occurred to her. Looking over to Izael, she frowned. "What'll happen with him when we're away?"

"I have hired a bogle to come and tend to his needs."

"A bogle?"

"Like a brodle or a boggart but not as big as a broog or a bogun." He waved his hand as he explained. When she stared at him flatly, clearly not understanding a single thing he was saying, he chuckled. "A small shade. Harmless. Flits around in dark corners and tends to move people's belongings about for fun. Mostly keys."

"Huh." She shook her head. She really knew nothing about the fae, past the obvious basics. Opening the fridge, she sighed. It was entirely empty. "Seems like Mr. Oil Painting Businessman didn't cook much."

"I'm not shocked."

"I think we're going out for breakfast." She shut the fridge again and thought it over. She really didn't know where she was in the city—but she expected probably downtown or near Newbury Street. Izael would probably get a kick out of all the shops on that strip of town. "Let me get dressed." She made it halfway to the bedroom before doubling back. "You're not going to be a problem out in public, are you?"

"Me?" He placed a hand on his chest, looking offended. "Whatever do you mean?" His innocent act lasted about half a second before he snickered. "I promise not to cause a scene. I won't even eat any bones if I'm served them."

"Great." With a sigh, she headed back to the bedroom and rustled around for her clothing. Black jeans, a striped purple and black top with fishnet sleeves, and knee-high black boots. She brushed her hair, put on some makeup, grabbed her bag, and slung it over her shoulder. When she went back to the living room, Izael was sitting on the floor, chatting with Pumpkin.

"So, you see, she—" He looked up and paused.

"She what?" Arching an eyebrow, she leaned her shoulder against the wall and folded her arms.

"I was simply explaining to him the new situation." He stood and brushed off his legs. "That's all."

"What were you really talking to him about?" The fact that Izael could talk to the cat was probably the least weird thing she'd had to grapple with that week. She was rather proud of herself for taking it in stride. "The truth, please."

"That…uh…" His shoulders slumped. "That I believe you are extremely lonely and could use some company when I am not at your side. As much as I would love to spend every second with you, I am a duke with business to attend to." He watched her, waiting, clearly wondering what her reaction to that would be.

Pushing from the wall, she headed to Pumpkin and crouched down to scratch his head. "I won't bother denying that. But just remember"—she jabbed a thumb toward Izael—"he's an egotistical asshole who might try to eat you someday."

"I am not going to eat your cat!" Izael huffed indignantly.

"You just got him because you wanted to prove to me that 'being owned' isn't a big deal." She shot him a look.

"How do I know you won't eat him if you win the contract?"

"I—" He blinked. "First of all, yes, *fine*, that's why I got him for you, but second of all, I'm not going to eat *your* cat because that's cruel." His expression fell. "Do you honestly think I would do that to you?"

Shit, did she just hurt his feelings? She straightened and watched him for a moment. "You're Unseelie. I don't know. I don't think so, but how do I know you won't change once you have what you want?"

He studied her for a moment in silence, those blue-green slitted eyes flicking between hers. "I do not want to hurt you. You can trust me, Alex."

Could she?

Could she *really*?

Never trust the fae. That was rule number one. But damn it if she wasn't tempted to try. Letting out a breath, she shook her head. "Sorry. I have a lot on my mind this morning. Let's go get breakfast."

When she went to walk past him, he caught her by the arm and pulled her into a hug. She went along with it for two reasons. One, it was kind of pointless when he could just manhandle her. And two, it honestly felt nice. He kissed the top of her head before resting his cheek there.

"I brought you the cat as a gift. Did I want you to see that ownership does not equal cruelty? Yes. But I also wanted to ensure you were not alone when I had to leave you be—that you were protected."

"Pumpkin is just a cat."

"He is far more than that if you wish him to be. You are a witch. You have been to Tir n'Aill and returned—there is true magic in you now." He leaned back to tilt her head up to him. "I could teach you how to use it, if you want."

"I'm not going to make that my wish."

"I didn't say that." He smirked. "Simply another gift from me to you, no strings attached."

She narrowed one eye at him.

"I swear!" Laughing, he reached down and squeezed her ass. "You'll reward me in exchange soon enough."

She slapped his chest and wriggled out of his grasp. Plucking a pair of keys from a bowl by the door, she headed out into the hallway. "Horny jerk."

"Guilty as charged." He followed her, grinning like the cat who ate the canary. "So, what do you say to some magical tutoring?"

"No strings attached?"

"None."

"Then that sounds fun. Maybe I can learn to protect myself against horny jerks."

"Hah, hah."

Smiling, she locked the door behind him before heading to the stairs. When they got outside, she quickly recognized where they were. The building was, as she suspected, in one of the richest areas of Boston right by Arlington Street. There was a great breakfast spot on Newbury that she had in mind.

He was going to have a blast in all the stores.

He's going to buy so much random shit, isn't he? She couldn't tell if she was looking forward to that or not. He was adorable when he lit up. Suddenly, she knew exactly where she was going to take him first. It was going to rack up one *fuck* of a bill, but it wasn't really her money, after all.

And maybe if he had shiny toys to distract him, he wouldn't be so focused on her. Breakfast first. Then? She was going to take a fae into the Apple Store.

She couldn't help but snicker at the idea.

"What's funny?" He strolled alongside her.

"Oh, nothing. You'll see."

"My songbird is plotting. I don't know whether to be proud or worried."

She smirked at him. "Why not both?"

"Why not both, indeed." He draped an arm over her shoulder.

The sun was shining. The weather was warm, and people glanced at the weirdest goth couple in the city, but otherwise ignored them. It wasn't like they would be the only freaks on Newbury Street.

It felt…normal. Well, no. That was the wrong word. It felt *natural.*

She was walking alongside a man-eating, murderous, insane, covetous Unseelie fae—who was loudly and proudly declaring his intentions to take her soul and keep her like a pet.

She should be screaming. She should be running for her life. She should be hiding in a church and begging for sanctuary. But instead? Instead, she was walking next to him willingly, and found herself looking forward to buying him expensive electronics. Sure, maybe because it would distract him. But mostly because it would make him *happy.*

And there was the thing that scared her most of all.

She didn't just care if he lived or died.

She wanted him to be happy.

I am so absolutely fucked.

CHAPTER SEVENTEEN

Alex managed to survive the majority of the day without having the cops called on her and her extremely strange "boyfriend." *Shit, is that what we are?* Oh, she really was so doomed. But she couldn't help but find it charming the way he pored over every little thing like it was a brand new marvel.

She had managed to pry him away from the Apple Store with only a shiny high-end iPad and a pencil. It took about half an hour of convincing him that Tir n'Aill did not have electricity *or* internet, so most of the functionality of a laptop was going to be pointless if he took it home. At least with an iPad he could draw or play stupid games.

She wondered if she could put child safety settings on it before he noticed what she'd done. The absolute last thing she needed was the deranged, murderous, hyperactive snake fae discovering *internet porn.*

She'd never hear the end of it.

And would probably be very sore as a result.

Definitely putting child settings on it.

For the safety of the realm. And my own ass.

Literally.

That sent her off into a laughing fit. Luckily, Izael was too distracted playing with his bags of toys—much of it being literal toys from Newbury Comics—while they sat on a bench in the public gardens and simply enjoyed the nice weather.

He had donned a pair of octagonal, dark blue-green sunglasses. And he still squinted when he looked up from his bag of goodies.

"Not used to the sunlight?"

"Hm? Ah. No. Unseelie are only allowed to reign in Tir n'Aill when the sun has set. And Seelie only reign when the moon has done the same. We take turns. If I were to venture out in the sun, I would be captured and likely executed. I don't go out in the daylight much." He shrugged. "Which is a shame—I do love how warm it is."

"So, you all take turns?" She blinked. "How does that work?"

"Complicatedly." He grinned. "Lovers are allowed to share the homes of the other, but not venture out. Places like the cities simply…shift, as the light fades. Twilight and dawn are something to behold in my world."

"I'd like to see that."

"Consider it done." He wrapped an arm around her shoulder and hugged her to his side. "Tomorrow, we shall return to Tir n'Aill before sunset, and we shall watch the change from somewhere safe." He leaned his head close to her. "Dear me, songbird, are you starting to enjoy our time together?"

It took all her patience not to elbow him in the ribs for sounding so smug. Screw it. She elbowed him in the ribs. He grunted in false pain, but she took the satisfaction from it anyway. "Don't push your luck, fae boy."

He chuckled. "You would make a wonderful Unseelie—you are so wonderfully violent and indignant."

"I'll try not to take that as an insult." She crossed her legs, kicking her booted foot as she watched the people wander around the public gardens. People would occasionally stare at them—and honestly, she didn't blame them. She was used to getting glances because of her dark purple hair, tattoos, and choice of clothing. But now that she was seated next to a man with bright turquoise hair, wearing a very expensive and eccentric matching-toned suit, and a perennial grin that screamed *I'm totally fucking insane*, she really didn't hold it against them.

They must look hysterical together.

The people in the various stores they had visited clearly didn't know what to do with the manic weirdo who was playing with everything like he hadn't ever seen a smartphone before. And to be fair, he really hadn't. But that was hardly normal. She smiled apologetically behind his back and tried to gesture that he was a little bit off in the head, but harmless.

Harmless.

Right.

Except for the fact that he had murdered at least two people in the past three days. And probably more that she didn't know about.

"What is troubling you?" He nudged her side.

"Hm?" She glanced at him for a second before going back to watching the strangers walking around the park, many of them on their way to work or running errands, blissfully unaware of what she was going through. "Isn't it obvious?"

"No."

Laughing quietly, she sighed. "You're after my soul, Izael. It's not that I have a problem with you—"

He grinned in victory.

She resisted the temptation to elbow him again. "But I don't want to be *owned.*"

"I know. But I insist you will come to terms with it in time." He leaned his head down to kiss her on the temple. "You will be free to do anything you wish. Go anywhere. You'll be freer now than you were before, for all intents and purposes. I can open up whole universes before you, wonders the likes of which you've never seen."

"Don't start, Aladdin."

He chuckled. At least that joke made sense to him now. "I could even gift you a flying carpet, if you wished."

"Sounds dangerous, honestly. I mean, I don't know a single person who ever went down that death trap slide at the county fair and went 'yeah, this would totally be a great idea at sixty miles per hour and airborne.' I'd fall right the fuck off and die." She smirked. It was fun to joke about it, but the fact that he could *actually* give her a flying carpet was still something that she was getting used to.

"At least you are a human smart enough to think about the ramifications of their requests." He grunted. "You would be astonished how foolish people are with their wishes. Tossing them about like they were meaningless and never thinking it through." He paused. "Wait. Death trap slide? I want one of those. What is it? Can we get one? I want two. Three."

She laughed harder than she should have. "I'll take you to the Topsfield Fair this year, if we're both still alive. You can experience all the chafing for yourself."

"Well, I plan on going nowhere. And I protect the things I own." He scooted closer to her until their legs were touching. "And you, as we have discussed, are mine."

"Not yet."

"But you will be."

"I really don't want to keep arguing about this."

"Then make your wish, and let us get on with it. You don't need to wait for the deadline. That's simply the cutoff, as contracts cannot go unsealed forever."

"They can't?"

He grimaced. "No. It is part of the treaty. We have a maximum of a week to seal any deals we brokered with humans. To keep us from 'unduly influencing the mortal world,' or some such nonsense." He waved his hand dismissively.

Hm.

That was good to know.

She didn't know what she'd *do* with it yet, but that was good to know. "Can I read the whole treaty?"

"I could procure you a copy of it, but you could hardly read it. It is in a language I doubt you understand." He smirked. "And I'd read it to you, but I would likely fall asleep halfway through."

"I wouldn't trust you to tell me what it actually said, anyway." She leaned her head against him. "You'd probably start editing things to make it play more in your favor."

"Oh, you're most certainly right." His lips were curled in that thin, lopsided smile of his. Goddamn it if he wasn't immensely handsome. There was something about that edge of lunacy—that manic danger that came with him—that she found way more alluring than she should.

"So. I thought you wanted to go to a club tonight? Or do you want to go watch the sunset in Tir n'Aill?" She needed to change the subject and get her mind out of the gutter.

"What do you wish to do? Either is fine by me. We have your whole life ahead of us, after all."

"I—" She paused and promptly glared at him. "Nice one, asshole."

His look of false innocence shattered after a second. "You can't blame me for trying."

"Yeah. I can." She rolled her eyes and went back to resting her head against him. "Tonight, let's go to the club. Then tomorrow, I *want* to see the sunset."

He snapped his fingers. "Darn. Very well. As you wish."

"Just promise me you aren't going to murder anybody at the club."

"I will do my best." He ran his fingers through her hair. "But I hardly understand what the big deal is. Humans place such a high value upon their lives. They believe that it is only something they receive once in this world. That after that, their chance to experience the glory of existence is gone forever." He shrugged. "We fae understand the truth of it—that we come and go, that we are part of nature. That we, like the grass in this field, will grow again, even if we are cut low."

There was beauty in that. Peace to it, as well. She had long since tried to hold on to that belief herself, that life was just part of a cycle. It was why her arm was decorated with spooky tattoos—to remind herself and everyone else that death walks beside everyone, even if the thought of it was uncomfortable.

But wanting to believe something, and *actually* believing it, were two different things. "I don't fear death, I just…don't want to die."

And she didn't want him to die, either.

That was the problem.

The big problem.

"Of course. You do not feel the truth of it like we do. Humans are too…loud. You drown everything else out. But it is part of your genius. Look—" He gestured at one of the cars that went down the street. It was an all-electric. "Look at that! See? When last I was here, all cars were stinky, belchy, rumbly things. Now you are trying to fix that. Slowly but surely, your kind always change. Always advance. My kind…

never do. We are stagnant. Content in our ways. We will never have *electricity* or *internet*."

"Probably for the better. We just use it to fight with ourselves, kill each other, and find new ways to make ourselves miserable. And to watch dumb videos of cats." *And porn.* But she kept that last bit to herself.

"And you don't think we fae fight and find ways to make ourselves miserable? Please. That is our entire purpose— bickering about things that don't matter. Playing games to amuse ourselves through the ages. Imagine what would happen to you lot if you were truly ageless, like we are."

She wrinkled her nose. "At least the only saving grace when assholes exist in this world is they only last for so long. Even if their damage can live on long after them."

"I never expected you to be a philosopher, songbird." He hugged her tighter for a moment. "I look forward to staring at the night sky and discussing heady topics with you. After, of course, I have fucked you raw."

She laughed. What else was she supposed to do? "Are you ever not horny?"

"No-*pe*." He popped the last bit again. "Neither am I ever not hungry. Is it time for dinner yet? Can we get more of that terrible Chinese food?"

She grunted at the idea of more fried grease. "Fine. But tomorrow, can we get something else? Like sushi or a pizza or something?"

"Sushi?" He blinked. "What's that?"

"Oh, man, we're totally getting sushi tomorrow." She could even afford to get it now. What a concept. "It might not be filled with enough bones for you, though. How do you feel about raw fish?"

"Raw…fish. You humans have begun eating raw fish?"

"It's a traditional Japanese style of food. I'm surprised you've never had it before."

THE UNSEELIE DUKE

"Your people were still very closed off from each other when I last visited. And the Americans and the British were not exactly on speaking terms with the Japanese in 1945." He tucked his new toys back into the bag that was nestled between his feet.

"That's a good point. I forgot." She smiled. "You'll like unagi."

"What's that?"

"Oven-baked eel. Or is that too close to eating family for you?" She nudged him in the side playfully.

"Peh. I am not an *eel*. Don't insult me." He stood and offered her his hand. She took it, not like she needed help standing up. But it was a charming gesture, anyway. "Besides. I would have little qualm eating even one of my own kind, if need be. I am not exactly…picky about my meals." The grin he gave her sent a shiver down her spine.

Sometimes it was easy to forget that he was a man-eating monster. Sometimes it wasn't. "Sushi. Let's just focus on the sushi. We can get it to go and eat it after watching the sunset tomorrow. But tonight, we'll get more Chinese food before going to the club."

"What a wonderful couple of 'dates' you've planned for us. I'm quite flattered. I think you may be trying to woo me, songbird. Are you actually looking forward to this?"

"If you want me to keep spending time with you, stop making fun of me when I'm not miserable about it." She poked him in the chest before she started walking back toward the condo he had gotten for her. "Pro tip."

He jogged a little to catch up before falling in stride beside her. "But it's so much fun to tease you!"

"Yeah, yeah, whatever." And truth be told, she didn't really mind.

And if she were really being honest with herself?

Yeah. She really was looking forward to it.

CHAPTER EIGHTEEN

Alex went light on the greasy food before they hit up the jazz club that night. It was a cute little place in Cambridge, and they decided to walk there as the sun was setting. Izael agreed it was worth skipping a night in Tir n'Aill for some swing music and good drinks. And for once, she could order off the cocktail menu without having to worry about her tab.

Having money was…nice. Really nice. She hoped she never started to expect it and always appreciated it.

For however long she lived, anyway.

Izael was beaming as they walked into the jazz club. They must have had a smoke machine or a hazer running to give it the good, old-fashioned look, as smoking indoors had long been banned in the city. Music and the chatter of people filled the air. And all at once, she knew she had brought the fae to his element. This was clearly where he belonged.

She almost wished she could have seen him strolling around New York City during the war, dapper and smooth and unstoppably charming.

They procured a booth after talking to the hostess—how,

she didn't know and didn't want to ask. The place was pretty packed. But within minutes, they were seated on a leather U-shaped booth that was far too large for just the two of them.

The waitress came over, and Izael *started* by handing the young woman a hundred-dollar bill. "Hello, darling. My lovely date and I are just so happy to be here. How are you tonight?"

"I—uh—" The woman stammered. "I'm—great, thanks?" She smiled nervously. Nobody tipped at the beginning of the night. But it wasn't like she was going to turn down the money. Alex didn't blame her. Izael would probably wind up making sure the waitress could pay her rent for the month off one tab alone. "What can I get you folks?"

"Two Manhattans, kindly." He leaned back on the crimson leather upholstery and draped his arms along the top of the bench. He looked like he was born for a place like this. "And a sampling of appetizers, if you have them."

"Anything in particular?"

"All of it." He grinned toothily, his voice turning low and sultry as he added, "I am a man of many vices. Food and drink only scratch the surface."

The woman blushed a little, nodded, and then scampered away quickly to put in the orders.

Alex glared at Izael.

He blinked. "What?"

"First of all, take your damn sunglasses off. You look like a fucking Blues Brother." She reached up and plucked them off his face. Folding them, she tucked them into his coat pocket. "Second of all, don't make the poor lady nervous."

"I don't think that was nerves, darling." That fiendish grin spread wider across his features. "Oh, goodness, songbird, are you *jealous?*"

"I am not jealous."

"Mm-hmm." It was clear he didn't believe her. And now he was gloating.

"I'm not." She rolled her eyes and turned her attention to the stage and not his smug-ass expression. "And I'm certainly not surprised."

"If it makes you feel any better, I prefer to keep one lover at a time." He stroked a sharp nail through her hair and tucked the strand behind her ear. "I would not worry about my wandering gaze. I simply cannot help being a, what's the phrase?"

"A flirt?"

"Exactly." He chuckled. "I've been known to engage in my fair share of fucking, but only when I am not otherwise committed or engaged."

That was weirdly a relief. And she didn't want to touch the reasons with a ten-foot pole. "I figured you fae were all swingers."

"Oh, we certainly love to love, there's no denying that. But I am a covetous creature. I do not like to share my things. And, therefore, I expect to be held to the same standards."

"So, you're saying you're an equal-opportunity asshole. That's nice, at least." She shook her head.

"Precisely." He cackled. Their drinks came a second later —the waitress clearly was prioritizing them over everything else. "Ah, those look wonderful, dear!"

"The food'll be along shortly."

"No troubles. We plan to be here for some time." He smiled.

Once the waitress had gone, she picked up one of the Manhattans. "I also should be annoyed you ordered for me."

"Would you have requested a different offering?"

"No. I like Manhattans."

"Then why be annoyed?" He blinked, honestly confused.

"The fact that you don't get it tells me there's no point explaining."

He shrugged. "At least you're learning to pick your battles." He took his own glass and lifted it toward her. "To us, songbird."

Letting out a breath, she clinked her glass against his. But she refused to answer his toast. *To us. Sure. For however long we last.*

The food came a little while later, and she picked at it while Izael downright inhaled it. "Are you ever not hungry?" She laughed.

"No. And I'm never not horny, either." He shoved a chicken finger into his face. "Why is fried food so damn *good?*"

"Because it's terrible for you, and the gods want us to suffer." She shrugged. "I don't know."

He cackled. "You're probably more right about that than you'd think." He was humming along with the band that was up on stage. It was a piano, an upright bass, a drummer, and a trumpet. She could have sworn she went to college with the guy on the piano, but she couldn't be sure.

"You should get up there and sing."

She snorted. "Fuck no."

"Oh, come on!" He nudged her shoulder. "Why not? I'm sure you're fantastic. Unless you're not, in which case, I may have found the problem as to why you weren't successful at it."

Shooting him a withering glare, she sipped her Manhattan. "Don't make me dump the ketchup in your lap."

"And ruin this suit?" He pouted. "Peh. But really, why won't you sing?"

"I'm not a wind-up toy. I don't perform on command." She decided to glare at the stage instead.

"You're no fun at all. Can I trade you something for it?"

He leaned in closer to her. *"Pleeeeeeeeeease?* Anything you want."

"If you agree to cancel the contract, sure. I'll go sing." She smiled at him, calling his bluff.

He huffed. "Fine. If you won't go up and sing, *I* will."

"What?" She blinked. But he was already up on his feet. "You can't just storm up there and—"

His grin was lascivious and wicked. "Watch me."

She slapped a hand over her eyes as he marched through the crowd and hopped up onto the stage like he owned the place. Nobody questioned him, not even the security guards who were stationed by the walls. Hell, they didn't even glance at him. Maybe they thought he was a performer—he looked eccentric, and he matched the vintage flair of the evening, with his dated-style suit and fancy brogue shoes. Or maybe it was magic.

The pianist did a doubletake as Izael leaned over him to talk quietly in his ear. At first, the man was confused, but then he simply smiled broadly, laughed, and nodded.

Now she was really suspicious that there was magic involved. But the fae were charming. That was their job, really, wasn't it?

Being charming and tricking people into falling for said charm. *Like me.* She sighed and sank back against the leather. The waitress came over, but she was also staring at the stage. "Um…"

"It's a long story." Alex shook her head. "Two more whiskey cocktails, whatever your bartender likes to make best."

"Sure thing." The waitress walked off, clearly perplexed.

Izael took center stage, plucking the microphone off the stand. The music faded, and he flashed a dangerous, wicked smile at the audience. Alex wasn't sure what to expect. But when the band started to play "Let's Misbehave," she groaned and rolled her eyes.

Of course.

Of course, that was what he picked.

Jackass.

When he opened his mouth to sing, she was honestly impressed. Izael had a great voice, even if the song wasn't terribly demanding as music goes. The audience clearly loved it, the dancers quickly falling into step with the tempo.

When he finished the song and rolled right into a song she didn't recognize, but was pretty certain it was by Bing Crosby, she blinked in surprise. All right. Izael really could sing. Damn. She sat forward, resting her elbows on the table, watching him as he soaked up the attention and lived in that spotlight like he had been born in it.

She didn't even notice as the waitress set down the drinks and walked away.

It was hypnotic. When he finished his second song, the audience applauded, and it took her a second to catch up and do the same. He hopped off the front of the stage, winked at a table of women who were clearly out on a girls' night, and headed back to the table with her.

He flopped down next to her, triumphantly. "Can we at least dance later?"

"Y—yeah. We can dance." She smiled at him. "I didn't know you could sing."

"You never asked." He shrugged but was clearly beaming with pride. "Now it's your turn."

"I…can't follow that act. Sorry." She picked up the drink. It was an old fashioned. "Maybe next time."

"Suit yourself." He picked up his own glass and tinked it against hers. "For tonight, we will dance, we will drink, and we will be merry."

There were worse ways to spend an evening, she had to admit.

She made it through her second drink before Izael dragged her onto the dance floor. He was as good a dancer as he was a singer—moving with a fluid grace she found herself a little jealous of.

But she couldn't stop smiling or laughing when he spun her around. It was clear he was having an absolute blast, and his joy was contagious. They stayed until closing, and he whined when they announced it would be the last song. He must have tipped their waitress a thousand dollars, judging by the stack of bills he dropped on the table as they headed out into the chill night.

Boston was surprisingly quiet at one in the morning—the subway stopped running before the last bars closed, which Alex was convinced was a con by the taxi companies. Izael decided he wanted to walk and enjoy the scenery.

There she was, arm in arm with him, as they headed back to the condo he had given her. She was a little buzzed, but the cool air was helping settle her head.

"Did you have fun?" He smiled down at her.

After a pause, she nodded. "Yeah. I did. That was a blast."

"See? It's not so bad, is it?"

"What is?"

"Being mine." His smile turned toothy. "It could always be like this."

She sighed. "Can we not have this fight tonight, please?"

"Fine, fine. I—"

"Hey, pretty boy," came a voice from behind them.

Oh, no. Boston was pretty damn safe, all things considered. But now and again, things happened. Like in any major city. Turning, she saw a group of four guys come out of the alleyway toward them.

Izael was grinning like the Cheshire cat—full of insanity and malice. "Time for a late-night snack."

"Please, don't," she murmured to him. "Just leave them alone, Izael."

The lead guy who had spoken pulled up his shirt to reveal that he had a pistol tucked into his belt. "All the jewelry and all your money. Now." The man looked at her and made a kissy face. "Maybe we'll take your girl too."

She did her best. "Izael, don't—"

But it was too late. He took a step toward them, as casual and debonair as ever. "Good evening, gentlemen! What a lovely night, don't you think?"

"Run," she tried to warn the four men. "Just run. He's insane, and he's going to kill you all."

The four men only laughed. The lead goon pulled the gun out of his belt. "Back off, fag. Just give us your shit."

Izael looked down at himself. "Why are you calling me a cigarette?"

Alex slapped a hand over her face. "They're calling you gay."

"Huh. Well, that's odd—I mean, yes, I am having a lovely night, but—" Izael's confusion at the derogatory slang ended when the lead goon pointed his gun straight at the fae's face. He laughed, low and quiet. "I will, for the benefit of my lovely date, give you four gentlemen the count of three to walk away. If you do not, I will not be to blame for what happens to you."

The three men laughed.

"One," Izael began to count. He clasped his hands behind his back.

"Get on the fucking ground, asshole—" the lead goon snapped.

"Two." Izael smiled.

"That's it. Fuck 'em up." The three men went toward Izael.

"Three." The Unseelie Duke cackled. He held his hands up in front of him, and all at once Alex learned why he was called the Duke of Bones.

It wasn't just because he ate them.

It wasn't because of that at all.

He bent his fingers.

And a horrific *crack* filled the air. It was the sound of a hundred bones breaking at once. A loud snap that resonated through Alex and made her jump back. The would-be muggers' limbs were broken at odd angles, each of their legs, arms, and even their hands and fingers twisting and taking unnatural, bent-back shapes.

They couldn't even scream. Their mouths were agape through shattered jaws, their eyes wide in agony and terror as they fell in heaps, limp and motionless, to the ground.

Izael sniffed. "I won't even dignify you all with becoming my meal."

Alex was covered in a cold sweat. Four muggers had been turned to discarded marionettes, their limbs bending in every direction that shouldn't be, and in places where there were no joints. And they were still alive—though she could only pray they were going into shock.

Izael turned to face her and smiled as if nothing had happened. "Anyway. Where were we?"

Taking four steps away from him, she couldn't help it. She retched, losing her dinner onto the pavement beside her, leaning heavily against the building to keep from falling over.

She was shaking like a leaf.

"Are you going to faint?" His hand rubbed up and down her back.

Yeah. Yeah, she figured she was. The world was getting that fuzzy, far-away feeling, like she was sinking down a tunnel.

He picked her up in his arms, carrying her easily from the

scene. She rested her head against his shoulder, needing something to lean against. He was talking to her quietly. "I am sorry you had to see that. But it had to be done. Tomorrow, we will get this sushi of yours, and we will watch the sunset in Tir n'Aill. And it will be lovely."

He was already on to the next thing. Like he hadn't just snapped people like twigs and left them in limbless piles to slowly die. That meant it wasn't anything new or interesting to him. It meant it was *mundane.*

This was going to be her life now, wasn't it? Watching him murder people?

"Take deep breaths, songbird. You'll be all right. I have you. I will never let anyone hurt you." He began to hum a tune from earlier in the night.

She didn't remember the rest of the walk back. He carried her the whole way, and she must have been fading in and out. Everything felt like a dream. Or a nightmare. As real sleep came for her, she had a new question to add to her endlessly growing list.

Could she cope with who he was? A murderous, dangerous Unseelie?

Did she even have a choice?

CHAPTER NINETEEN

Alex woke up the next morning alone, with a note on her dresser from Izael saying he would be spending the majority of the day in Tir n'Aill attending business, but that he would be along before dinner. It gave her some time to think, and she was kind of grateful for it.

She needed to process not only that he had murdered four people, but that he had broken them into tiny pieces. She kept waiting for the cops to knock on the door, or for the news to report on security cam footage of what had happened.

She wondered what the cops did with supernatural stuff, now that she knew it was real. Were there also vampires? Werewolves? Ghosts? There were demons, apparently, since one of them sired Valroy. Did the rest of the world know? They had to—right? She couldn't be the only one being tossed around like a chew toy by a deranged supernatural puppy.

Maybe there's a support group I can join.

Pumpkin spent most of the day on her lap, or chewing on her fingers, or happily chasing a laser dot around the living room. Izael had bought a cubic fuckton of toys from a pet store, clearly going for the "more is more" approach of caring for the fluffy animal. Which was fine by her, and certainly fine by Pumpkin, who had gone from street cat to king of an expensive condo in record time.

But how was she any different than the cat? Just a pampered pet of a fae. Fed, kept, given attention and amusement. There were two halves of her head warring for supremacy. One half was shouting that she was *not* a pet. That no matter how nice it was to be spoiled, she was a goddamn person, and she should be able to make her own decisions.

The other half said pets were sometimes more family than family, and it didn't mean she couldn't do whatever she wanted. What was freedom, really? How did one define it? The ability to go anywhere, do anything, say anything, be anyone? She doubted Izael would ever tell her "no" to a single thing she wanted.

So, what was the big deal?

Why did it feel so wrong?

Why did the fact he was a murderer not bother her more? It really should be terrifying to her. She should be screaming and throwing things at him when he showed up. But he was a wolf, and the goons had been sheep. Right?

She didn't have a shockingly iffy moral compass. Right?

It was an hour before sundown when she put in the order for sushi, and half an hour after that when Izael appeared in the living room. It was time to go. Time to go see the sunset in Tir n'Aill. Time to dig herself an even deeper grave.

After procuring several *very* heavy bags of sushi—she ordered him one of everything and then some food for her—she patted Lord Pumpkin on the head and headed through a portal to Tir n'Aill with Izael.

It was like any other Thursday in the world to him, it felt

so casual. Every now and then she had to mentally slap herself as a reminder of what was really happening. But it was hard not to admit she was enjoying herself. Enjoying spending time with Izael.

When they arrived in Tir n'Aill, the sun hadn't set yet. Sort of. Izael's home—with the black and white marbled flooring and ringed with ruined walls and oddly floating architecture—was still dark. It was like there was an umbrella over everything. The huge ash tree in the center that stretched a hundred feet overhead wasn't *that* densely packed with leaves. There was no explanation for the perfect darkness that covered his home.

Except, of course, for magic.

Right on the other side of his home, the world was illuminated with the late afternoon sun. She could even see the glow of the orb through the other branches. Leaves drifted down from trees, and she could hear the chirping of birds and the rustle of other animals in the underbrush.

But where she was standing, it might as well have been midnight.

"Huh." Was the best she could do.

"Like I said. The Seelie rule in the daylight, and we rule when it is gone. We are allowed to make ourselves little… pockets like this. Otherwise, they would slap me in irons and haul me away." He smiled. "Let me put these wonderful things away, and we'll have our dinner!"

"I get the feeling it won't be meaty enough for you."

"I'm sure I can rustle up a snack later if I'm still hungry." The fae went about secreting away his toys, putting the objects in boxes and footlockers before taking his true form. His long tail—which really must have been twenty or thirty feet long from his waist to the tip—curled lazily around her on the ground. "Come. I know just the spot to watch the sunset. But you'll have to trust me."

"Trust you *how*, exactly?" She arched an eyebrow at him.

"For me not to drop you." He turned. "Climb on my back."

"Wait, what?"

"We're going up." He pointed, as if she didn't know which direction *up* was. "To watch the sunset."

She looked up at the giant tree. "You're going to take us up the tree?"

"Precisely. Now, climb on. And hold on." He chuckled. "I won't drop you, but if you let go, I make no promises about how quickly I can catch you."

"Can't you just carry me up?"

"Not with the bags of food, and wine, and glasses, I can't." He huffed. "Now, climb aboard, songbird."

Letting out a long sigh, she walked up behind him. It was weird, trying to figure out how to climb onto his back when he had a tail. "Can I step on you?"

He flashed her a sinful smile. "Oh, *please.*"

She stared at him flatly.

He finally gave in and chuckled. "You won't hurt me."

"This is so fucking weird." She rested her hands on his shoulders and stepped up on the thick cord of muscle that was his tail. It at least served as a great stepping stool for climbing onto his back like he was giving her a ride. She wrapped her legs around his waist and hooked her arms in front of his throat. "Please don't drop me."

"Like I said. Just don't let go." He picked up the bags of food in one hand and moved toward the tree.

She squeaked and ducked her head close to his as he began to climb, using the coils of his tail to scale the barky surface. "Ooh, shit."

"Are we afraid of heights, songbird?"

"We're afraid of falling, actually." She cinched her grip tighter, clasping her hands onto her wrists, clinging on for dear life.

He chuckled. "Well, then? Do not fall."

"Shut up. Just shut up."

"You are so indignant sometimes." He kept climbing higher and higher. She refused to look down—she refused. She knew it was just going to terrify her even worse.

"How're we going to eat sushi in a tree?"

"I thought you wanted me to shut up?"

She sighed.

He laughed. "You'll see." The trunk of the tree was getting thinner as they climbed.

She dared to look down, and they were *easily* sixty or seventy feet off the ground now. Groaning, she squeezed her eyes shut and tried not to be sick. "Shit, shit, shit—"

Izael was snickering at her, but she didn't bother getting angry about it. She was too busy focusing on not puking, or slipping, or thinking about how high up she was and how much it would suck if she fell.

"You can let go now."

"You're insane." She clung harder to him.

He nudged her leg. "Just look, will you? Silly human."

She realized they had stopped moving. She opened her eyes and let out another quiet "huh."

The tree had grown into...well, she didn't really know how to describe it. A balcony? The floor beneath them was made of a hundred different branches, all tangled together and woven to form a solid object. He was "standing" there—if snakes could stand; she wasn't quite sure what else to call it—on top of the solid balcony. Branches continued like normal farther up to the tip of the tree, but they were very nearly at the top of it all.

She could feel the slight sway of the tree. It was a little alarming, but not too terrible. She very carefully, very slowly, let herself down from Izael's back before promptly sitting down. The front of the strange balcony had no rail-

THE UNSEELIE DUKE

ing, leaving it open to the view beyond. Which also meant falling.

Izael was still grinning like an idiot, clearly amused at her antics. "Poor songbird. I suppose we shouldn't work at getting you wings, then, eh?"

"I'm fine if I trust what I'm standing on. I don't trust this tree." She paused. "No offense to the tree, if it's listening."

"It is. And it's an old friend of mine—probably the only one I truly have." He shrugged. "It takes no offense."

That was weirdly sad, and yet she couldn't say she was surprised either. Izael lowered himself and placed the bags of food on the balcony.

It gave her the chance to focus on the view. And oh, what a view it was.

It took her breath away. She had no words for it. This was the land of the fae—and now she knew why there were so many stories told about it. The land that stretched out before them was lush and green, and every single shade of nature. Trees were pink, red, green, yellow. She could see creatures soaring over them, dipping down low or flitting about like giant insects. And off in the distance, by a large river that glistened in the setting sun, looked like a fair or a marketplace.

"What's that?" She pointed.

"Hm?" Izael looked up from where he was setting out all of the food. And there was a *lot* of it. "The City of Dawn. Where the Seelie capital is, if you can say it's anywhere. It moves. Once the sun sets, it becomes the City of Dusk. I would take you there, if it were safe for you. But even if they mistook you for a fae with your glamor, you would be gobbled up in seconds."

"Why?"

"Because we prey on each other, just as much as we prey on humans." He set out two glass goblets and uncorked a bottle of wine. He poured her a glass of red. Not exactly what went with sushi, but she wasn't going to complain. "We are far crueler with our own kind than we are with you, believe it or not. We are not so fragile."

She grimaced. "Great."

"When you finally belong to me, no one will dare touch you. Then I will be free to take you anywhere you like. Even to the Din'Glai, the Moonlit Court." His grin was indulgent. "How wonderful it will be to see the others drool over my new toy."

"You're not helping your case, here, buddy." She fished out a pair of chopsticks and split them where they were joined at the back.

"What on literal Earth are those?"

"Chopsticks." She held them between her fingers and wiggled the ends closer and farther apart. "You eat with them."

"But…why?" He scrunched his nose.

"Why use anything? This is what they use for utensils over there. That's all." She picked up a dumpling with it and popped it into her mouth. "See?"

"I demand you teach me. Now." He grabbed for her chopsticks.

"Hey, hey! There are plenty." Laughing, she handed him another unwrapped pair of chopsticks. The sushi place had given them like twenty pairs, assuming they were feeding a small army. Not one extremely hungry snake.

Izael unwrapped his pair and mimicked what she had done—cracking it in half. He struggled to hold them correctly but managed to figure it out after a little while. She showed him the basics and then left him to practice picking up rolls as she gazed out over the beautiful world of Tir n'Aill.

There were low hills in the distance, rolling mounds that

THE UNSEELIE DUKE

were covered with fields of perfect green grass. It felt like every time she had gone out to sit in the grass and watch the clouds go by. Gods, she could spend hours sitting there and watching the view. She sipped her glass of wine, occasionally nibbling on a piece of sushi as Izael tried one of everything first before deciding on what to eat.

He loved the fried squid. And the unagi. And anything that was meaty and savory. She snickered as he picked up a piece of sashimi and wiggled the slab of raw fish, cackling at it before gulping it down. Turned out he figured out chopsticks just fine but quickly decided eating it with his fingers was faster.

The air was warm, even in the shade, as she watched the sun creep toward the horizon. The sky began to turn amber and gold, instead of the bright, cheery blue, as it dipped lower and lower.

"Now the fun begins." He scooted closer to her to enjoy the view as well, even as he kept reaching over to shove a roll or some nigiri into his face every few seconds. "Watch."

For a moment, she wasn't sure what she was supposed to be looking at. But then, as the sun dipped a little lower and a shadow formed at the base of one of those rolling hills, the places where the darkness touched…changed.

Trees that were once green were now pale shades of white, purple, and blue. Creatures that flitted about like insects now had the wings of bats. But only where the darkness touched. As the shadows grew longer and changed, the world shifted back and forth, as if she were seeing two different worlds that were layered on top of each other.

And maybe that was what they really were like—not one world, but *two.* They just shared the same space. As the sun continued to set, the darkness overtook the City of Dawn. The tents changed from carefree, gaily colored things to far more somber and twisted structures, waving flags of crimson and navy instead of pale pinks and greens.

It wasn't until the moon began to peek up over the horizon and the sun had fully faded that she could manage to tear her eyes away from what she had seen. She downed her glass of wine.

How can I ever go back to normal, knowing someplace like this exists?

Even if I "win" this contract and I stay on Earth and keep my soul?

Izael refilled her glass. He had demolished about three quarters of the sushi, though it was clear edamame or any of the vegetable-heavy items weren't his cup of tea. That was fine; she loved edamame. "What do you think?"

"I...don't think I've ever seen anything so beautiful in my life."

"Why, you flatter me." He flashed her a lopsided smile.

"I meant the view, asshole." But she couldn't help but smile back at him. Damn it. His stupid sense of humor was like a plague. She looked back out at the world, now cast in the shimmering moonlight. *I just wish...*

No.

No.

There would be no wishing. None at all. Not ever. Not now, not in a week, never.

"This could be your second home. And Earth could be mine." He kissed her shoulder. "Would that be so terrible?"

"Yeah, kind of. Because anything and everything here wants to eat me to various and sundry literal degrees." She sipped the wine. "Izael?" She turned her head to look at him. "Remember how you said you'd teach me how to use magic?"

"Yes."

"I have...a little bit more specific of a request to make."

This was going to get worse before it got better. But it was the only way forward that she could see.

"A favor? You are asking *me* for a favor? A very dangerous thing..." His expression split into a cruel smile, his sharp canines showing. "Do tell."

"I need you to teach me how to protect myself."

He titled his head to the side slightly. That seemed to have surprised him. "Explain."

"Well, between Puck showing up and randomly teleporting me away, to Anfar arriving, to that spy—there might be a time when I can't rely on you to protect me. I need to have some way to try to keep myself safe." She turned her attention back to the view. "Because I don't want to be scared of this place."

"You would not stand a chance against the likes of Anfar or King Valroy." He stroked his fingers through her hair, combing the strands before tucking some behind her ear. "But I see sense in this request of yours. I will give you the means to defend yourself, my pretty witch. We will unlock whatever power beats in your heart and set it free. But it will come at a price. It will change you. And it will require a sacrifice."

"What kind of sacrifice?"

"Oh, not much...just half your life." He kissed her shoulder again.

"Half my—what does that mean?" She leaned against him. "And no bullshit, please."

"There is an underground lake where the waters are said to speak to the soul of those who bathe in it. And for those who drink the water, it can break down the barriers between the soul and the world beyond. Its liquid has been given to aspiring human magicians by my kind for centuries. But anyone who drinks from it is linked to this place—now and forever. There will be no ridding yourself of it once it is done." He wrapped an arm around her and pulled her closer to him. "But it takes as much as it gives in exchange. No matter what comes, you will be a part of this place, and it will be a part of you."

She hesitated. But who was she kidding? After everything she had seen? After everything she knew?

"This place is already a part of me." She turned her head to Izael, and for the first time, *she* kissed *him.*

His shoulders went slack as if she had knocked the wind from him. When she pulled back, the expression on his face was soft and vulnerable. He smiled, almost dreamily, and rested his forehead against hers. "Then it shall be done. Drink your wine, my songbird. When this night is through, you will be happy you did."

Lifting her glass to him, he tinked his against hers. She chugged her glass and coughed. "Fuck it."

He chuckled and hugged her close with one arm. He refilled her glass a third time. "Fuck it, indeed."

CHAPTER TWENTY

Izael was about to do quite easily the most insane and stupid thing he had ever done in his life. And that was saying something. This was nonsense even to *him*—it was beyond dangerous. It was playing with a lit fuse and blowing on the flame to get it to burn faster.

But what was life without a little excitement now and then?

He could hear the voices of all those he had known throughout his years, screaming and begging and pleading with him to think again—to change his mind—to not bring Alex to the Hartsblood. Yet, as always, he did as he always did.

Said thank you to those voices in his head.

And then promptly told them to, in Alex's own words, *fuck off.*

Because this was going to be fun!

It could possibly lead to an immense amount of chaos. But that, in its own right, was exceedingly entertaining. He hadn't lied to her when he had described the purpose of the "underground lake." But he had also been sparse on the details.

Yes, the Hartsblood was known to unlock the true power of a soul, regardless of whether they be fae, or demon, or human, or whoever drank from it. And yes, those who bathed in it could hear the whisper of Tir n'Aill and know what it was to be connected to the world.

But it also could do terrible things.

Terrible, wonderous, *amazing* things.

He warned her that it would leave her changed. And it would. But it would not make her into something she was not—no, it would merely give her the gift to become what she was meant to be. What her soul would be like, if unbound by mortal flesh.

If either King Valroy or Queen Abigail found out what he had done, he would be skinned, tarred, feathered, turned into leather, and then eaten as a feast. One did *not* bring mortals to the Hartsblood. The last time anyone had done that, the idiot fool had nigh become a demigod who could see all that was, and all that is, and used his gifts to go off and help some fool knight pull a sword out of a stone.

Whatever. Izael hadn't paid much attention then. He didn't see the problem with it. What was the fun in a world where the scales never moved? No, he liked to drop a boulder on one side or the other now and again. Shake things up. Keep things interesting.

And he hoped this was going to be just that.

He could not say precisely why he wanted to take her there. But there had been something in her expression when she asked for a way to protect herself—a determination in those steel blue eyes of hers.

She wanted to stay in Tir n'Aill. She wanted to stay with him.

The kiss she gave him—the first real kiss anyone had ever

THE UNSEELIE DUKE

paid him, and not the other way around—had proven that to him. He had plenty of lovers in his life. Scores of them, in fact. But they were always with him for the dangerous joy of what he could bring them. Not because he had many allies or those who cared for him.

He had not been searching for sympathy when he said his tree was one of his few friends.

Insanity tended to do that.

But here she was, fighting against what she wanted and what she felt she should want. She might not want to sign away her soul to him just yet, but she…clearly desired to *be* with him.

How could he say no?

How could he deny her anything?

After all she had seen, she was choosing to become bound to Tir n'Aill, and by extension, him. She was choosing to say goodbye to the boring life she had known. Perhaps she realized it was already too late. Perhaps she was wise enough to see the truth of it.

That she was already his.

He could give her a bauble to protect herself. An iron knife, perhaps. Or some magical trinket. But those things were flawed. She was right to assert that she stood no chance against Puck or Anfar, let alone King Valroy or the Queen. Izael figured he could defeat Puck in a fair fight—if he could convince a Seelie-serving half-breed to fight *fair*—but the others? Not a chance.

So, the only option he had was to see what she was truly capable of. To try to unlock power in her that he could not.

To the Hartsblood it was.

He helped her climb onto his back once they had finished their meal, and he wound his way back down the tree, careful not to spook the poor thing. The fact that she was afraid of falling was immensely entertaining, and he was tempted to tease her by false dropping her a few times. But she seemed lost in thought, likely considering her choice, and he didn't want to push her too far.

When he reached the bottom, he brought her around to stand in front of him before kissing her. Slowly, this time. Without his usual starving demeanor. This time, it was a simple expression of affection. His songbird. *His witch.*

"Once you do this, there will be no turning back. Do you understand?" He cradled her cheek in his hand. "There will be no returning to the mortal world without the magical one harassing you for all your days. Myself notwithstanding." He smirked. "Whether you win this contract or not. You will be bound to Tir n'Aill."

She furrowed her brow, that cute little line appearing between them, and she studied the center of his chest as she searched for an answer. Taking a deep breath, she nodded and let out her one-word answer in a heavy sigh. "Yeah."

He chuckled. "You don't sound so convinced."

"What'm I supposed to do? Seriously? Just go back to working in a coffee shop, making shitty espressos for people? How can I forget all this?" She gestured to the forest around them. "How can I go on, wondering what could have been, if only I was brave enough?"

"A boring life is no life at all." He paused. "And a life without wishes is without direction."

"I know, I *know.*" She turned her back to him and paced away a few steps. "Isn't there another way, Izael? Some other deal we could make?"

"No." He supposed it couldn't hurt to finally tell her the truth. "The contract is binding to us both. I couldn't cancel it even if I wanted to." He shrugged. "But all you need to do is make a wish, and your soul will be mine, and you will have whatever in the world you desire."

"What if it's a wish you can't grant? Like, if I asked you to blow up the moon or something?"

He snickered. "As amusing as that would be, remember—your wish has to be *truthful.* I'll know if it's real or not. And I don't see you wanting anything that is so beautifully irrational as that."

She sighed and rubbed her hands over her face. "This is stupid."

"I agree! Why don't you get it over with already?" He grinned. "Just tell me that you wish to have both of my giant cocks shoved deep inside your—"

She turned and shot him one of those withering looks that entertained him far more than they should.

"Fine, fine." He reached out to her. "Five days more, and it will not matter. You will have to tell me your wish, whatever it may be. But for now, I have a favor to grant."

"We never did set what you were going to ask in return."

"Hm. Don't you want to see what it'll do to you first? I know I'm dying of curiosity."

She folded her arms across her chest. It was that look she got when there was going to be no convincing her otherwise.

With a dramatic sigh, he threw his hands up. "Fine! Very well. In return for this immense favor I am about to grant you, I request…" He tapped his chin and debated his options. Sex was the obvious choice, but it was too easy. And he wanted to win that through his own merits, regardless. He snapped his fingers as it came to him. "I request that you sing for me."

"You want me to sing for you?" She arched an eyebrow. "Why?"

"Because I have yet to hear you. And you seem ashamed of it. Why?" He turned the question around on her, overly pleased with how clever he was being.

"Because I regret—" She shook her head. "It doesn't matter."

"No, it does." He slithered closer to her, wrapping his tail on the ground around her in a lazy circle. Not constricting, just enclosing. "What do you regret?"

"I regret going to school for it. For pretending that I had a chance in making music my life, that's what." She had that hollow tone to her voice again. That emptiness that he despised. "Either I was a wind-up toy that my family could snap their fingers and demand I perform for them, or I was useless. Just a kid with no skills who was going to work at a coffee shop the rest of her life because she didn't serve any real purpose."

His heart, or whatever he had in the place of one, broke a little at her words. He drew her into a hug, even if she was rigid and resisted at first. "No wonder you bristle at the notion of being owned. I am not them—this family of yours, these destroyers of dreams who bent you low." He kissed the top of her head. "I am here to set you free."

"On a leash."

"Well." He paused. "Yes. But—don't look at me like that! It's *my* leash. It's different! So—*ow!*" He groaned in exaggerated pain as she punched him hard in the stomach. No, it didn't really hurt. But it helped her to feel like they were on a level playing field.

And that was all he wanted.

Oh.

Oh, my.

He laughed. He laughed hard and long. She was watching him now like he had truly lost his mind, and perhaps he had. Because what just occurred to him was a terrifying realization that put his whole life on the scales next to what he was about to do.

"What?" She looked puzzled and a little worried.

"Oh, nothing." He straightened and let out a long, contented breath. "Simply that I am, what's the phrase? Batshit insane."

"Apparently."

He smiled and held his hand out to her. "Let us go see what the Hartsblood holds for you."

"What just happened?"

"Nothing. Nothing important." And it was true—what he had just realized was nothing important to her. Well, not precisely. It might become important eventually, but it wasn't now, and therefore it wasn't a lie. Hah! He had managed to eke out another conversation with her without lying.

"Right. Okay. Sure." She shook her head and then placed her hand in his.

He opened a portal for them both. It was time to unleash her soul—and see what dwelled inside his little songbird.

Because he wanted her to be his pet, his toy, his belonging —*and his equal.*

And that, right there, had the real potential to end his life as he knew it.

He couldn't think of anything more exciting than that.

ALEX FOUND herself standing upon a smooth, rocky shore. The kind of surface that was worn smooth by thousands of years of water coming and going, plus a slick coating of algae. Algae that was glowing…red.

"Whoa." She looked down at the ground beneath her. "Gross." It was squishy and strange, and gave off an eerie, otherworldly glow. In fact, the whole chamber was lit with it. Izael had warned her that it was an underground lake. He hadn't warned her that it was the color of blood and *glowing.*

"The Hartsblood has been here as long as Tir n'Aill has

existed. It is the beating blood that fuels us all. It runs beneath all of this realm, feeding the roots of everything that grows." Izael wandered up to the edge of the shore but didn't go any farther. His white, opalescent scales glinted red in the uplighting. "From this source that is us all, we come and go."

"So, it's…like…primordial magic?" She crept up to the edge of the lake. The liquid was still and unmoving. "What'll it do to me?"

"It will take half your life. I pray it does not take it all."

"Could it do that?" He never mentioned dying was on the table.

He shook his head. "I honestly do not know, songbird. Humans are banned from coming here by law."

"You left that part out."

"Meh. Rules exist to be broken." He shrugged. "Otherwise, why have them at all?" He flashed her that toothy, manic smile that made her worry.

"I don't think they're meant to be fun, you nutjob."

"Peh." He waved his hand dismissively. "Then I care about them even less."

She slapped a hand over her eyes. "You're going to get me killed, aren't you?"

"Most certainly, eventually." He cackled. "But right now is likely not that time. Hop on in. The water's fine."

"You just told me it could kill me!"

"If you had no magic, sure. Maybe. Possibly. Potentially." He tapped his chin. "And maybe even not, but you—again, stop glaring at me like that. It doesn't solve anything." He waggled a finger at her. "You wanted this."

"I wanted to defend myself."

"And this is the surest way to guarantee that. Everything else is fallible. Any gift I could give you would be useless against the likes of those who might seek to harm you. Including myself." He smirked. "Now, we shall see what you were meant to become in your truest state." He gestured at the water. "In you go."

"But…" She sighed. There wasn't any point in arguing with him. This was what she asked for. "What will I come out like?"

"Who is to say? Only you could know. And most aren't aware of themselves to see their own soul in such a way." He settled down onto his tail, sitting on the thick coil of muscle, and smiled. "I will be waiting for you on the other side."

She took off her shoes and her socks.

"Oooh, are you going in naked?" His expression was so hopeful she would have laughed if she wasn't probably about to die.

"No." She rolled her eyes. "I just hate squishy socks."

"Damn." He snapped his fingers. "Maybe later?" There was that hopeful expression again.

"Yeah. Sure. Fine. If this doesn't *kill me*, we can go skinny dipping in your hot spring."

"Great!"

"You're impossible." She shrugged out of her light jacket and tossed it aside. No point in soaking through whatever she didn't need to. Her phone was still on Earth, but that didn't stop her from checking her pocket. She had left it on her dresser. Why take it to a world with no cell signal?

Cracking her neck from one side to the other, she took a deep breath in and then let it out. "All right. Here goes…well, possibly everything."

She took a few steps into the water. It was uncomfortably warm. No, to be specific, it was an uncomfortable *body temperature.* Like it had no temperature of its own at all. And it was squishy. Just a little viscous. "Oh, this is gross." She worked her way slightly deeper, until the glowing liquid had reached her waist. She waited.

Nothing happened.

"Are you sure this is supposed to work?" She turned to look back at him.

He scratched his head. "I don't think there's a second glowing lake of primordial ancient magic."

She shrugged. "Well, it's not working, so I guess I ruined my clothes for no r—"

Something grabbed her by the ankle and dragged her underwater.

CHAPTER TWENTY-ONE

Izael watched as Alex was yanked beneath the surface. "Alex?" He blinked. Was that normal? Was that supposed to happen?

He honestly didn't know. It wasn't like he had ever done this before. "Alex! *Alex!*" There was no answer. Not like he really expected one. What good was it going to do to shout at a lake? Grumbling, he fidgeted. Seconds ticked by.

How long could humans hold their breath?

Another thing he didn't know.

Fear began started to creep up his spine. Was she dead? Had it taken her? He glowered at the surface of the glowing lake. "Let her go. Give her back."

Silence.

It was a lake, after all. Snarling, he made up his mind. "She's mine, and you will not take her from me!" He was going to go in after her. Sliding into the water, he reached out and immediately hissed in agony.

It burned!

Reeling back, he fell onto the stone, curling his tail protectively around himself. Baring his fangs, he watched the skin of his hands turn red and blister. It had burned him like acid even just after a split second of exposure. His scales were singed. It had touched his stomach as well, and the skin was already exposed to the muscle beneath.

There would be no going in after her.

Hissing at the lake in fury, he paced at the edge of the glowing lake. "Let her go! She's mine! *Mine!*"

He tried again in desperation, only to make matters worse. His skin seared and dissolved wherever it touched the glowing liquid. He made his way in deeper, ignoring the agony. He had to have her. He had to save her! Howling in frustration, he decided he was going to go in there one way or another—even if it killed him.

I would rather die in there with her than be without what is mine.

Luckily, he didn't need to go that far.

Just as he was certain she was dead, Alex burst up from the surface of the water, hacking and coughing. She floundered for a moment before she stood, reappearing roughly where she had been taken. She retched liquid out of her lungs, still clearly struggling to breathe.

"Alex!" What wonderful timing. He gathered her up in his arms and quickly undulated to shore, putting her down on the slimy stones before collapsing beside her.

He looked down at his hand where the bones were exposed on the back of it. Well, that hurt a great deal. His head spun, and he had to lower his head back onto the stone.

His vision reeled. He was hurt worse than he had thought. "Well…shit."

Everything went black.

THE UNSEELIE DUKE

"I—" She coughed. "Fucking hate—" She hacked. "Everything." But she could breathe, even though she had swallowed the wrong way and her stomach and her lungs were trying to remind her to breathe air and drink water, not the other way around.

Something had snatched her and yanked her under the water. She wished she could remember anything about what happened afterward. It was just…blank. Missing. Water surged into her lungs, and she had been convinced she was going to drown.

And then she could breathe again. Izael had grabbed her and yanked her out of the lake. He was now suspiciously silent.

Blinking, wiping the water out of her eyes, she peered at him. "Iz!" There was his nickname again. And again, for the same reason. He was hurt—really hurt.

He looked as though he had been entirely doused in battery acid. Sections of his torso were burned away. She could see the muscles of his ribcage and the bones in his hands. His tail was in worse shape. What had caused it?

The water?

It hadn't hurt her…

"What the fuck—" She shuffled closer to him, still coughing occasionally, but her own near-drowning already forgotten. "Iz? Iz! Wake up!" She shook his shoulders where he wasn't burned. But he just lay there, unconscious and unresponsive. "I can't get out of here without you. I don't know where I am, and—you can't die. Iz!" She threaded her hands into her wet hair. "Fuck, fuck, *fuck.*"

What was she supposed to do?

Taking a deep breath that still felt a little hitchy and wet, tried to calm down. Panicking wasn't going to do her any good. She had to find a way to patch Izael back together. But how was she supposed to treat third degree acid burns on a goddamn fae snake?

Think, Alex. Think.

It was in that silence that she realized something.

There was music playing. She knew for a fact there hadn't been before. She furrowed her brow and tilted her head, trying to figure out where it was coming from. It was like the cavern itself was…it wasn't singing, it was instrumental, but the source was all around her. It was quiet, but it was undeniably there.

And there was something else in the music around her. A terrible discordant series of notes. It sounded like a C, C♯, and a D all played at the same time. It made her teeth hurt. "What the f—" Then it hit her.

It was Izael.

Those terrible notes were coming from *him*. It was like he was resonating with it, and the more she paid attention to him, the louder the notes became. Was…was this her power? To hear music?

Could she do anything with it?

Maybe—if she just tried. Magic was just the force of someone's will, right? She shifted to kneel beside Izael, focusing on his wounds. That was definitely where the sound was coming from.

Holding her hand over him, not touching him, she just…*tried* to change the notes. C could stay where it was. That D, however. She hummed a G. And sure enough, it shifted. Now it was that C♯ that had to go. Maybe it didn't have to go far. She hummed a E♭, turning the discordant half-steps into a C-minor chord. She held it there, forcing the music to stay in tune. And she watched to her amazement as the wounds…began to heal.

It was like watching it happen in reverse. Muscles and tendons grew back over bones. Skin grew back over muscles and tendons, still pink and raw. She held it until the redness faded. She dropped her hand, laughing in disbelief. "Holy shit. Holy fucking shit."

The music around her was back to normal, missing the discordant notes. "Izael!" She nudged him. "Wake up."

He groaned. "I don't wanna…"

"Izael, get the *fuck up* so we can get out of here."

He opened one glowing turquoise eye. "What happened—I—" He sat up and looked down at himself before rubbing his hands down his chest. "Alex? What happened?"

"I. Um." How the hell was she supposed to explain? Best to jump right in. "I healed you."

"You—" He cackled in laughter and hugged her tightly to his chest. "You healed me! My little witch. How?"

"I—I can hear music, and you were playing terrible notes, so I just…fixed it." When she focused on him, she could *hear* him. Like a soundtrack. It was a waltz in the minor key. Of course it was. "It's super weird."

"My songbird's gift is music. How perfect. How absolutely wonderful." He kissed her. "And you cared enough about me to heal me."

"I don't know how to get out of here without you." It wasn't a lie. It just wasn't the whole truth.

"Naturally." He poked the end of her nose. He curled his tail under him to stand, helping her to her feet. "I will let you keep your dignity this once in exchange for saving me."

"Whatever. I—" Her head spun. She suddenly felt extremely weak. Her knees went out, and if he hadn't caught her, she would have fallen.

"My poor witch. Magic uses power, and it will exhaust you if you aren't careful." He picked her up in his arms. He looked so damn proud of her that it made her cheeks go warm. "Come. Let us go back to Earth. We will sleep in your bed where it is safe. I think you have earned a good night's rest."

That did sound awesome. "I need to shower and get this gunk off me. I feel gross." She leaned her head against his chest. He was right; she felt like she had run a marathon. And she wasn't a runner.

A portal opened beside Izael, and he disappeared through it, taking human form as he did. Probably for the best. The condo he had stolen for her wasn't exactly sized for a giant snake. He walked her into the bathroom and set her down on the edge of the tub before turning the water on.

"I can bathe myself." She smirked. "I'm tired, I'm not dead."

"Can't risk it. You might fall and crack your head." He put his hand in the water, testing the temperature then flicking the stopper for the drain. "Besides. Allow me to spoil my songbird."

When the world spun dangerously around her again, she leaned her head against the tile and decided it was probably for the best. "All right, fine."

He began to strip her clothes off her, peeling the wet garments off and tossing them into the sink. She didn't fuss when he reached behind her to unclasp her bra. For once since meeting him, he wasn't being a horny jackass about it. He might actually be concerned.

Once she was naked, she slung her legs into the bath and slipped into the water, groaning at the warmth. Little bits of red algae, now dark and not glowing, floated off her into the water.

"What do you remember?" He lathered up a washcloth and handed it to her as he started to carefully pour water over her head.

"Literally nothing." She shook her head. "I was pulled under, and then I was back on the surface. I remember the water getting in my lungs, and then…just…nothing. Scene redacted. I don't know."

"Hm. Perhaps what you learned was not meant for you to remember."

"That doesn't make any sense."

"It makes perfect sense. Some things in this world are grander than we can comprehend. To see it and to remember it might drive you insane. And we can't have two lunatics bumbling about, now, can we?" He chuckled and began shampooing her hair.

"I guess." She shut her eyes and relished the sensation of him tending to her. It was just so wonderfully comforting. When she listened, she could hear the music around her again. It was more muted on Earth, far less vibrant. But it was still there. "I have real magic now."

"You had real magic before. Now what was meant to be has simply been unlocked."

"When you said it took half my life, what did you really mean? Am I going to die in like twenty years now?"

He snorted. "Hardly. You may not even die of old age at all now. Which I can only hope. It would make our situation far less tragic. No, when I meant half your life, I meant what I said. It took half your life force, and you became part of the Hartsblood. And in turn, it gave you half back. Some infinitesimal part of what was given in exchange was part of you, incorporated into the whole. That is what frees you to be wholly what you were meant to be."

"Huh." She would try to wrap her head around that later. Right now, she was exhausted, and the sensation of him pouring water over her head and rinsing out her hair was lulling her into a sleep. He worked in conditioner—how thoughtful—and repeated the gesture. And the entire time, he kept his hands to his damn self.

When he was done, he drained the tub and helped her

out, wrapping a towel around her. She felt half-awake as she went through the motions of toweling off and then changing into her pajamas.

One night in college she had stayed up for forty-two hours straight to get some work done before a deadline, and that was what this felt like.

"It will get easier as you go. But you shouldn't try to rewrite reality if you can help it." He kissed her cheek. "Small steps."

All she could do was grunt in acknowledgement as she crawled beneath the covers. Pumpkin jumped up, purring like a motorboat and kneading the blanket beside her.

"Hey, bud." She scratched his head. There was music in him, too. A solo violin. Maybe she could actually have him as a familiar now. How cool would that be?

She had magic. Real magic. And that was incredible.

Izael nestled in close to her, wrapping an arm over her side and holding her close.

She wanted to thank him for everything but knew better. Instead, she lifted his hand and kissed his fingers. "This was a wonderful day."

"That it was. Well, acid burning and near drowning notwithstanding." He chuckled quietly behind her and kissed the back of her head. "Sleep, songbird. You have earned it."

It wasn't like she had much of a choice. Sleep took her seconds later.

Izael wondered what kind of cataclysmic chaos he had just unleashed upon Earth and Tir n'Aill. His songbird could hear the music of life and change it to suit her needs. That was… an immense amount of power for a human to wield.

Something told him he was going to get into a great deal of trouble for what he had done.

If anybody finds out.

Maybe he could sneak this under the table. Pretend she simply had that gift from the beginning. He bit back a laugh to keep from waking her up. That was unlikely, to put it mildly. No, the others would learn what he had done. And he could only hope their strength combined could fend off what would follow.

Because he had wanted an equal.

And he might have created a demigod.

And she is all mine.

CHAPTER TWENTY-TWO

Alex stared blankly at her mug of coffee as she stirred it endlessly with a spoon. She had ordered groceries—which felt *weird*, but she could afford it now, so great, she supposed—and Izael had yet to wake up. The fae had rolled over, mumbled something about hating mornings, and dropped the pillow over his head.

So, she changed, made coffee, and was now sitting at the dining room table of a dead man's home, entirely lost in thought. She had a hundred thousand questions going around in her head. And none of them were getting her anywhere.

What did I do?
What can I do now?
Am I even still human anymore?
What does this mean for the future?
Am I going to get in trouble for this?
Is Izael going to get in trouble for this?
How do I use this to get out of the contract that means he'll die either way?

She had to think of something clever. Some way to nullify

the contract and escape it entirely. But how? There had to be some way out. Some chance. Some string she could pull, some loophole she could use. But *what?*

If she had a wish by the end of the contract, he would grant it and her soul would be his. If she didn't have a wish, he'd bury her in money for the rest of her life. Either way, he'd die. And she decided she officially didn't want that to happen.

Izael was a man-eating, death-cursing, sneaky, snaky fae. But…damn it if she wasn't growing extremely fond of him and finding herself enjoying it when he was around. Taking in a deep breath, she held it for a long moment before slowly letting it out.

"Bad morning?"

She yelped. Sitting across the table from her—appearing out of nowhere—was Puck. "Damn it, fucking—"

"Sssh, or you'll wake up Sleeping Beauty." He leaned his arms on the table and reached over to steal her coffee before sipping it. "Thanks for the mug, kid."

"You're an asshole." Standing, she headed to the coffee pot to pour herself a new mug. "Help yourself, I guess."

"Already did." He snickered.

Goddamn fae.

"Sooooo," Puck drew out the word. "I hear you had a wild night, huh?"

"Who else knows?"

"Currently, nobody. I just know things." Puck sipped the coffee as she walked back to the table with hers.

"Great." She sat down. "I don't even know what really happened. I just hear a constant soundtrack now." She looked off and let her focus shift to the music she could hear playing from the world around her. Softer on Earth than in Tir n'Aill, and it only seemed to come from living things. Which made sense, she supposed.

"And you can change that soundtrack, which is the dangerous part. If you could just hear it, I'd say congratulations and go on my merry way." He frowned. "As it stands, this is bad. Very, very bad."

"For who?"

"Everybody." He sniffed. "Mostly you."

"Fun. Why?" She sipped her coffee. "Please be specific."

He snickered. "Too much time around Izael already, huh?"

"I'm catching on."

"Good. I hate slow learners. So boring." He shifted in the chair. "Here's the thing—you have real magic now. Serious magic."

"I don't know what I can do and not do. I'm not really a danger to anybody." She shrugged. "And I have no desire to control anybody's lives."

"That's great, but do you think they'll trust you?"

Point. "No. I don't."

"Exactly. And the others will get wind of this someday—both the Seelie and Unseelie. Maybe not today, maybe not tomorrow—but if Izael gets his way and takes your soul, he will have power over you. And therefore, *he* will also have your magic." Puck stared at her, knowingly.

Grunting, she leaned back in her chair. No, she couldn't imagine that anybody would want Izael wielding whatever wacky superpowers she had now. They seemed to tolerate him only loosely at best. "Shit."

"Now you've got it." Puck lifted his mug to her in a salute.

She turned her attention out the front window of the dead guy's condo—it really wasn't hers, and she wasn't sure it'd ever feel like it was—to think for a minute. "One thing isn't adding up. Why do you care?"

"About you? I don't. No offense. I mean, you seem like a fun girl and everything, but no—I don't give a shit about you, specifically."

THE UNSEELIE DUKE

At least he wasn't lying; that was nice.

Puck shifted, crossing one leg over the other and draping his arm over the back of the chair. "What it is, though, is that I'd rather not see this world and mine come to an end. I tried warning you off by just saying Izael was going to die if this contract ran to completion. I'm afraid it's much worse than that."

She arched an eyebrow at him. "You're telling me that not only does he die, but I somehow cause a total apocalypse of *two* worlds?"

"Yep. All your fault." He snickered into his mug as he gulped down more of the coffee. "I mean, you can kill anyone now with a thought."

"I—what?" She blinked. "No, I can't."

"Yes, you can. All you have to do is tell the music to stop. You can change the notes. You can even change the instruments. But you can also tell it to shut up."

"I…" She didn't know what to say to that. "But…"

"So, you can kill *anyone.* In large numbers. Izael. Me. Even Abigail." He paused. "You'd probably struggle with Valroy, though."

"Not that I'm planning to, but why?"

"He's—well, he's—" Puck narrowed one eye in thought. "Complicated."

"That doesn't help." She lifted the mug to her lips. Hot coffee was lovely. Cold coffee was acceptable. Room temperature coffee was gross.

"He's a tree."

She almost choked on her coffee on that one. "I'm sorry, *what?* The Seelie Queen is married to a tree? I guess that gives a new meaning to 'morning wood,' huh?"

Puck snickered quietly. "Okay, I'm starting to like you. No, I mean, well, yes, it does, but not like *that.* See, Valroy has a body, like you or me—but his beating heart is actually a large tree at the center of a moving, impossible maze that is actually his subconscious. Yadda-yadda, eldritch monster from beyond the void given flesh, etcetera and so-on." He waved his hand dismissively as if it were no big deal. "Long story."

"Apparently." She watched Puck for a long moment. "So… what do I do?"

"I don't know, honestly. Every timeline I can see that goes forward from here ends poorly. But you seem clever. I'm hoping you figure it out." He flashed her a cheeky smile. "I'm rather dumb as a brick, all things considered. Hey, at least you have five more days, right?"

"Right. Sure." She rubbed a hand over her face. "At the rate Izael and I are going, I'll have made it to day three before I've caused a double apocalypse and the downfall of two civilizations."

"Oh, probably." Puck huffed a laugh. "It's not your fault. Izael is an impatient lover."

The way he said it made her wonder. "Not that I care, but you sound like you speak from experience."

"Look." He blew a lock of his hair out of his face. His silver hair was short and cut at odd angles, as if he just attacked it with scissors whenever it got annoying. "Don't you start getting judgmental."

"I'm not. As far as I can figure, fae swing every which way." She shrugged. "He just doesn't seem like the sharing type."

"He isn't when it's something he thinks is his. When it's just a casual fling, he'll jump into the party like any other self-respecting fairy." Again, with that cheeky smile. "And he's clearly decided he's keeping you."

"How many others have there been before me? Or, hell, currently?" She didn't *think* Izael was the type to leave out a

THE UNSEELIE DUKE

mystery closet full of human lovers, but fuck if she knew that for certain.

"Oooh, jealous?"

"No, simply trying to figure out where I stand."

Puck snapped his fingers. "You're no fun. I love messing with jealous lovers."

"Just don't turn my head into a donkey's, okay? I'm having a fucked-up enough week as it is." That really would be the last thing she needed.

"Nah. I only did that the one time, anyway." Puck sighed. "No, there aren't any other pets he has stashed somewhere. And I can't remember the last time he wanted to *keep* someone. He doesn't usually…take good care of his toys."

"What do you mean?"

"I mean he's violent, insane, eats people whole, and somehow manages to have an ego bigger than the other Unseelie courtiers, and that's saying something." Puck got up from the chair to go make himself a second cup of coffee. Not like the guy needed more caffeine—he was always moving. "He gets, well, easily *bored.*"

Bored.

She sighed. "And I can guess what he does with toys he's bored of."

"Omnomnom." Puck found the creamer without a problem, which told her that he either somehow already knew where it was or had been rooting around her home without her knowing. Fifty-fifty shot.

Yet another thing to worry about. What would Izael do once he either won or lost? Would he get sick of her in a week? A month? A year? Did it matter? Why did that hurt her feelings?

God damn it all.

"What's your plan, then, *chica*?" Puck plucked a spoon out of a drawer, stirred his coffee, and at least had the presence of mind enough to drop the spoon into the dishwasher when he was done.

"I don't know. I'm trying to figure out a loophole to this contract, but I haven't come up with any bright ideas yet." She shook her head. "And now that I apparently have scary musical *death magic,* I have to deal with that too."

"I'd try to spend some time learning how to control that." Puck wrinkled his nose. "All we need is you going off by accident."

"I'm not a bomb."

"You kind of are." He smiled. "Don't worry, though—I like bombs. Especially those big, silly, Acme ones they use in cartoons." He drew the shape of one of the comically rounded bombs from *Looney Tunes.* "I'd love to see one in real life someday."

"They don't actually exist."

"Don't ruin my fun."

"I'll do my best." The fae were exhausting. And she already had enough to deal with. At least Izael was still asleep, for now. "You should probably get out of here before he wakes up and tries to murder you. Again."

"Fair. Well. Do your best not to wreck everything, hm? And here's hoping you're smarter than I am. Because if you aren't?" He smiled cheerfully. "We're all gonna die." With that, he blinked out of existence. Just one second was there, the next wasn't.

Fucking fae.

Getting up, she refreshed her mug of coffee and opted to go sit on the sofa instead, wanting the cushy leather surface instead of the hard dining room chair. Pumpkin hopped up next to her, purring, rubbing his head on her leg.

"Hey, buddy." She scratched his chin. He purred louder, kneading the sofa beneath him, his eyes shutting as he basked in the affection. "I have to say, of all the dumb things Izael has done—like cursing a man to be an oil painting to get me a better apartment—getting you was a wonderful idea. I'm glad you're here." She didn't know if the cat could understand her, but it didn't really matter. "I had cats growing up, but never had the money to have one on my own."

Pumpkin just purred and rubbed against her as she petted him. "What do you think I should do?"

"Feed me?"

"Geh!" Jolting, she lifted her hand from the head of the cat. "Um…" Oh, great. Great. Just fucking great. Now her cat was talking to her. "Holy shit, you can talk."

A louder purr and a head bump to the thigh. *"Can't. Silly."*

Great, now her cat was basically calling her stupid. He wasn't talking, his lips weren't moving, but she could just… understand him. She wasn't sure if there was even a voice behind it, or if it was just that she somehow *knew* what he was trying to communicate to her.

Right. Familiar. He was meant to be her familiar.

There was a fae asleep in her bed, another one who came over for coffee with warnings of *total apocalypse,* she had magic that could apparently kill anything in its tracks, and now a talking cat. And a ticking clock attached to a very non-cartoony bomb hanging over her head that was going to run out sooner rather than later. A ticking clock that only she could stop. And she had absolutely no idea *how.*

Fuck, she hated Tuesdays.

CHAPTER TWENTY-THREE

Alex flipped the ninth burger on the griddle, the sizzle of the meat as it cooked providing some weird sort of comfort. It was simple. Normal. Cooking burgers was easy. *Human.* Something that her life had abandoned, in large part because of her own stupid choices.

It was two in the afternoon, and she was hungry. She figured the smell of the grease and beef would be what finally inspired Izael to get out of bed. Even after three cups of coffee, she had dozed off on the sofa for a while, waking up well past noon with Pumpkin curled up on her chest.

Her familiar.

That, she could understand now.

The cat in question was kitty-loafing on the counter, watching her cook.

What am I going to do?

The thought went around and around in her head because she couldn't find an answer. And no matter how many roads she went down, trying to plan out different approaches, they all ended in failure. Which would apparently cause the downfall of two entire worlds.

She was just a failed-singer-turned-failed-barista. What kind of sick cosmic joke was it that she had all that importance on her shoulders? Let alone that she had managed to somehow wind up with the power to murder people.

One thing was clear, though—Izael couldn't know. He couldn't know what Puck had told her or the seriousness of the situation. Or be told in any way shape or form that she could drop people like flies if she wanted to. Because if she failed—which was almost certain—in finding a way out of the contract, he was going to wind up with her soul and have that power for himself via proxy.

And she liked Izael far more than she should, but…she could see why giving that lunatic that kind of ability would be *extremely* problematic.

"What is that wonderful smell? Oh! *Burgers!*" The madman in question cackled as he walked into the room. "I didn't know you cooked!"

"I mean, yeah. I think anybody can figure out how to make a damn burger." She set the cooked patties aside. The fries were already out of the oven. "I made you eight. You think that's enough?"

"We'll see." He sat on one of the stools at the kitchen counter and pulled the tray over to him. Watching him inhale a burger in only a few bites was disturbing and yet weirdly fascinating. "So! How about going back to the jazz club tonight?"

"I don't know that it's safe for me to be around that much music or that many people right now." She frowned at the sizzling hamburger patty. "I might go haywire and, I don't know, turn everybody into shrubs or something."

"Exactly! It'll be fun. What good is life without a little mayhem in it?" He was already on to burger two. He picked up a bottle of ketchup that she had put on the counter and squeezed a huge puddle of it onto his plate. He dipped his burger in it before taking another bite, which was more proof that he was a complete lunatic.

"Izael, I don't want to hurt people."

"Changing someone's life is not hurting them. They'd be just as alive as a shrub as they would be as a person. And in fact, you'd be helping! There are far too many of you folks these days." He dipped the burger into the puddle of ketchup again and took another enormous bite. "Saving the world, one human-bush at a time."

She sighed. "Izael, no. Can't we just stay in? Watch a movie or something? We could go to a museum—I don't think there's much damage I could cause there."

"You'd be surprised." He was now on to burger three, which got the same sin-against-nature, ketchup-dipping treatment. "We had fun last time, didn't we?"

"Yeah, until you magically crushed, like, four guys."

"They deserved it. Besides, you promised you'd sing for me. What better place than that jazz club?" He smiled.

"First of all, no, it won't be fun. And second of all, I agreed to sing for you, however," she waved her spatula at him, "you never specified *when*. I'm sure I'll sing for you at some point in the future." If they both lived that long.

He opened his mouth to argue before shutting it again. "Damn it." He grumbled as he shoved another giant bite of food into his face. "I was excited, and I didn't think it through."

"That's not my fault." She took her burger off the griddle and put it onto a bun. She sat down across from him at the counter and, like a normal *civilized* person, put the ketchup on top of the patty and then put the bun back on top.

"You're just scared."

"Of course I am." She took a bite of her food. The greasy meat helped her mood. "Who wouldn't be? I don't know what I'm capable of, and I'm afraid of screwing everything up. Besides, if we're trying to be incognito, going full *Jumanji* on a bunch of fucking randos in a jazz club isn't the way to do it."

"I understood a third of that."

She chuckled. "*Jumanji* is a movie. You'd actually really like it. The original, anyway. Not the reboot travesty." She took another bite of her burger. Izael was on his fifth. She lost track of when he had eaten the fourth. "And rando is just short for a random person."

"Hm." He picked up a fry and swirled it around in the now veritable lake of ketchup on his plate before eating it. This time, he chewed and swallowed before speaking again. "Regardless, you have a point. I certainly don't want to pull Anfar's ire or alert the Seelie of what we've done. So, let's teach you. Then, *tomorrow* we go back to the jazz club, and you sing."

He grinned in that devious way that told her that he already had something planned. She sighed. He was impossible.

"Fine." She ran a hand over her face. "How do we train me?"

"Simple. We go find a quiet, private place in the woods somewhere, and we let you wreck the place until you figure out how to control yourself." His tone was extremely casual, as if learning to rewrite the natural order of things was a daily event to him. Maybe it was. Hell if she knew.

She pondered it for a moment. What other option did she have? "We'll go to the Arnold Arboretum. That way, if I end up…accidentally creating some sort of weird, out-of-place species, it'll look somewhat intentional there."

"Fantastic! Can we take snacks?"

She rolled her eyes but couldn't fight her smile. "Yes, we can take snacks."

Izael hummed to himself as he walked along with his songbird through the human-kept woods. The arboretum in question was large and private, with an extensive collection of plants and trees from all over.

His beautiful, amazing, and now very powerful songbird seemed rather lost in thought, though he couldn't say he blamed her. While he was excited to unleash her potential upon the world and see what she was capable of, that kind of magic must be terrifying to someone already overwhelmed with her situation.

It was the sole reason he hadn't already bent her over every piece of furniture in her new home and had his way with her in every conceivable fashion. He wanted to spoil his new pet, not break her.

It troubled him how quiet she had become since the trip to the Hartsblood. He had hoped she would revel in her newfound gifts. But instead, it seemed to make her even more distant, even more worried.

Could there be something else troubling her? Some other reason that she was so morose?

He needed to find some way to cheer her up. Some way to rekindle that fiery spark in her that he adored. He shoved her shoulder as they walked, sending her veering off for a few steps. "What is wrong, songbird?"

"I can hear a constant soundtrack around me. Everything is playing music. The *world* is music. It's beautiful, but…it's scaring me. I don't want to ruin everything." She shoved her hands into her coat pockets. It was a warm day, but she still wore a light jacket.

"How do you even know you can do any such thing? So far, all you've done is heal me." He was beginning to grow suspicious that something else had happened. "What are you

THE UNSEELIE DUKE

not telling me?"

She shook her head and didn't respond.

That confirmed it.

She knew better than to lie to him—he still had the spell that would tell him when she was. He balled his hands into fists. "It was that little *shit* again, wasn't it? What is that half-breed bastard lying to you about now?"

"Izael, please, just let it go."

"No." He took her by the upper arm and tugged her around until she was facing him, stopping in the middle of the dirt path through the woods. "You are mine, and I will not have him meddling in my affairs! What has he told you? I will not be patient this time."

She shut her eyes. "Can it wait?"

"No. No, it cannot." He flicked his other hand, summoning to his palm the orb that looked like it was made of pure crystal. "And do not lie to me, remember."

Letting out a long, ragged sigh, she pulled her arm from his grasp and walked off into the woods. "Let's at least find somewhere to sit down."

She was stalling. Buying time. But he put up with it, following on her heels. She found a large enough rock to suit them both and sat down. "Puck told me that no matter the outcome of the contract—whether I win or lose—you're going to die."

The glass orb did not glow. He scoffed. "And you believed him? Oh, Alex—what a silly thing to be so bent out of shape about! Yet, I find myself flattered." He knelt on the ground at her feet, not caring if he got grass stains on his clothes. She was staring down at her lap, and he crooked a finger under her chin to urge her to meet his gaze. "This is why you have been so eager to find a way out from our contract."

"I mean, yeah. I'm also not so thrilled about you owning my soul if I lose, either, but. Yeah." Her cheeks went just a little red. She was embarrassed. Oh, the poor thing. She must be conflicted over feelings for him.

Which meant she had feelings for him.

He laughed.

Which made her glare at him.

"I'm not laughing at you, pretty girl." He picked up her hand and kissed her fingers, vanishing the glass orb from his hand. "I am…happy."

"You're happy you might die?"

"I'm happy that you care if I do. That is all." He kissed her knuckles again before placing her palm to his cheek, leaning into her touch. She was so wonderfully warm.

"You really think Puck was lying?"

"This is what he does. He *meddles.* For as insane as I am, he is far worse. He delights in destroying the happiness of others, unraveling schemes and foiling the plans of anyone he deems amusing enough. Even if he believes he has seen the outcomes of those futures, we make our own paths. Not him." He smiled up at her.

And she smiled faintly back. But there was still something troubled in her eyes. She didn't believe him. "Yeah, okay." She sighed.

"In five days' time, you will see that it is all for naught, when I win and grant your wish—and take your soul." He kissed her palm.

"You say that like it's supposed to be comforting."

"It is."

She sighed again.

Laughing, he stood and planted his hands on his hips. "Come, now. We came here to test out this new magic of yours! And it seems like you have found a private enough place for us. Shall we, then?"

"I guess." She still didn't sound convinced.

Puck's prophecy was vaguely alarming, but he would

figure out a way to skirt around it and avoid the death the half-breed time traveler had predicted.

But honestly, he did not care. Because one thing was starting to become clear to him. He might not yet own Alex's soul…but perhaps he already owned her heart.

And that was a far harder prize to earn. And one that he hadn't expected to steal for quite some time. Yet here they were! How exciting. He hadn't even been *trying* very hard.

I'm a genius.
A sexy genius.
This is gonna be amazing.

CHAPTER TWENTY-FOUR

Alex wasn't sure if she should be relieved or worried that Izael took her at face value with her explanation of what Puck had told her. It had been, after all, only half the story. But if he dismissed Puck's warning of his impending death, he certainly wasn't going to take a double Armageddon any more seriously.

But the moment had passed, and now he was grinning to himself like an idiot because she had confessed that she didn't want him to die. Which was true, but also embarrassing. She shouldn't want to fall in league with someone like him. An Unseelie fae. He could be tricking her—conning her into falling for him. She didn't *think* that was the case. But how could she really know?

He was hundreds of years old.

And she'd only known him for a matter of days.

But those were all things she would have to to deal with in the very-quickly-approaching future. Right now, she had to figure out how to use her new, scary magic.

Izael sat down on the grass and patted the spot in front of him. "Sit."

With a heavy sigh, she got up from the rock and obeyed, sitting in front of him.

He pointed down at the grass in between them. "Do something."

"Seriously?" She arched an eyebrow. "That's your version of training me? 'Do something?' I'm pretty sure I could have gotten that far on my own."

"Really? Because you seemed pretty content to hide in your new flat." He smiled. God, sometimes she wanted to smack the smug expression off his face.

Shaking her head, she gave in. "Whatever." Turning her attention down to the blades of grass, she focused, trying to allow herself to tune out—literally—the rest of the world and only hear the individual strands of green.

They were quiet, but pervasive. The trees around here were a deep hum, like the pull of a bow over the lowest strings on a cello or a bass. Something that resonated through the ground beneath her. But the grass was a higher-pitched sound, singing in harmony with everything else around her.

Maybe she could change the note they were playing. She kept it in harmony with the rest of the world around her but tried to focus on shifting it down a half an octave.

The grass began to grow. A single strand reached up, going through its normal cycle in fast-forward. When it was about a foot high, she stopped and smiled. That was *cool.*

Izael stayed silent, simply watching her, clearly not wanting to interrupt for once.

Now, she wondered what would happen if she changed the instrument. Instead of a string instrument, she shifted it to a flute. The grass changed into a tiger lily in full bloom, its orange petals with their black spots opening to the sunlight above. "Whoa…"

"See? Hardly terrifying."

"What if I try to make it an animal? Like a mouse or something?"

"I honestly do not know. Try it."

"But…plants don't have souls, right? And I assume a mouse does?" She looked up at him, turning her attention away from the flower. "Like, if I turned a tiger lily into a human, would they just lay there with the lights on and nobody home, or would we have a very naked very terrified new person running around the woods?"

"There's only one way to find out." He cackled. "Either way, it sounds like fun! Don't worry. I'll eat them if it's a problem."

"I…that is not a good solution."

"But it *is* a solution." He sat back, resting his hands in the grass, looking pleased as punch. His octagonal sunglasses were hiding what she knew was a devious and probably slightly evil expression. "Try it. Make it a living creature. Do a field mouse, as you said."

"But what if the plant doesn't want to be a mouse? I don't want to hurt it."

"You aren't hurting it. You're changing it. We are all a part of life—we are all one organism, really." He gestured one of his hands aimlessly. "An instrument in the orchestra. You're just rearranging who sits in what section."

Shutting her eyes, she scratched her head. She didn't know how to feel about the whole thing. Everything he was saying made sense, but it was just…overwhelming. And way more responsibility than she had any right to have.

But it was worth a try. She didn't even know if she *could* change a plant into a mammal. If she could, that meant the opposite was also probably true. And at least he wasn't asking her what might happen if she stopped the music—told the orchestra to go silent. Yet. She was sure he'd get there eventually.

Opening her eyes, she looked at the tiger lily and ran her fingers over one of its leaves. It was beautiful. Maybe she could make it a bird. It might like to be able to fly. Looking up at the tree over them, she caught sight of a sparrow chirping away in the branches. She focused on the music that it made—a happy little melody on a piccolo.

She made the song of the lily match.

And before her eyes, the lily changed into a goddamn bird.

It hopped around on the ground for a moment, turning its head to look up at them both, confused. It pecked at the earth for a second before flapping its wings and flying up to the tree to join its more naturally-made friend.

"Holy *fuck.*" She laughed. "I made a fucking bird! I—whoa!"

Izael tackled her, sending her flat on her back with him over her. Before she could ask him what the hell he was doing, she had her answer. He silenced her protests with a kiss that was harsh and needy, almost bruising in its intensity.

He cradled the back of her head in his hand, his sharp nails pricking her skin, as he deepened the embrace, invading her mouth with his forked tongue that eagerly wrapped around hers.

She grasped the front of his suitcoat, needing something to cling to. He was a wild storm, and she was just a raft lost at sea, being tossed about in waves that didn't care if she was going to drown in them.

When he finally broke the kiss, she was breathless, her chest heaving. He grinned wickedly down at her. "It is nearly sunset. Let's return to my home, unless you prefer I take you here, in the woods, where anyone could find us."

"I…" Why was she nervous? Why did that feel like it was a step over some point of no return?

He parted her legs and pressed his hips against hers, miming the dance he was clearly hinting at. She gasped at the feeling of him there, at the sensation of him grinding against her. He was going to be a lot to handle, even in human form.

Her stomach twisted into a knot of nervous anticipation and excitement. Gods, she wanted him. Gods, how he clearly wanted her. She let her eyes slip shut as he repeated the gesture, relenting from the pressure only to redouble it.

"Fuck," she said through an exhale.

"That's the intention, yes." He snickered. That earned him a glare that turned his snicker into a laugh. "Come, songbird. There is no need to be shy. You need this just as badly as I do. I will not make you take me in my true form—not yet." He rutted his hips against hers and groaned, shuddering as he caged her in. *"Damn it."*

She slid her hands to his hips, hooking her fingers into his beltloops. It felt so good, having him there over her. His sharp cologne coupled with the scent of fresh grass and an earthy, woodsy smell mixed with the music all around her— she felt drunk. Swallowing down the lump in her throat, she knew there was nowhere to run. Nowhere she could hide. And she didn't want to.

Nodding once, she surrendered.

Izael wasted no time in hopping up to his feet, the proof of his need for her outlined very clearly in his trousers—and scooped her up in his arms. The familiar but no less jarring sensation of being taken through a portal followed a second later.

This might be a huge mistake.

No, it was *definitely* going to be a huge mistake.

But what did it matter, really? The world was going to end soon—two of them, actually—and all because of her.

She might as well enjoy it while it lasted.

Finally, finally, finally!

He put his songbird down and shoved her roughly toward his hot spring. She yelped and took a wild swing in his direction to try to fend him off. He didn't care. He was going to have her—in human form, *fine*—but he was going to have her!

"Hey! What're you—"

He pushed her again, sending her screaming and falling into his hot spring, the steam rising from the surface curling away like smoke in the splash.

She came up, sputtering, pushing her dark purple hair from her face. "I've already nearly drowned once this week. Can we—"

He was already stripped and in the water with her. He was not a patient creature; he knew this. She let out a cry as he fisted her hair and devoured her angry complaints with an equally furious kiss.

If she thought he was going to go easy on her simply because he would have her with only one of his cocks, not two, she was sorely mistaken. *Heh. Sore.* Yanking her shirt up, he slipped his hand underneath her brassiere and roughly squeezed her breast. They were so soft, so supple—they fit so perfectly into his palm. He wanted to squeeze them together and fuck them. He wanted to bury his head in them and sink his fangs into their yielding flesh.

He was not one who denied himself what he wanted.

She was gasping when he broke the kiss long enough for him to rip her shirt off over her head and strip her topless. He pushed her back against the edge of the pool, arching her backward over a rock.

She tried to protest. "Izael, wait—"

Like he was going to listen to a silly little thing like the word *wait*. Especially when he had a wonderful, beautiful, tempting sight like her helpless before him. He put a hand around her throat, pressing her head back, forcing her to arch those beautiful breasts up closer to him.

He descended on one of her rosebud nipples, already pert, and bit down. Hard. She shrieked, slamming her fists into his shoulders, trying to deter him. But as he curled his tongue around the injured flesh, her cry turned into a low moan.

Pretty girl. Don't worry. I know what you like.

Too ashamed to ask for him to take her. Too embarrassed to admit how much she liked it rough. He would relish watching his new impertinent and indignant toy unravel on him. He squeezed his hand around her throat, just a little—enough to put pressure on her but leave her plenty of room to breathe. It pulled another moan from her chest, her hands on his shoulders now clinging to him instead of trying to push him away.

He bit her again, just as hard as before. She cried out, squirming and writhing, but didn't fight that time. He continued the pattern, biting and soothing, nibbling and licking, lavishing her with the attention he had been so desperate to give her since the moment he saw her.

Mine, all mine.

He switched sides, lest her other breast become concerned he planned to neglect her. Her heart was racing, her breath coming fast and shallow. And they had only just begun!

Flicking open the button of her jeans, his other hand invaded her panties. Vanishing his sharp nails, he plunged two fingers deep inside her without warning, renewing her wailing and pointless pounding of her fists onto his back.

But the proof of what he found was all he needed to confirm his theories. She needed this *desperately*, the sweet nectar of her body quickly coating his invading digits. He broke off his attentions from her reddened nipple to loom over her, grinning in triumph as he watched her writhe and whimper.

"Pretty girl…look at you. You like this just as much as I do, don't you?" He let go of her throat only to press his thumb past her parted lips. "I'm going to have you in every way a man can have you—do you understand me?"

She closed her lips around his thumb, sucking on it, rolling her tongue along the pad. Yes, she did understand. And she seemed just as eager as he.

"Yes, that's it. Just like that." His voice was thick with lust and need, barely more than a growl. He wanted to slam himself past those plump, perfect lips of hers—to fill her throat and pump his seed deep into her. But that would have to be her dessert. Right now, he was far more focused on the main course.

Plucking his thumb from her mouth, he nearly tore her pants from her, tossing her soaked boots and socks and finally leaving her as naked as he. She watched him, wary and curious, with half-lidded eyes dazed from her own desire.

If she thought he was going to take her gently, she was a fool.

Snatching her by the hair, he yanked her up from the rock only to turn her around, her back to his chest, and snarled in her ear, "I am going to make you *mine*, do you understand? Once I'm done with you, songbird, you'll never be able to take another lover and be satisfied."

Any attempt at a reply was cut off as he bent her over the same rock, his hand on the back of her head, pinning her down. The water was up to their thighs, and the extra height for her was exactly what he needed. He picked up her thigh with his other arm, hooking it over his elbow, exposing her to him.

He should probably ease himself into her. He was no slouch in his human form—he got to choose how he appeared, after all. He *probably* should be nice and let her get used to his considerable girth and length.

That would be the gentlemanly thing to do.

He laughed.

Nah.

Without even a stutter, he buried himself to the hilt in a single stroke.

And knew she wasn't going to be the only one left changed forever.

Ecstasy crashed over her without warning as he rammed himself into her with one violent thrust. It felt like she had been hit by a car. She let out a cry that was half a scream and half a choked wail as her muscles clenched around him in her release.

Izael snarled over her like an animal—like an actual wild beast. He leaned his weight against her, his hand pinning her head to the rock, as he throbbed inside her. He was huge. It ached in the most perfect way. Her head was already reeling.

"*Mine—*" he growled, primal and unyielding. This wasn't just fucking. This was *claiming.* He wanted her soul. He probably already had her heart.

And now her body was his, too.

He began to piston inside of her at an almost inhuman tempo. She couldn't speak. Couldn't ask him to slow down. Couldn't do anything but try to breathe and feel him ram home inside her like he wouldn't ever leave.

The pleasure was unreal. It could drive a person insane. And it would be entirely worth it. The sound of his body slapping into hers and his furious grunts and moans of pleasure over her tangled with her mewling whimpers each time he bottomed out inside her.

He pulled her thigh higher, splitting her wider, and she let out a sharper cry as he somehow managed to find a way deeper, forcing it all in, straining what already was almost too much for her to take. But he seemed to want to prove otherwise.

There were no words. Just the seemingly unending tempo as he did as he promised—and *took* her. Claimed her. Made her *his*. She knew his claims that she would never be satisfied with anyone else weren't mere egotistical boasting.

This was ecstasy. Pure and utter violent ecstasy. Pain mingled with bliss, and she needed more of both. How long it went on, she couldn't say—but he seemed unstoppable. Maybe he wouldn't ever stop. Peak after peak, release after release, it seemed like he wouldn't ever let her body down from the razor's edge.

Until she knew she just couldn't take anymore. "Please—" she gasped, the first word she had been able to summon since he began.

The hand that pinned her down suddenly fisted in her hair, yanking her head up from the stone, arching her back. "Surrendering already?" He laughed, cruel and taunting, as he rammed himself to the hilt and held himself there, using all his weight to increase the pressure, making her wail. "Yes, that's it—sing me your song, little bird. *Beg.*"

"Please—Izael—I—" Her head was spinning.

His arm wrapped around her throat, yanking her back to his chest. He squeezed, tightening his grip as he buried his head in her hair close to her ear. "Yes. Beg me. Plead with me." He pulled his hips back only to snap them forward again. The angle made it all the more intense.

She cried and clung to his arm. "Please—Izael—I can't—I can't take any more—please—"

"You're mine. You belong to me. Now and forever. *Say it!*" Another ramming thrust had her seeing stars. He had truly lost his mind, and she was about to join him if he didn't stop.

"Yes—yes!" She dug her nails into his arm. "Please —Izael—"

"Good songbird." His thrusts became erratic and somehow more brutal. "My songbird. *My* witch. *Mine.*" One final impact and she felt him surge, throbbing as he spent himself inside her.

It sent her into another catastrophic peak of pleasure, and she wondered if she might die from it. What a way to go.

He roared, releasing her thigh to wrap both arms around her. With a hiss, he dug his teeth into her neck. She had no clue if he had broken the skin. It didn't matter. It was all too much. The hot water. The overwhelming sensation. The pleasure that threatened to consume her. The pain that somehow only served to make it all the more intense.

She felt him gather her up in his arms. She must have blacked out. Soft pillows were underneath her, and someone was kissing her sweetly. But her head was too busy trying to catch up from whatever wild rollercoaster had decided it wanted to have its way with her.

Someone whispered to her as she slipped into unconsciousness.

"I love you."

But it must have been a dream.

Because that couldn't have been real.

CHAPTER TWENTY-FIVE

Tzael wrapped Alex in loose coils of his tail as he held her close. They were buried under multiple blankets. He wasn't particularly tired, but he understood why she had decided to pass out.

I hope I didn't break her.

He doubted it. She was a resilient creature. It felt so good to have her naked body next to his. He had whispered to her words of truth, knowing she had already slipped too far out of consciousness to hear him.

By the Morrigan, was this what love was like? He had not recognized it for what it was at first. How would he have? He had never been in love before. She had been a splendid lover, but something about it had been…different.

It had *mattered.*

It wasn't simply a wanton lust that had been sated. It was something else entirely. He kissed the back of her head, her hair once again damp. He did not care. It was his fault for having thrown her into his hot spring, after all.

All he could do was focus on the simple fact that he was in love. This songbird had stolen his heart long before she had even considered giving hers in return. *You devious witch. This was supposed to be my conquest, not yours.* But how could he hold it against her? His lonely nights were over. He would have to find a way to make her ageless like him, to ensure she never left his side.

Because now that he had tasted what it felt like to love someone, he never, *ever* wanted to let it go. He would fight the gods themselves if it meant keeping her. He smiled, shutting his eyes. Now he had to simply convince her that her true wish was to live forever by his side.

How hard could that be?

Surely, she must already want it. She was simply being stubborn; that was all.

"Izael."

And there went his good mood.

Grimacing briefly, he slithered out from under his blanket and pillows and, forcing a false beatific smile, he draped himself over the edge of the boat that hung from his tree. "Uncle Anfar! To what do I owe this pleasure?"

"I am *not* your uncle." The sea monster was wearing his human guise and glowered up at him with those fully black eyes, his expression fixed into a dour and unapproving one. Izael wondered if he was ever in a good mood. Honestly, he could not fathom what the cheerful selkie Anfar had gained as a mate saw in the curmudgeonly, grumpy beast. "You missed a gathering of the Din'Glai. There were important matters to attend."

Izael shrugged. "I am sure the Moonlit Court got along just fine without me. Usually, you beg me to stay away from official matters." He moved from the bed and down the tree, leaving Alex unconscious and hiding where she was. It was for the best. She was still his wonderful little secret, after all.

"Yes. I do. We managed to settle our agenda with far

less…manic interruption. But it was suspicious. Where were you?" He narrowed those inky black eyes.

"Asleep." He smiled and pointed up at his boat. "As I was right until you woke me."

"At this hour?"

"I was tired from a strenuous bout of lovemaking. I have found myself a new dalliance—she is a sweet thing. Lovely purple hair. She tastes like coffee and spices. Would you like to try her?" He grinned wide, flashing his fangs. "We could share."

Anfar made a face of disgust. "No."

That was precisely what Izael had been counting on, of course. "That is where I was. I fear I must have missed the summons while I was busy stuffing both of my cocks into her—"

"Stop." Anfar turned his back on Izael and began to walk away. "I do not need to hear the details."

Izael cackled. "Oh, Uncle Anfar. You're no fun at all."

Anfar only growled in annoyance as he disappeared into a puddle of water on the ground, choosing not to reply to Izael's taunting. It was probably for the best. It had been a while since Anfar had taken Izael to task, and he had no desire to be beaten that night.

But Anfar's curiosity as to his whereabouts was an annoying reminder that his absence was not going unnoticed. He sighed. He knew Alex's glamour was a flawless one—but taking her out into the world of the Unseelie was… risky. While no one would be able to see through her guise and discover her as a human witch, the odds that his songbird blew her cover were extremely high. She was not fae—she did not know how to *act* like one. One wrong move, and it would be over.

But he had promised to show her his world. Perhaps he

could kill two songbirds—*heh*—with one stone. Tapping his chin, he did what he did best.

He schemed.

ALEX WOKE up feeling like she had been run over. No, she felt like she had when she was a late teen and decided to take up horseback riding for a brief second. She felt *pummeled* in places that shouldn't be that bruised.

Groaning, she rolled over onto her stomach and buried her face in the pillow. She must be in Izael's boat-bed-of-pillows. It was a weird arrangement, but she had to say she enjoyed it. It was oddly comfortable and not as lumpy as she would have predicted.

And it smelled like him.

She was under several fur blankets, and she was cozy, even if she was battered.

"Did you have a nice nap?" Izael crooned from beside her.

"Fuck you."

He laughed quietly, kissing her cheek. "Let us eat. I think you might need some protein after what we did."

"After what *you* did to *me*. I had little to do with that massacre." She opened an eye and lifted her head to shoot him an unhappy look. "You're an asshole. You couldn't have taken it easy on me?"

"You wouldn't have enjoyed it half as much if I had." He poked her on the end of her nose. "Come! We have to dress you like a true fae and get your glamour back on so we can go join the feast."

"Join the...what?" She blinked away the grogginess and rubbed her hand over her eyes. "What do you mean?"

"I promised to show you Tir n'Aill. It's time to see how you do in public."

THE UNSEELIE DUKE

"But…I'm not supposed to be here. What if I fuck up? I don't know your customs." She sat up, not caring as the blanket slipped down to reveal her breasts. They were covered in red marks and straight-up hickeys. "Izael, I look like I've been in a car wreck."

"Badges of honor!" He scooped her up in his arms. "And I have a plan for that."

She wriggled but put up with it as he carried her out of his bed and back to the ground. It felt weird to be butt-ass naked in a place with no actual walls, but whatever. "Which is?"

"We pretend you are entirely mute. And perhaps a little dumb." He poked the end of her nose. She was getting used to that—she figured it was an affectionate gesture from him. "You are beautiful enough that my interest in someone who is hardly a…mental match for me would not be out of character for me enough to raise suspicions."

Rubbing her temples then squeezing the bridge of her nose, she tried her best to remind herself to be patient with the bastard. "So…I pretend to be a *mentally challenged and mute* Unseelie fae version of arm candy for you?"

"Arm candy?" He blinked. "Oh!" Cackling, he hugged her close, pressing her naked body against his bare chest. He was in his true form. She figured wearing a shirt with a tail would be kind of weird. "I love that. Yes. Exactly. You will be my dumb and mute arm candy."

"You are way, way too proud of yourself." Shaking her head, she gave up. It was clearly unavoidable at this point. He had *that look.* "Fine. Whatever. I'm hungry."

Laughing in triumph, he pushed her away a few inches and repeated the same glamour routine he had done before, stealing a few strands of her hair and enchanting it into dust. When he was done, she looked the same as she had before. Her skin was whitish-purple, her hair was somehow even more vibrant, and she had pointed ears.

"Each night as the moon begins to set toward the horizon, we convene for a feast. All are welcome to join, but many are too afraid to do so for the…predators that dwell there." His toothy smile told her all she needed to know.

"And I'm not going to get yanked into some epic orgy by a pack of *other* horny Unseelie?" She arched an eyebrow.

"Oh, I'm certain others will try. And try their damnedest." He summoned a gossamer dress, the sheer black fabric appearing in his hands as he gestured like he was flicking out laundry. He dressed her. A second later he was braiding her hair. She just put up with it. It was weird how much he liked to pamper her.

Weird, but enjoyable. She just wasn't used to it. "And what do I do when somebody tries to get me into a foursome or moresome?"

"Well, two choices. You can either give me a wink and enjoy the rampant fucking, or you hiss at them and hide behind me. I am notoriously covetous of my lovers." He was extremely dexterous as he wove her hair into a complicated pattern. "If you feel so inspired, however, you could always straddle me, and we could give them all a fantastic show."

Christ, he was exhausting. "I don't know if I'm into voyeurism."

His hand slipped around her throat as he pulled her back against him, his long fingers tightening. It sent her stomach cinching into knots. "Did you know you were into this?"

She shivered. There was zero point in denying what that did to her. "No."

"What is the human phrase? Keep an open mind." He kissed her cheek and lowered his hand. "Now. Let's take a look at you."

His tattoos shifted again into a new position. He stepped

back and turned her about, studying her. "Hm. Something is missing. Ah! I know." Quick as lightning, he shot over to his wardrobe. Pulling open a drawer, he began to dig through it. She couldn't see what was in it, but it looked like a massive pile of different pieces of jewelry.

"How much jewelry do you own, man?"

"Hm? Oh. This is just my disposable stuff." He picked up a silver necklace, studying it in his palm. She couldn't quite see the details from where she was. "My truly valuable items are stashed away." He slithered back to her before holding up the necklace in front of her.

She felt her eyes go wide as she took in what he had. Disposable. Right. Sure. It wasn't tarnished at all, despite looking like a vintage Victorian piece. It was probably platinum. It was inlaid with mother of pearl, sapphires, and amethysts in a large medallion that would sit just at the beginning of her cleavage, and underneath the bone Ouroboros necklace she never took off.

With how sheer and low-cut the gossamer dress was, she knew it would show off her, well, assets.

I'm going to get into so much trouble tonight.

He unclasped the end of the chain and draped the necklace around her, clipping it back into place and pulling her hair out from under it. "You look flawless."

"This is a really, really stupid idea. This could get us killed."

That maniacal, devious grin split his features as he watched her with hungry, glowing, turquoise eyes. "Those are precisely the best ideas."

Yeah. She was doomed. Totally fucking doomed.

He took her arm and tucked it into his elbow. "To the feast!" A portal opened before her, and he half-dragged her through it as she fought to keep up with him.

She pulled in a breath of surprise as she saw what was on

the other side. He had taken her to a feast, all right. The table that stretched before her was at least twenty feet long—and it wasn't the only damn table. It was overflowing with roasted meats of all kinds, several of which she couldn't identify and was probably happier not knowing what they were.

Before her was every kind of monster and creature she could have ever imagined in any of her most vivid dreams or nightmares. One man had horns curling from his head like a deer, his legs matching the species. But he had long, terrible, bony spines protruding from his back and sticking out like a porcupine. He was laughing and drinking with a woman who had a fish's tail. A literal mermaid! She was sitting in a chair, smiling, seemingly unconcerned with the fact that she was out of the water.

Alex clung tightly to Izael's arm, standing closer to him as she took in the sights around her. Another man looked to be made of shadows—like black smoke coalesced into a shape that could have been human. He was sitting with another man who was *made entirely out of bees.*

Holy shit.

Holy fucking shit.

She was so out of her league it wasn't even funny.

Another man resembled an ice sculpture, his hair sticking out from his head in literal sharpened points. Another creature, whose gender she couldn't identify, looked like a stick bug if it was enormous and crossbred with a horse who walked on two legs.

Izael leaned over and kissed her temple. "Breathe, songbird," he whispered. "This would be no new sight for you."

She pulled in a breath, forcing herself to calm down. Right. Right. She could do this—she could absolutely do this. This was normal. Totally normal. Totally, absolutely, one-hundred-percent normal.

She was an Unseelie fae. Right? Right. Straightening her

back, she smiled at him. She couldn't speak, after all. This was all just an act—maybe if she just pretended it was a dream, she'd survive, and they would both get out the other side of this in one piece.

Maybe.

Unlikely, but it was worth a shot.

"If it isn't the Duke of Bones! We were beginning to worry about you," boomed a voice from the table. She looked over to see who had spoken. It was…a man who was also a goat. He stood from the table, his long black coat falling around him and nearly reaching the floor. From the waist down, he had goat's legs that were covered in jet black fur. From his head curled two black horns. His face was human, a dark black goatee—of course—covering his chin. His black hair was pulled back in a crimson tie. He only had one arm; the other sleeve of his coat was tailored to a stump. But he gave off a regal demeanor all the same.

He looks like Baphomet. If Baphomet fucked Dracula and had a kid. She blinked. *Goatula.*

"Aaah, my Lord Bayodan. So sorry to have worried you. I fear I have been distracted with my new bauble. This is Alaeni," Izael introduced her. "My newest find. Isn't she something?"

Bayodan watched her, his crimson eyes sliding up and down her form. "Indeed. A pleasure to meet you, Alaeni." He bowed, folding his one arm in front of him.

"I fear she is mute. The perfect woman."

She shot him a look that could have melted the ice man who was currently eating roasted chicken.

Bayodan chuckled. "And a fire in her, I see. Yes, I could see why she would be a distraction."

Turning her attention back to Bayodan, she smiled at him as if to beg for his forgiveness, and curtseyed. He seemed nice enough, if…intimidating.

He reached for her hand, and she gave it to him, letting him kiss her knuckles. "Will you join me and my mate, Duke? We would appreciate your company."

"Of course! We are both *starving* after the day we have had." Izael laid the innuendo on thick. She rolled her eyes. She couldn't help it.

Bayodan chuckled. "I like this one." He gestured wide with his one hand toward the table. "Come, friends. Let us feast."

Well, she could pretend to be mute. Dumb, however? Not so much.

Yeah, this was a really stupid fucking idea.

CHAPTER TWENTY-SIX

Alex found herself sitting between an Unseelie snake and an Unseelie goat man at a feast attended entirely by monsters. It was one of those moments that was so jarring it made her reflect on the series of idiotic choices she had made that had wound up putting her smack in the middle of a situation that was probably going to get her murdered.

Bayodan seemed perfectly nice, his deep voice always carefully metered and strangely soothing, especially in comparison to Izael's far more manic demeanor. The goat even poured her a glass of wine and passed her a plate of roasted chicken legs—she really hoped they were chicken—to help herself.

Izael was chattering away with whoever was sitting across from him at the table. She looked like a literal ghost, her eyes empty and hollow sockets, her long, flowing hair a translucent, eerie shade of greenish white. It would have been terrifying to see if she wasn't smiling and laughing along with everyone else.

Izael's tail, however, was wrapped around her left ankle as an assurance that he hadn't forgotten about her.

"Allow me to introduce my mate, Alaeni." Bayodan leaned back in his chair and gestured to the person sitting to his right. "This is Cruinn."

Alex blinked. The person sitting beside him was…something else entirely. They were made entirely out of what looked like *broken glass.* Shards of crystal that shifted and changed, sometimes forming smooth surfaces, but most of the time they were fractal and caught every glimmer of the firelight around them like a prism. She couldn't tell if they were a man or a woman, but Alex had the suspicion that they were neither. Or maybe both. Or maybe, in this case, it really didn't matter.

Cruinn reached out a hand to her, the pieces smoothing out. "What a pleasure! You have come here with the duke. I'm not sure if we should be offering you our condolences." They chuckled.

She smiled back at them and shrugged, as if to say she wasn't quite so certain either. She reached out and put her hand in theirs and watched as they leaned down to kiss her knuckles. They were cool to the touch—not unlike the glass they resembled.

But something seemed a little off about the fae made of glass. She noticed chunks were missing here and there. Holes where a shard should be. And there was a strangeness to their smile that made her think of the elderly in a nursing home. Like something wasn't quite all there.

An arm draped around her shoulder. It was Izael. He pulled her close and kissed her temple before whispering in her ear. "Bayodan and Cruinn were once loyal advisors to King Valroy. They betrayed him for Abigail's sake. Bayodan lost his arm, and Cruinn…lost far more than that, though they are getting better."

Bayodan smiled faintly, clearly knowing what Izael was telling her. He bowed his head slightly. "We paid our price and do not regret what we have done."

She frowned at them, feeling sorry for what had happened. She had no idea if they deserved it, but it sounded like it was awful all around.

"We appreciate your kindness." Bayodan reached for his goblet of wine and lifted it to her. "Open hearts are rare amongst our kind."

Oops. Did she fuck up? She hoped not.

"She is young. She'll learn in time." Izael chuckled and leaned back in his chair, loosening his arm from around her shoulders. "Eat, Alaeni. Enjoy."

And she tried to do just that. She took in the conversations around her, glad she had agreed to pretend to be mute. She wouldn't know what to do, trying to keep up with what she heard around her. It was just a sea of references to people, places, and events that she could only begin to fathom what they were.

It felt like a fever dream.

All the food was delicious. She didn't even stare at Izael as he gobbled down both a turkey leg and the bones involved. The evening went on, and soon she couldn't possibly put any more food into her face, preferring instead to nurse her own goblet of wine. She was probably on her second or third glass, but it had only served to make her a little comfortably fluffy.

The music that filled the air made it feel all the more dreamlike. She knew it was not really there—not for everyone else, at any rate. But it was just the music of the life around her, of the Unseelie fae and of Tir n'Aill. It wasn't helping her stay out of a hypnotized state.

Luckily, Izael snapped her out of it before she zoned too far out.

"Ah, and there is my dear Uncle Anfar," Izael said as he gestured with his fork. "The one at the edges. The dreary undead sea captain. That charming man beside him is his mate, a selkie named Perin."

It was easy enough to spot them in the crowd given Izael's description. Sure enough, Anfar was…fucking terrifying. He had long, dark blue-green hair that was soaking wet and hung limply around his stern, sharp features. His eyes were pitch black from lid to lid. His skin was a grayish hue that reminded her of a dead body, his lips purplish. His clothing looked like a captain who had been dredged up from some sunken seventeenth-century frigate. Now she had a face to match the voice with, and she rather wished she didn't.

Sitting behind him was a young man with short, rakish brown hair and an easy smile. He was twice Anfar's size, looking much more like a living sailor, not a dead one. He was laughing with another man who resembled an elf with blue skin and stark white markings on his face.

The fae were fascinating but strange—each one somehow unique from the next. Although these were all seemingly high-ranking courtiers, so she figured they were somewhat more spectacular than most.

The whole scene was something out of a dream. She was glad she was just acting as Izael's date for the night—that made her small and unimportant. It was easy for her to be ignored. Bayodan did his best to be a good dinner "neighbor," but he was constantly being pestered by others for conversation. That was fine by her. Not like she was supposed to be able to speak, anyway.

She sat back in her chair with her goblet of wine and simply took in the surreal sight. It wasn't helped by the constant music that swirled through the air. The trees, the grass, the animals, the fae around her—everything sang together like an orchestra. She could feel the mood of every single person at the table if she focused on them, hearing how they either played in harmony with those around them or didn't.

The farther away the person was sitting from her, the harder it was to hear them.

Izael's tail slipped farther up her leg, curling around her calf and ending just below her knee. He didn't even seem to realize he was doing it. She wondered if it had a mind of its own. The moon was bright, casting a pale glow across the table and its contents, glinting off the silverware they used.

Wait.

She furrowed her brow and picked up an empty saucer in front of her. There was Latin inscribed along the edge, and as she turned it over, she saw a seal on the bottom with a cross emblazoned in the middle.

They were all eating off communion silver.

Izael leaned over to whisper to her. "King Valroy has a penchant for stealing human objects that amuse him, the more blasphemous the better. I am not the only one with a love for humanity, though he masks his fascination through focusing on *things,* whereas I prefer the people."

She shrugged. To each their own, she supposed. She put the saucer back down.

The party began to wind down after a while, as the food on the table was picked clean, although the wine never stopped flowing. Different fae began to stand from the table and wander off to the edges of the party, sitting on large collections of pillows and blankets. Apparently, hoarding them and turning them into mattresses or seating areas was a thing that wasn't unique to Izael.

It was when the pockets of fae all started fucking that she had to try not to laugh. Or stare. Or to laugh and stare. *You knew they were horny. He warned you about the orgies. What did you think was going to happen, stupid?*

Izael caught her staring. "Do you want to join in?"

Seeing as one guy who was basically a lizard was stuffing a woman who looked like she was made out of mist with a dick the size of her arm, it was hard not to stare. But it was also not exactly something she figured she'd enjoy. Or survive. Mostly survive.

She shook her head.

"Suit yourself. Come, let us find a place to sit and enjoy ourselves."

She shot him a glare.

"For once, I'm not being euphemistic." He chuckled and stood from the chair. He grabbed a bottle of wine and his goblet. "You are too sore from earlier tonight."

That was very true. She picked up her own goblet of wine and followed him to an empty spot a little way away from everybody else. Close enough that she would still be "treated" to the sight of everybody railing each other, but at least it was a proverbial balcony seat and not the front row.

He lay back on the pillows, propped up by a larger collection of them, his mother of pearl tail sprawled out around him in lazy loops and spirals. She stepped over several coils to sit beside him.

It was super hard not to stare at the…uh…entertainment. She sipped her wine and shook her head. She had to give up on thinking these creatures operated like humans. And to be fair, this was probably what human royals used to do. Or that rich people still did. Hell if she knew.

She had just never been to a full-on orgy before, that was all. Not like she really cared how people enjoyed themselves. Everything seemed consensual, so whatever.

"I'm impressed at your ability to withstand temptation," Izael folded an arm behind his head and shuffled lower into the pillows, but not far enough that he couldn't easily drink his wine. "Any one of these groups would gladly welcome you. They simply know better than to approach because you're with me. I get…bitey when people touch what is mine."

And she knew he meant that literally. She shrugged. She didn't know how to communicate to him that it was fine by her. It wasn't really her thing to jump into a big fuck-fest and get spit roasted by strangers.

"Will you kiss me again, pretty girl?" He reached up and stroked his fingers through her hair, toying with a lock of the purple strands. "It was so wonderful the last time."

She arched an eyebrow at him, silently asking two things. *Just a kiss?* And *why do you make it sound like it was something special?*

The look on his face made her glad she couldn't actually ask the questions aloud, however. He looked…vulnerable, for lack of a better phrase. As if he was really asking her for something that mattered to him.

Holy shit.

Did people not ever kiss him first?

Her shoulders slumped as the reality of that hit her. Was Izael *lonely?* She leaned over him and kissed him, stopping before it went too deep or too passionate. She really was too sore to go another round with him.

The sleepy smile he gave her was adorable, she had to admit. Then it had to go and get feisty. "I mean, your *jaw* isn't sore, right?"

She slapped his chest. It only made him laugh. He hugged her to his side, nearly making her spill her wine. She shuffled a bit to get comfortable.

"But seriously, your jaw isn't sore, so you could—" He stopped. In fact, the whole party stopped. Everyone turned and stared as someone walked up to the party from the woods. He was tall, with pale skin and dark blue tattoos that ran down one arm, the symbol of a maze emblazoned on his chest.

His long hair was the color of the sapphires she wore. As were his enormous *bat wings.* They were tipped with three fingers that were like the talons of a great bird. The membrane between the bones was almost translucent, still tinted that dark blue.

He had a smile on his face that was condescending and cruel, fiendish, and just downright *evil.* He was looking out at the party with equal parts contempt, disgust, and pride. That was a man who delighted in the pain of others, she was certain of it. She'd mistaken Izael for a bonfire, but now having seen a real one—she realized the Duke of Bones was just a fire in a hearth.

That creature was truly dangerous. She fought the instinctual urge to hide. Or to run into the woods and fuck right off from this whole nonsense before the newcomer noticed her.

Because there was no wondering who he was. There wasn't even a question in her mind, even if he hadn't been wearing the silver crown on his head that looked like tangled twigs and dead vines.

That had to be Valroy. King of the Unseelie.

And she was a human witch with magic she wasn't supposed to have.

The night had suddenly become much, *much* more dangerous.

CHAPTER TWENTY-SEVEN

Alex fought back panic. It wouldn't do any good—none at all—and she had to focus. Turning her back to the party so nobody could see her lips move, she knelt beside Izael. "We need to leave. We need to leave *right now.*"

Izael grimaced, baring his teeth. "It will be fine, songbird." But it was clear he didn't quite believe his own words. "He already knows I have taken a human witch."

Keeping her voice a harsh whisper, she tried to insist otherwise. "No, you don't understand—what if he finds out about the magic? What I can do? If he—"

He smiled in that manic, beatific way when he was putting on airs. "My king! What a pleasure! Do join us."

Shit, shit, shit! She turned to face Valroy as the creature approached. Holy shit, he was terrifying. Least of all because she knew what he could do to her. She scrambled back to the edge of the pillows but couldn't go any farther without having to climb over Izael's tail.

Valroy sneered at her obvious fear. "Hello, duke." He tilted his head slightly as those faintly glowing sapphire eyes of his raked over her. "A convincing glamour. Not even I would have noticed."

Her heart was pounding in her ears. She wanted to run—wanted to hide—but there was nowhere to *go.*

"I am flattered by your praise, my king." Izael pulled himself up, coiling his tail around her, as if sensing her urge to flee. Or maybe to signify that she was under his protection. "I assure you she is just as beautiful in her true form."

"I am certain she is." Valroy didn't take his eyes off her.

She stood, deciding she very much didn't want to be on the ground if he decided to lunge at her and rip her throat out.

"Come here, child." Valroy held his hand out to her.

Shit, shit, shit! What should she do? She couldn't very well refuse the guy, could she? He was a fucking king. She wanted to scream. Putting her hand in his, she couldn't help but notice she was shaking. Whatever. She figured her terror was plain as day anyway.

Valroy tugged her closer, forcing her to step over the coils of Izael's tail. "So, you will be the one who frees us from this interminable treaty? I thought you would be taller. Or at least more impressive."

She tried real hard not to take that personally.

Izael frowned. "I am not breaking the treaty with this arrangement. She has a willing contract she signed with me." Izael was tense, his shoulders rigid. "We have done nothing wrong."

"No, you have not." Valroy chuckled. "But if you believe I am going to let this opportunity go, you are sorely mistaken." He hooked a claw through the ring of the Ouroboros pendant she wore and used it to pull her even closer. "The treaty calls out the punishment that *I* would suffer if *I* took action to defy it. It says nothing of what would happen if a *human* caused such chaos."

Valroy was going to use her to break the treaty. Breaking her silence, figuring at this point it really didn't matter, she had only one question. "How?"

The king laughed, cruel and unfriendly. "And why would I tell you? It would spoil the fun."

Izael took her by the upper arm and pulled her back to him. "My king, I must protest—"

"And what will you do, snake?" Valroy cut him off. "Her soul is not yet yours. She is still, what's the phrase? Up for grabs? I can do with her whatever I like."

Izael growled. "The contract is unbreakable, even by you."

"Yes, yes. And what are the details of it? Ah. That you will spend seven days on Earth and seven nights in Tir n'Aill. After which, you must make your wish." Valroy grinned. "It will only take me one night of torture to ensure that she truly *wish* for the treaty to be broken."

Her stomach twisted in knots as adrenaline flooded her system. So that was his game. Torture her until she wished for the treaty to be nullified. She'd like to think she wasn't weak enough to succumb to it, when war was on the line—but she'd never been tortured before. She'd probably break like a twig.

"No." Izael pushed her half behind him. "She is mine, and you shall not hurt her."

"Then the game is simple. You have four days and *three* nights to convince her to make a wish for the treaty to be broken on your own. If you do not? Her final night belongs to me." He turned from them, clearly done with the conversation. "Oh. I will let you have her when I am done with her. Whatever is left, that is." He laughed.

Alex was shaking. Fear and anger—fight *and* flight at the same time. She felt lightheaded. Izael said nothing as he took her hand and led her through a portal, taking her back to his home. She leaned against one of the ruined walls as he changed his shape to his human form, if simply to be able to pace.

He was raging. Absolutely fuming. "How *dare* he? Who does he think he is? You are mine! *Mine!* I care nothing for any of this!"

"He's the king. He can do what he wants." She shut her eyes, putting her hands over her face. She had to think. There had to be a way out of this. There *had* to be.

"I will not stand for this! I will not allow it!"

Sure. Right. Like he had a choice.

Izael was suddenly in front of her, her upper arms in his hands. "It is simple. Make the wish, right now. Wish for the treaty to be broken. Your soul will be mine—he will have what he wants, and we can move on from this." He smiled as if it were the most obvious thing in the world.

"I have, like, eight problems with that plan."

His expression fell. "It's the only way out of this, songbird. Do you want to be tortured? Broken?"

"Of course not!" She nudged him away from her. She was still shaking. She needed a drink. She needed to get away from all of this. "But I'm not going to be the reason war breaks out again. What if he succeeds this time? What if two worlds end because of me?"

"Who told you about Valroy's plans?" Izael's expression twisted into one of rage. He put it together the second after he asked. *"Puck."*

She took a step away from him.

"What else did he tell you? Hm?"

"That I'd be the reason two worlds ended. I don't—I can't —I can't be involved in this anymore. Let me out of this contract, Izael."

He laughed, sounding just like Valroy had a few minutes prior. "I cannot. Contracts are binding to both parties."

"Fuck." She shook her head and backed away. "No. This

can't be real. This can't be happening. I won't be a part of this!"

"You have no choice. Make the wish. Give me your soul and let Valroy burn the Seelie and the humans to dust. There is nothing we can do to stop him." Izael stalked after her. "Do it, Alex—or do you wish to have your skin peeled off and your fingernails ripped away? And that is simply how he will begin torturing you."

"I—no. No. I won't. I won't. I'd rather die than know I was responsible for the deaths of billions. I don't care what happens to me." She kept retreating, even if he kept advancing.

"Do you think he will give you a choice? No. Once he's done with you, you'll do anything he asks, just to make the pain stop. Save yourself the torment. Please." He was starting to look desperate—and then she realized what it was. He was also terrified. "I do not want to watch this happen to you."

"This is your fault. If you had just—if—" She cringed. "No. I won't! I don't care."

"Then you leave me no choice." His expression turned hard. "I will make you. I will be far kinder, far gentler than he. You might heal from the pain and torment I will bring you in time. You will never mend what he is capable of doing to you."

Her eyes went wide. "You wouldn't."

"To save you from him? To ensure you are mine forever?" His lips turned up into a horrible, sadistic smile. "I will do anything."

When had she started crying? Did it matter? God, she hated crying. It was so useless. So pointless. It made her so angry whenever she started and couldn't stop. But she figured she had a decent excuse.

What was she supposed to do?

She couldn't make the wish. She'd be lying.

She couldn't go back to Earth on her own. And even if she could, where would she go that he couldn't find her?

Where could she go anywhere, where she'd be safe from Izael and Valroy?

There was only one answer.

And it was probably going to get her killed. *But at least then I'd just be dead and not responsible for double Armageddon.* But what other choice did she really have? None besides being tortured by either Izael or Valroy. One sounded beyond horrible, and the other sounded like it would be worse than death.

Taking a breath, she let it out slowly.

Then, turning on her heel, she ran as hard and as fast as she could into the woods of Tir n'Aill.

IZAEL HAD HOPED she would simply understand that what he was offering to her was, given their current predicament, a kindness. Sure, he didn't want to torture her—she didn't want to be tortured—but the other options were far, far worse.

She clearly did not see it that way as she ran into the woods as fast as she could.

It took him a second to process what she had done. "Alex? *Alex!*"

She ignored his shouting.

Where did she think she was going to hide from him? Where did she think she was actually going to go? She had nowhere to run, nowhere she could wedge herself that he could not find her.

Fear. That must be it. Blind fear. Simply running like a terrified deer, not realizing she was heading for the edge of a cliff. His poor songbird. She would come to understand this was for her own good.

Perhaps this could be a fun diversion. He did love a good hunt. He would give her a head start, let her get a few hundred feet away, before he chased her. He smiled. Perhaps she'd even let him fuck her when they were done. Nothing made for a glorious round of lovemaking like a little bit of life-ending fear, right?

It was a perfect plan. An absolutely flawless plan. This would all turn around, and they could laugh about it when the sun came up and they—

The sun.

He looked up at the sky.

He hadn't noticed it was turning brighter out. The moon was already gone, and the *sun was rising.*

Now he was the one who felt a fresh wave of fear spread over him. She wasn't simply running away. His songbird was too smart for that. She had a goal in mind.

And the goal?

Was the Seelie.

Now he screamed and ran after her. He did not have much time to save her life. To save her from her own foolish choices.

"Alex!"

CHAPTER TWENTY-EIGHT

Alex ran. She ran as hard and as fast as she could. All she had to do was make it until dawn. That was it. Maybe they'd take her prisoner and she'd be somebody's goddamn pet. Maybe they'd end up torturing her, too. But it didn't matter.

Because staying with Izael was a guarantee of both those things.

There was also a really good chance she was going to die. She didn't want to be murdered by any stretch of the imagination, but laying down her life to save two worlds seemed like a thing you were just supposed to do without question.

I should have known better.

I really should have known.

Never trust the fae. Never make deals with them. And never, ever trick yourself into thinking you might have actual feelings for one. Izael had promised not to hurt her. And that lasted exactly seven seconds when push came to shove.

She jumped over roots and tried not to run smack into a tree or trip over rocks or whatever. She could hear Izael shouting for her in the distance. She knew he'd catch up with her. She didn't think she'd actually manage to escape him on foot—she wasn't a total fucking idiot.

She was just buying time.

Time until the sunlight was high enough that she was officially an Unseelie-looking-motherfucker in Seelie town.

Bursting through the underbrush, she skidded to a halt as she found herself standing on a dirt road. Cool. She could run faster on dirt than through trees. All she had to do was pick a direction, and—

"What do you think you are doing?"

Fuck. Izael.

She turned to face the fae who was standing there, glowering at her. In his hand was clenched that glass orb he had made from her blood—the one that was supposed to tell him if she was lying. But now, she guessed it had another purpose. "You lied to me," she said through a hard breath. She was not meant for cardio.

"About what?" He took a step toward her, and she took one back.

"That spell. Wasn't just for lying, was it?" She pointed at his hand. "You can find me using it."

He chuckled. "I did not lie. I said that the spell would do nothing to harm you. And it hasn't. Does it allow me to see you, wherever you are? Why, of course." He held it up, perched between his pointed claws. "Shame on you for not being more specific."

The phrase *I should have known better* kept playing around in her head in a loop. Now she just kept adding reasons to the list. "And you promised you wouldn't ever hurt me. Now you're threatening to torture me."

"But the lesser of two harms that would befall you." He stretched out his other hand to her. "Come here, songbird—I can make this all better. Just wish for the treaty to be over and we can forget this ever happened."

"No." She turned and started to run again. But she made it only a few feet before something hit her hard from behind and knocked her to the dirt. Her head spun from the impact for a few precious seconds. When she finally realized where she was, and what was happening, she was already caught in the coils of his tail. He clenched down on her, inspiring her not to struggle. "Let me go!"

"Never." His words were a snarl. "You are *mine*! And no one—not even the Unseelie King himself—will take you from me!" He grasped her by the necklace she wore—the one she'd had since she was a child. "This marked you as mine long before we met. I am simply taking what belongs to me."

Glaring a hole into him, she held firm. "Let me go, Izael. You can't do this."

He chuckled, clearly thinking she was a fool. "And who will stop me? You? The *Seelie*? I know why you are running. I know what you think to achieve. If you think what the Unseelie will do to you is cruel, you have no concept of what they are like—what they are capable of!"

"Oh, like torturing me until I agree to let Valroy destroy two worlds?"

"You do not know he will be successful."

"Puck told me he would use my power to end two worlds. Valroy just wants to torture me, thinking I can wish the treaty away—what the fuck do you think he'll do when he realizes I have real magic now?" At least she could catch her breath, even if she was trapped. "What do you think he'll do to me when he finds that out? Do you really think he'll let you keep me?"

Izael grimaced, clearly having not put that together. "Then I will take your soul. He cannot touch you—cannot do

THE UNSEELIE DUKE

anything to you if you are mine. That is the law of our people."

"Yeah, 'cuz he looks like a guy who gives a fuck about laws." She rolled her eyes. It was his turn to be an idiot. "No, Izael. Let me go. If you can't let me out of this contract, I have nowhere else to go that's safe."

"Nowhere is safe for you. Not now, not ever."

"Then kill me."

"No!" His coils tightened around her. "You are mine, and I will not let you go!" He seemed desperate now, like he was on the edge of a precipice.

But she couldn't care. She couldn't let herself care.

Instinct told her to reach out with her magic. Something in her told her how she could use her new gifts to escape. She listened to the world around her, to the soundtrack that surrounded her, and she…skipped tracks. Just willed herself to be listening to something else, somewhere else.

She yelped and staggered as everything around her simply changed. Izael was gone. She was no longer in a forest, but on the edges of a grassy field. She had to laugh a little bit—it had worked. Her stupid instinct had worked. "Holy shit." She shook her head. Yeah, that was cool. She could *teleport through music.*

She wished she could spend some time to appreciate that—to really let it sink in. But the night was slowly giving way to dawn, the faint blue sky slowly turning orange and yellow as the sun crept closer to the horizon.

There was nothing left to do but wait and hope the Seelie weren't just as bad as their brothers and sisters, and that they might take pity on her dumb ass.

"Alex!" It was Izael. He was standing on the edge of the forest, hiding in the shadows. He had a wild look on his face of pure desperation and panic. "Come here this instant—you do not know what you are doing." He reached for her.

"I think I do know what I'm doing for once." She sighed. "I'm sorry, Izael. I really am. I did really enjoy our time the past few days. I hope you did, too."

"Alex, come back to me. Please. Do not do this. You do not have to resort to this. We can talk this through—we'll find another way. Come here." He stretched his hand closer but wouldn't put it into the slowly growing sunlight. "Alex—" His voice cracked.

Was he going to cry?

Well, he'd have good company. She wiped her cheeks. Shit, she hated crying. "I'm sorry, Izael…I'm so sorry." She smiled faintly. "But you're lying. There isn't another way, and you know it."

He roared in anger and slammed his fist into the tree beside him. It splintered and cracked from the strength of the blow. "Come back here *now!*" Begging hadn't worked. So, he resorted to fury.

The sun was starting to warm her back as it crept higher and higher above the horizon. She watched as the grass around her slowly shifted from a silvery-blue to warm greens and yellows. She shut her eyes for a moment and, taking a deep breath, slowly let it out. This might be the last time she saw Izael.

"I care about you, Izael. You tricked me into thinking there—there might be something between us. A future, even." She kept her eyes shut. She didn't want him to shake her resolve. "I had so much fun with you. More fun than I've had in eons. Take care of Pumpkin—please don't eat him."

"Alex—please, my songbird, look at me—please—" He was pleading now, his voice shaky.

That finally got her to look up at him. He was on his knees, having once more taken human form, right at the edge where the darkness that clung to the forest met the field. He was, in fact crying, tears streaming unchecked down his cheeks. He was still holding out a hand as if trying to reach her as she slipped away down river rapids. And maybe, to him, she was. "Please, my songbird—do not leave me."

Her heart broke. She wanted, with all her heart, to run into his arms. To use her wish to give Valroy what he wanted. But it would never end happily. It wouldn't last. "I'm so sorry. I…I just can't."

"You don't understand." Izael's shoulders shook. "I—I love you, Alex. I love you. You cannot leave me. I have never loved *anyone* before. Please…"

He had promised he wouldn't ever hurt her. He had promised to keep her safe.

Through blurry eyes, she smiled at him the way she smiled at her grandma when she was lying in her casket—the sadness of a final farewell. "I'm just so sorry."

And before he could say another thing, the sunlight overtook the forest, and he vanished as he fled to keep from joining her in the light.

He was gone.

She was alone.

For now.

Sinking down into the grass, she put her head in her hands and wept. The Seelie would come for her. They would find her. Only one question remained—

What would they do with her when they found her?

Izael destroyed the furniture in his home in a violent rage through sobs of grief and loss. She was his! *His!* He had even told her how he felt—confessed his love for her.

But she had not believed him.

And even if she had, it was not enough to convince her. He was not enough for her. She should have forsaken everything, both worlds, the sky, the moon, *everything*, for him. Why wouldn't she?

He would have done that for her.

He fell to his knees on the stone and placed his head in his hands as he wept. His songbird was now the prisoner of the Seelie—or perhaps she was dead. He could use his magic to spy on her, but…part of him did not want to know. Did not want to see her being brutalized, tortured, seduced, or maimed by another.

No, that was supposed to be for him.

Love is terrible.

I hate it.

I hate this thing in my chest that feels like I have been gutted like a fish.

But what was he to do?

Sit there on his floor like a child and let the world take his songbird away from him? No. No, that was not the way of the Duke of Bones. He was *Unseelie,* and he would have what belonged to him.

Slowly pushing back up to his feet, he straightened his clothes and smoothed back his hair. Taking in a wavering breath, he calmed his shuddering sobs. Alex belonged to him. One way or another. Now and forever. In life and in death.

Izael began to laugh. There was a tragic humor to the whole thing, wasn't there? He would find a new solution to this mess.

Or he would burn down all of Tir n'Aill out of revenge.

Either way, I win.

To be continued in book two…
The Unseelie Wish

ABOUT THE AUTHOR

Kat has always been a storyteller.

With ten years in script-writing for performances on both the stage and for tourism, she has always been writing in one form or another. When she isn't penning down fiction, she works as Creative Director for a company that designs and builds large-scale interactive adventure games. There, she is the lead concept designer, handling everything from game and set design, to audio and lighting, to illustration and script writing.

Also on her list of skills are artistic direction, scenic painting and props, special effects, and electronics. A graduate of Boston University with a BFA in Theatre Design, she has a passion for unique, creative, and unconventional experiences.

Printed in Great Britain
by Amazon